A NEW PRINCESS

A SWEET FANTASY ROMANCE

THE DANCING PRINCESSES
BOOK ONE

ALEA HENLE

ISBN: 978-1-952735-26-4 (print, as Alea Henle), 978-1-952735-10-3 (inactive print, as A.R. Henle), 978-1-952735-08-0 ebook

Published by Crabgrass Publishing

Editing by Rare Bird Editing.

Cover design by Augusta Scarlett

❀ Created with Vellum

CHAPTER 1

Gisela followed a trail of sunlight from the village.

Her toes dug into warm earth still damp from the recent downpour. She held her green tunic well above her ankles. The pose made her belt rise along her torso and slip under the band wrapped around her breasts rather than rest around her waist. The serpentine brass pin securing her tunic at the shoulder chafed where it brushed her skin.

Only her hair remained in place. A green cloth wound around her head to hide the purple streak marring her otherwise black locks.

She left the village behind, from the hustle and bustle to the buildings of wood and brick with their thatched roofs. The smoke rising from squash and peppers roasting in the ovens, as the cooks and their assistants labored to prepare the one meal all ate together. The runners dashing back and forth from the potting sheds to the fields, bringing seeds and young sprouts to those planting the summer's crops in earth made soft by the rain. The songs of the weavers at their looms crafting lengths of linen for use or trade.

At least the songs offered some cover for the bright chatter of the young as they streamed naked from the nurseries out to play in the mud. Called to each other. Yelled. Screamed. The nursery guardians egged them on, all showing an edge of relief at this break in the spring rains that had kept everyone pent up so long.

By the time Gisela walked a dozen paces from the village perimeter, she gave up and let her skirt fall about her ankles. Her tunic was a hand-me-down, and her errand worth the mud even if others might disagree, in particular the elder who'd turned the tunic over to the common stores because she had no time for mending.

Gisela had time, little though she wished it. Given a choice, she'd take more work—the better to lay aside personal concerns and focus on duty. Alas, the only additional task she'd been offered, subtly enough she pretended not to recognize the invitation, was to become a nursery guardian. Maybe someday she would embrace such labors. Much as she used to love watching the children play, she could not bear it yet.

Better to get away, take anger and bitterness and earth them where none else might witness.

The latest rain had left the fields and woods damp. Passing through the still air slicked her skin with sweat. Such a good, steady fall of water nourished crops poking up through the dirt. It cleansed the layers of grime adhering to stone chimneys, thatched roofs, and the woods that lay between the village and the charcoal burners' kiln. All appeared cleaner and brighter as the sun reflected off wet foliage.

Nevertheless, she retreated away from people. Drank in the earthy scent of oils wafting up from the greenery, and the hints of white, yellow, and various shades of purple blooms growing along the wide path toward the next village over.

At first she wandered without purpose, knowing only where she did *not* wish to be.

Yet keeping to the trail raised the risk of meeting someone. Anyone. The few Escalli remaining held only a few villages in which to live, laugh, and cry. Although spread across rough hills, the people kept in regular contact. Many lived and worked in one village but had close friends in the others. Moreover, a number of traders found the path a convenient route even though the villagers were known for trading away more than they ever acquired.

How much did she wish to avoid people, known or unknown?

She turned aside onto a narrow, overgrown track that led to a once-fertile field. No one would think to find her there, should any even miss her. So long as she had made a clear escape from the village, her absence should not be noted until twilight. The elders had called a council for the evening fires, and her presence would be desired to enter the deliberations and decisions into the village rolls, but until then she was free.

Her damp skirt swished around her ankles as she passed by a large, old tree. She brushed the smooth bark. No one had cleared the way since the summer storms began, or perhaps even earlier given the number of fallen twigs, branches, and leaves.

Head down, she picked her way with care. Within moments she emerged from the woods into a desolate scene. Lines of caked earth showed where plows had passed in earlier, better times. Despite lying fallow for several years, the field had yet to recover.

The afternoon sun filled her with warmth and eased the chill that lingered in her since winter. Field birds flitted along the rows, pecking at the earth. Tree rats raced along limbs stout and fragile to chitter at her.

Few signs of burgeoning life surrounded her. Although the rain's recent glaze on leaves and stalks had begun to dry, scarcely any tender shoots budded. Only enough to show growth persisting in drained earth.

This was something to celebrate. No need for words. She desired movement. To feel life in her veins.

As well, to celebrate evidence that lying fallow did not mean death or ending: merely a different type of existence. Renewal might take time, but it came to pass sooner or later.

She tapped the earth to announce her presence. Gentle on the toes as she lifted her foot and then a firm touch with the heel.

Only birds and bees noticed.

No matter, she expected no response. It was a matter of courtesy, or so she'd learned from the old, frail sire who once spent time in the nurseries teaching children to dance, back when she was a youngling.

Many of the children laughed at him for the finicky ways he'd picked up during years spent roaming the land before settling back down with the Escalli—or so the gossip ran.

Gisela had joined in the laughter, then.

Yet when she was chosen to apprentice to the council scribe and learned to use a stylus to scribble notes on a wax-covered wooden tablet, and craft formal accounts in pen and ink on parchment, she appreciated the lessons on how to hold her body, maintain good posture, and respect her muscles and sinews. The practices helped keep her hale and healthy. She'd sought him out to sit at his feet and drink in lessons, though by then he spent more time watching children dance than instructing.

She tapped a second time.

Usually, the earth responded with a faint ripple of pressure, light enough she varied between belief and doubt that anything had happened.

This time a matching thrum jolted against her heel. Even her teeth hummed for a moment.

Her breath caught. She froze, hands out and left foot raised. Her right ankle wobbled and she stumbled to the side before she regained her balance.

Shock drove everything from her mind save realization that the land had accepted her invitation.

When the earth agreed to join the dance, a wise dancer consented at once. Her old teacher's advice ran through her, and she shifted her stance immediately.

Bending down, Gisela laid her palms against the warm earth. Her right sat flush against firm, cracked dirt between furrows. The left angled down as it rested on the side of a furrow. Her third and fourth fingers sank into the shallow mud at the bottom.

You choose the measure.

Each time she'd done this before, she'd waited a full five breaths before the faintest tremors rippled where skin met dirt.

This time, barely had she bent to touch when a firm, fast beat set her hands shaking.

Bam, bam, ba-da ba-da ba-da, bam.

She straightened as she assumed a start position. Clapped her palms together for several measures, until her whole body thrummed with the beat.

Then she danced.

Up and down the crooked trails between furrows. Leapt across the narrow trenches where weeds and remnants of previous year's crops sought to grow and flourish. Dipped her toes here and there, brushing new-green vegetation with the tips. There were more than she'd seen before, more than she'd thought.

Turned three times in quick succession. Then jumped across another furrow and rose onto her tiptoes. Energy crackled within her body. Her old, foul mood gave way to sheer pleasure in the dance. Every movement, even those that stretched her muscles, produced delight and joy.

She held her arms high, fingers flicking this way and that. As though she had dipped her hands in a bucket of water and sprinkled stray drops in her wake. Kicked high with one leg, then to the side with the other. Turning again, five times, she lifted her arms higher, stretching so her hands met in the middle, above her head.

Then she arched her back, let her arms fall wide, and dashed down to the end of the furrow to start up the next.

Her gestures and steps drew upon the dances favored at the quarterly village festivals, celebrations of life and fertility. She let go of any preconceptions as to what steps and gestures went with which. The fever of the moment captured her, and all her body—muscles, sinews, bones—combined to select whichever movements best expressed joy in warmth and sunshine after rain.

Sweat slicked Gisela's skin. Her tunic clung to her torso, belling out around her legs when she moved with vigor and sticking when still. Her open mouth dragged in deep breaths, filling her lungs. Her arms and legs ached, as did her neck, belly, and back. These were minor matters, for the same dance that caused them also eased the pain.

The more she danced, the better her spirits. Cares and worries fell away, unable to compete with the insistent drumming in her blood and bone.

Old, hard-baked earth softened beneath her, as though she brought life-giving rain with her passage.

Tree rats chattered from perches high in the trees, voicing the beat that resounded in her body. Small birds flocked about her, never approaching too close and yet mirroring her movements. Soft coos and bright cries added to the tree rats' drums to provide impromptu music.

After one startled glance, even a rabbit joined in—hopping across the furrows and tracing intricate patterns through the paw prints left behind.

Gisela's hair slipped, thick, black curls marred by the streak of purple falling half-loose. Without missing a step, she grabbed the slackening cloth around her head and pulled it off entirely. Her hair streamed free behind—and the length danced with her, floating and whipping as she whirled about.

At the end, when she had covered all the field, she raced around the sides. Arms back and head cloth trailing after her.

Until she reached the corner where she'd started.

There she stopped. The beat faded. Her pulse slowed, resuming a more restful pace. Her chest heaved as she dragged in air, lungs aching and breathing taking longer to return to normal. A light breeze wicked away sweat drying on her skin, leaving her chilled. Otherwise, a sense of wellbeing filled her body. Old troubles lurked at the back of her mind, but their weight had lessened.

Bowing low, she laid her palms against the earth in the exact spot as before—the mud still held the prints of her last fingers.

Thank you.

A last pulse across her skin, then nothing.

A green haze enveloped the field. Old, yellowed shoots and leaves now glowed green. The earth exuded a subtle glow.

The birds fell silent, scattering across the field to pick for seeds and bugs as did the rabbit among the new shoots. The tree rats ceased their chattering.

Sharp as a tree limb breaking, a harsh clap resounded in the sudden quiet.

The rabbit fled and birds took flight to join the tree rats up high.

Hands twisting the length of cloth in her hands, Gisela whirled around.

Five people clogged the narrow track. More passed along the trail behind them, given the thud of oxen, creak of wagon wheels, and distant chatter of voices.

All of which she'd missed.

So many people, all gaudily bedecked. Three carried swords or spears, and wore armor over knee-length tunics: boiled leather breastplates and arm and leg guards, all with gilded embellishments. Bright red cloaks flowed from their shoulders, and matching bands with gold embroidery decorated their tunic hems. A hint of sweat and leather tainted the air.

Helmets partially shielded their faces. She could not tell which might be dams, sires, or those who were both or neither. Nevertheless, there were visible differences between them. Serpentine blue tattoos wound up a pair of pale legs, a silver hand-chain stood out against the warm, ruddy hand of another, and a bracelet of red feathers circled the third's deep brown skin.

The fourth unexpected visitor was an elder by their long, braided white hair, and carried the aroma of sea moss, which Gisela only recognized because the village council had once confiscated a drunken peddler's goods, after he was found guilty of assault and destruction, and found a vial of it within. They'd sold it for enough to cover all the damage to property, if not the villagers.

The elder seemed to be a sire, though looks could be deceiving. As dark of skin as the soldier with red feathers, he wore a plain, ankle-length tunic over which he'd wrapped a long swath of deep green fabric woven with thin gold thread that caught the light and bent it. One end was thrown over his shoulder, weighted down with a band of heavy embroidery including several gold coins.

The bright dyes in those few pieces of clothes alone would require at least as many launderers as the village possessed to keep the garments in good order.

Yet all paled in comparison to the fifth and central figure. The one who had applauded. The dam stood tall, with a solid build yet delicate wrists bedecked with several bracelets. Her thin, gauzy tunic, visible at throat and hem, was dyed deep purple. She too wore a long, woven cloth wrapped over her tunic several times. The cloth bore an intricate design of birds and flowers in contrasting shades of blue. A matching band, narrow and only a thumb's length at its widest, kept black hair liberally streaked with gray back from her face.

What a face it was, long and narrow with deep-set eyes, thick black brows, and a thin-lipped mouth. Burnished gold skin with a brace of wrinkles. A profile near-perfectly formed for carving in stone or metal . . .

Or stamping on a coin.

How many times had Gisela seen council members test and verify metal coins? Sometimes she'd even handled them herself, and spent a moment tracing the features impressed in gold or silver—the land's rulers, the Terparchon and the Marchon. One of the palaces lay on the lake several day's journey to the northwest.

The Terparchon's eyebrows lifted.

Gisela held her head-cloth-wrapped hands close to her body, all too aware of her old, stained tunic and ill-kempt appearance. Her knees trembled, but her feet and legs remained connected to the earth and did not fold beneath her. The very dirt under her seemed to help hold her up.

She did, however, bow her head. Held her breath. Focused on having done nothing wrong. Even the elders of her village would likely accuse her of nothing more than foolishness in coming out to dance. She'd chosen a fallow field, so she hadn't damaged any crops.

Moreover, she'd danced. The royal family was well known for their love of dance. Indeed, the fame of the ruling family's Dancing Princesses spread far and wide. To see one walk out on promenade, or so traders told when passing through, meant witnessing grace unparalleled. Their dancing ranked as nothing less than poetry in motion.

Even allowing for the exaggeration storytellers invested into their tales, Gisela hoped her dance had not displeased.

The Terparchon stepped forward, movements marked by distant chimes. The folds of her tunic floated about her ankles, revealing gilded sandals and several anklets hung with bells.

Two of the guards followed close behind, the ones with the silver hand-chain and the feathered bracelet. Both held spears at the ready.

Laying a single finger under Gisela's chin, the older dam pushed her head up and back. She had enough height on Gisela to look down upon her even so. She grasped Gisela's chin and turned her head this way and that, then grabbed Gisela's wrists and twisted them so as to inspect work-roughened hands and ink-stained fingers.

As before, the earth supported Gisela as she let her body be turned this way and that.

"Where are you from, girl?"

Gisela blinked, drawing back. The Terparchon used the same language spoken throughout the land, but more quickly than Gisela was accustomed to, and rolled her rs.

Gisela's silence tested the ruler to the point she gave an impatient grunt.

"Do you not understand? Your village. Name it, child." The resonant voice gave the words a musical intonation and a beat not dissimilar from that to which Gisela had so recently danced.

"Foleilion, Great Ruler."

The Terparchon repeated the village's name, turning her head far enough for those behind her to hear. The mantled elder coughed, raising a hand to cover blue-tinged lips.

"Idan?" The ruler's eyebrows rose again, though her tone seemed polite.

Two steps brought the elder sire to her side, after which he raised a hand to his mouth for another cough.

"Foleilion was founded by the Escalli refugees your Excellence's mother allowed to settle here a few decades back. One of several communal villages, run by elders for the good of all. Some produce trade stuffs, most notably well-woven cloths, but they are largely self-sufficient among themselves." An odd sound, not quite a cough. "They pay their taxes on time."

"Interesting." The Terparchon dismissed the elder with a wave of her hand.

He bowed and slipped back. Lost his balance for a moment, but the guard with tattoos steadied him.

"Your foot." The older dam let go of Gisela's hands and gestured for her to raise a leg.

Gisela swayed on one foot as she lifted the other high. Muscles that hadn't ached in the dance began to hurt with star-bright pains that sparked unpredictably here and there along her thigh.

Grabbing Gisela's foot, the ruler tilted her head and inspected it. Pressed sharp nails into the calluses. Flexed it this way and that. Gisela gritted her teeth as her head swirled, hoping she wouldn't fall or faint . . . or lose the last remnants of her midday meal that now seemed so long ago. She bit her lip, the harsh taste of blood filling her mouth.

Just when she was about to give up, and plead for mercy or risk death by grabbing hold of the Terparchon, the feather-bracelet guard braced her. Well-shaped fingers with red-painted nails wrapped around her forearm, dark against her sand-colored skin.

Not content with inspection of one foot, the ruler insisted on seeing the other as well. The guard continued to support Gisela through further poking and prodding until at last the Terparchon let Gisela's other foot drop.

"Well, you're no elder." The Terparchon dusted her hands. Frowned at them, then wiped them on the skirt of the guard with the wrist-chain. "But you are a dancer, true and certain. Here of all places. I will remember you."

Without another word, she turned on her heels and walked away. The chime of anklets marked her steps, until drowned out by the creak of leather armor and tromp of four other sets of feet following behind. Then all melded with the ongoing sea of wagons and walkers proceeding down the track eastward.

The Terparchon took most of the joy of the dance with her when she left, leaving only a faint throb and pulse in Gisela's feet.

That, and the distant hope the dam would forget Gisela. After all, the ruler had inspected her closely but failed to inquire after her name.

CHAPTER 2

The formal ball inspired in Stevan nothing so much as a desire to sneeze.

The rulers allowed their courtiers much leeway in selecting attire in which to parade and flaunt themselves—resulting in a riot of different colored tunics and mantles of varying hem lengths and necklines—but mandated all wear the same perfume. Despite suppressing his urge, as sneezing risked unpleasant notice and disfavor, his nose continued to itch.

If only he were anywhere less formal. His lightweight tunic was fine enough for the occasion, but not his dark green mantle. His best, until he could afford to replace it. The fabric wrapped around his body fewer times than ideal. A good thing, as the heavy fabric was intended to keep a body warm in winter. Unfortunately, it was ill-suited to the sultry summer weather. He oozed moisture, so much so that his bangs clung to his tan-colored forehead and drops slicked the brown braid hanging halfway down his back. A hand-me-down from his third-oldest brother, the mantle fell to mid-calf on Stevan. It thus put on full display the lower portions of Stevan's tunic, with their attendant traces of mud stains despite repeated laundering, and his decidedly plain sandals.

Stevan's two-up sibling, who'd turned down the honor of receiving the mantle before it came to Stevan, claimed the color made Stevan appear sallow and sickly.

Little though Stevan cared for that, he disliked more the notion his clothing affected his fortunes. Making one's way in the world as the fifteenth child of an impecunious noble family was difficult enough. Before coming to court as an adjunct to an adjunct, he'd counted his ribs rather than muscles. Stretched meals as far as they could go.

He hadn't gone hungry at court yet, at least, but neither had he found any way to make enough of a mark to gain a competency. Enough to support a modest style of living would count as a success for one long expected to fail. He'd leave the grand pretensions and uneasy marital contracts to his other brothers and sisters.

As long as he managed not to sneeze.

The heavy, smokey perfume the rulers currently preferred triggered in Stevan no reflexive response such as some unfortunates faced. Some servants and guards suffered so much they would trade to get out of court duty on months when the proclaimed scents made their eyes burn or noses twitch. Or pay alternates to take their place, those that could afford it.

His new position as a clerk and aide placed him amongst the hangers-on at court, but did not allow him the possibility of paying someone to take his place—even had he enough funds, which he did not.

He lacked the excuse of ill-health.

Nor was he willing to explain his desire to be anywhere else.

He simply detested the perfume, which certain unlamented and not-missed members of his family had favored. Despite the passage of years, the little hairs along the nape of his neck stood stiff at the scent despite the weight of his mantle. His fingers twitched, except when concealed under the folds of cloth.

Ears waited for a whistle and snap, or a high laugh—but the only sounds were the muted chatter of other watchers around the room and the labored results of musicians anxious to impress. Harpists with predilections for rippling trills. Mellifluous flautists each soaring higher than the next. Drummers determined to ensure everyone felt the beat in their bones.

Lanterns blazed from every corner of the wide-open plaza, held by still, stiff servants dressed in simple white tunics and loincloths. Overhead, the sky was the roof—a glorious expanse of deep blue with slowly fading brighter colors reflecting on the water where the sun had vanished beyond the end of the wide lake.

Beneath their feet lay a wooden dance floor covering a wondrous mosaic portraying the first Terparchon's selection of the first Marchon to lead the armies. Couples, trios, and the occasional quintet danced to the lyrical beat of the court musicians.

Everyone—male, female, or eleee—wore thin ankle-length tunics covered with lightweight mantles and girdled at the waist with gilded leather belts or brightly embroidered sashes, the better to flutter their skirts as they preened and posed. Many flaunted wealth and status in circlets across their brows or broad circular collars over their mantles. The poor went without or made do with cloth alternatives. Only soldiers and servants were notable for simpler attire.

And everyone with any pretensions whatsoever shoved a half-dozen or more bracelets around their wrists and clasped bell-hung anklets above their sandaled feet.

Given the cacophony of so much chiming metal, the musicians did well merely to be heard above the dancers and the crowds mingling around the edge of the floor.

The princesses stood out with their circlets of gold twined with silver—for only they and the royal family adorned their heads with gold. The dancing had become general enough that anyone might dance within reason, or within the confines of custom and rank. The princesses had yet to dance with someone not bearing precious metal or jewels at brow or neck.

Hands clasped behind his back, he remained on the shady side of a marble pillar. Most of the court promenaded around. Music and movement always lured him, but he resisted the urge to join the crowds on the floor.

Too many posed rather than danced for pure enjoyment.

Moreover, joining in the dancing required finding a partner since no one asked him. Easier to remain unnoticed along the side walls—watching and guessing at the motives of those mingling around him.

Those who had power knew it. They stood, sat, or danced at the center of crowds. Others with less clustered around, divided into ever-changing groups. Those without any power formed sober, forgettable witnesses, such as the silent holders of torches.

Glitter, glitter, and more glitter. Fine colors, flashing jewels, coy glances.

All well and good for those who could afford such frivolous pastimes.

He preferred his day duties of shuffling papers and negotiating supplies. There he worked through tasks with right and wrong answers. So much simpler than the constant shifting and searching for power and influence.

"You're not so bad at this as you claim." Stevan's two-up sibling, Brenn, appeared out of nowhere. "You should give yourself more credit."

Stevan jerked, one arm grabbing hold of the marble and the other slipping to his waist. He lacked so much as a table knife. Only certain trusted individuals were allowed to bring weapons to the dance.

"How do you do that?"

"Do what?" A broad smile stretched Brenn's thick mouth wide. In ways that counted, he was the bigger person. Taller, broader, and wealthier, albeit not by much. He kept his dark-brown curls cut short, so as to offer little purchase to enemies should he ever be in a battle and lose his helmet. For this occasion, he'd donned a knee-length tunic rather than ankle, plus a flowing red mantle. The circlet across his brow, a length of blue enamel twined with copper only a hair darker than his skin and bearing the faintest green patina, attested to his rank as a captain in the guards, as did the subtle wings attached to the heels of his sandals.

"You always manage to sneak up on me." Stevan licked his dry lips, nodding at the sword and daggers hanging from Brenn's belt. "You should clang, with all you carry."

"I practice walking silently, the better to test sentries and catch those dozing when they ought not." Brenn clapped a hand against Stevan's back and nodded at the dazzling array of dancers at the center. "Why are you not out there dancing?"

"I wasn't asked."

"Piffle." Brenn lived up to expectations, clapping Stevan's back again. "That never stopped you at home. I recall dozens of times you snuck off to the village and joined dances on your own. You always wound up with plenty of partners by the end of the night."

"There it was a pleasure." Plus Stevan had known most of those he asked. "Here it is . . . performance."

"Ask one of the princesses to dance. Let them see your grace. How well you match them. That's a straighter slide to security than slogging with papers."

A good consortial contract was the fastest way to wealth for impoverished nobles, but Stevan had no mind to pursue it. Without a reasonable degree of affection—and sometimes even with it—such alliances tended to grow thorns that injured any who came near.

Even the power and connections that would flow from becoming a princess's favorite wasn't worth the risk. A sentiment he suspected his unmarried and uncommitted brother shared, though he teased Brenn nevertheless. "Straighter than swinging your sword, either. You're as good a dancer as I, so why not live your own words?"

"Kind words, though we both know that is not true. I clomp about too much." Brenn's voice turned tight, rising several notes from his usual rumble. "Stamp my feet with all the delicacy of an ox."

"A quote?"

"I tried. Asked one of the princesses to dance with me." The older man's brows lowered, but otherwise he gave no sign of unease. "It didn't work. But there's no reason it wouldn't for you."

The current dance spilled into a serpentine spiral as all on the floor joined hands into two immense chains and wove among themselves. Jewels flashed as half ducked and others leapt. The uneven slap of sandals against the mosaic tiles sent ripples of resonance throughout the hall.

Stevan's shoulders swayed, hips shifted, feet itched. His hands grew damp at the memory of serpentine dances past, when he'd vied with others to be the last knocked out, the last to break a chain. Shown his worth on the dance floor, if nowhere else.

Already, pockets of the serpents had broken into gales of laughter —or charges of trickery—as hands slipped and dancers fell away.

"Come, dance the next with me." Brenn nudged Stevan with his shoulder. "You took laurels at the festivals when you were young."

"Once." Stevan shrugged. Only on one occasion had he done better than place second or third, something his father had pointed out when he arranged for Stevan to apprentice as a clerk rather than expend money on a place in the guard or doing anything more than copying texts in a clear hand.

"More than that." Brenn frowned. "You outlasted near anyone else on a half-dozen occasions at the least. Show off your moves rather than hiding them in the shadows."

"What is this? A laureled dancer among us who does not favor the floor?"

Stevan straightened with a snap, laying an arm over his chest and bowing. Next to him, Brenn did likewise. An element of music vested in that voice, fitting, for it was music and dance that made the Terparchon who she was. The Marchon ruled in matters of war, and kept a keen eye on issues of justice and diplomacy as well, but in all else the realm belonged to the Terparchon. As it had to her mother before her and grandfather before that, and on back for generations.

This night, the Terparchon dressed in midnight blue. Her mantle rivaled the sky for depth of color and ability to drink in light without giving it back. A crown enameled in blue and set with deep sapphires rested atop her head. Bits of unenameled silver in the crown and the gray strands in her hair surrounded her warm, golden face with the illusion of a starry sky in contrast to the starless-sky folds flowing about her body.

An older woman in a silver mantle stood two steps behind. Despite unusual tan skin with lilac undertones and lovely white hair bound in a braid as long as Stevan's, she was thoroughly eclipsed by the Terparchon.

Two guards hovered behind the ruler as a precaution, but otherwise she had only one attendant. By preference, it was said, as she enjoyed mingling with crowds during dances. She had a gift for going unnoticed when she wished.

Stevan swallowed the sudden lump in his throat. "I took laurels on one occasion, Excellence, though I have shown a knack for movement. But I am still new to this court and enjoy watching the parades of those more skilled than I."

"New, but with no need to be so retiring, Stevan of the Silver Hills." She dropped his name with ease as she tilted her head back, eyes nearly level with his. "It is a sad commentary upon the court that we have not yet offered sufficient lures to bring you to the floor. But do not be so selfish as to rob us of the pleasure of your company."

A trio of rings and matching bracelets flashed silver and blue as she extended a hand, palm up.

Brenn kicked Stevan, but Stevan had already nodded and set his hand, damp and cold, on her warm, dry one. "The pleasure is mine, Excellence."

"We shall see." Turning, she led the way into the crowds mingling and reshaping into duos and trios for the next dance. He followed, body at ease and face calm—all except a sudden twitch in one cheek which started up and refused to stop.

His performance in the dance depended on many factors, not least whether his partner meant to show him up or show him off. Whether he recognized the dance and remembered the steps. As well, whether the steps allowed others to approach and lay obstacles in his way.

So many unknowns and pitfalls.

He had to take courage from his ability to move and let the music take him. Though he had not danced at court often, he found escape and relaxation outside the seasonal palaces—in lesser halls and common taverns. He was young and lithe, if poor and unfamiliar with such proximity to royalty. Though he'd also spoken true—he'd taken laurels, but only when dance prizes were awarded on grace and movement. Never more.

Never magic, such as the Terparchon and her attendants wielded.

It would be an interesting span of time before he could bow again and retreat back to the wall in disgrace. Or face multitudes desiring to dance with him in hopes that a little of his current partner's luster might rub off on them.

A bitter tang bloomed in his mouth, but he swallowed and set his jaw.

The Terparchon led him to the center of the floor. Around them gathered the twelve Dancing Princesses arrayed in a veritable feast of colors, each with a chosen partner.

In other courts, the title of prince and princess might denote close blood or marriage connection to a land's rulers, but not here. Not in Codaros, where dance ranked high and the greatest dancers held true power in their bodies.

Blonde, brown-eyed, fair-skinned Ylena in a daylight-sky-blue mantle over her tunic held hands with the Terparchon's son Todor, her second-born and a masculine version of his mother down to his preference tonight for deepest blue. Neither did more than glance at him from the corners of their eyes.

Red-haired Jola wore a harsh shade of yellow that enhanced the green undertones of her otherwise fawn-colored skin, giving her the appearance of one half-dead. She was known for curious color choices in her attire, but this did not put off Nefeli, the Terparchon's eldest, who wore an unusually eye-catching mantle of red that gave her golden skin a ruddy, fiery cast. A number of wrinkles fanned around Jola's eyes. Several years separated the two, but they were reputedly devoted to each other.

Short and slight, the Terparchon's younger daughter, Zora, stood next to the tallest person in the court. The gold circlet perched upon her black hair glinted next to her partner's upper chest, so much did they tower over her. Brown-haired and brown-skinned, Heron was one of six princesses who did not present themselves as women—two were men and four eleee. Both Zora and Heron wore shades of green, one light with a tinge of the sea and the other so deep as to verge on black.

The Terparchon smiled upon each and every one, a sparkle of mischief in her eye. Or perhaps only the joy of returning to the dance floor as she seldom did these days.

A remembered whip and crack resounded in Stevan's mind. He rolled his shoulders to ease the knot forming in his back. Settling into place opposite his partner, he mirrored her stance. He bowed, twisting his arm and torso in the traditional sign that he acknowledged her right to take the lead. Only the closest of pairings could tackle dances without a designated lead. Twice in his life, he'd been fortunate enough to watch dancers able to share the lead between them.

Under no circumstances was this the time or place. The Terparchon and her princesses led, without question, and their partners—even those of royal birth—followed.

The Terparchon accepted his acknowledgment as her due. Standing straight and tall, she did not glance toward the musicians as she lifted a hand in command.

"All present, attend the dance." The evenings master of events pounded a staff against the floor. The rills of conversation quieted enough for his voice to roll against the columns. "The tachino."

A drummer gave a fast roll, then slowed the beat down considerably.

"An interesting choice."

"A favorite of mine." The Terparchon smiled at him, teeth flashing white and sharp.

A line of sweat formed along his spine, but his mouth turned dry. A chill ran through his brain as he searched for every iota of memory about the tachino.

Performed within an invisible square, any careless step outside became cause for dismissal from the floor and, for those who did not last long, mockery. Solo sections where partners mirrored each other alternated with parts where arms snuck around waists as partners whirled in seemingly wild spinning that had to be carefully controlled so as not to leave the dancers dizzy enough to misstep.

The music started slow, and inexorably sped up.

"A second elimination dance in a row." Stevan managed a smile back, careful not to show his teeth. "Unusual."

"Do not disappoint me." The Terparchon positioned her arms for the start: upraised, palms facing him.

Instinct and a knack for mirroring had him align his body and arms opposite her, body a step ahead of his mind. Drawing in a deep breath and letting the air out slowly, he let his body slip into the movements.

He focused on her. Matched her, without ever taking the lead.

The flutes soared above the drum as the dance proper began. Past and future faded away. Only the present existed—only the dance.

A step to the right, curl the arm and bow. To center. To left, curl and bow.

Out and in—close enough to feel her breath hot on his throat. Eyes meeting, his careful not to risk a challenge. No touching.

In and out.

Heart-beat follows the drums, rises with the drums.

Wrap arms around waists—forget she could order his dismemberment with a word—and whirl. Pick a spot in the distance and look only there: Brenn, leaning against the column as though he had not a care in the world but his jaw clenched so tight he'd likely ache all night. Rely on the firm surface beneath. Resemble the mosaic floor: solid, stable, and decorative.

Whirl.

Whirl.

Back to stance. Ignore the rest of the world. Only the dance exists.

Speed.

Precision.

Speed.

Note the pleasure on the Terparchon's face when closing in for the whirl. Do not rest easy.

Do not stop to wipe sweat dripping from forehead, even when it runs into eyes and makes them sting.

Nor question the unexpected ripples of energy crackling in the air.

Familiar from a distance, watching the princesses dance with their partners —and now, for the first time, experienced up close.

Feel the energy as it wells from the earth, through her, then to him, and out until the air above the dance floor fills with sparkles that rival the stars above.

Taste the airy fizziness as though inhaling wine straight from the vat.

Only the dance matters.

Until a high scream cut across everything. Drums, flutes, and sandals slapping against the floor.

Stevan froze, muscles seizing at sudden stillness after frenetic movement. Opposite, the Terparchon's torso shook as she, too, stopped in place.

Everything stopped, as a second scream rang out and a deeper shout.

Then a thud and a cry of pain.

Stevan whirled around. Snapped out of his fizzy daze, breath coming in pants and sweat dripping along his body.

The Terparchon lurched, hands grabbing inelegantly at his thick mantle. Her shoulder pressed on his and hip dug into his side, as they watched her son kneel next to his writhing partner.

Ylena bent double, hands clutching at her leg. Sounds no longer escaped her. She rocked, mouth gaping open as though she were a fish, her face contorted in agony. Her movements dislodged her circlet. Blonde hair spilled free, falling around her as the circlet rolled over and came to a stop at Stevan's toes. It plopped half-on and half-off his sandaled foot.

A trio of healers in mismatched purple and orange mantles rushed over to cluster around the fallen princess.

The Terparchon knelt with her son for a few moments, whispering. Then bent and did the same for the writhing woman, albeit with no sign she heard.

Stevan retrieved the circlet of gold twined with silver, fingers curling around metal still warm from Ylena's head.

When the Terparchon extended an imperious hand his way, he

helped her up. All eyes fell on her. The dancers close by, and the watchers from the edge of the floor.

"The dance is over for the night." She stretched an arm toward the musicians. "Something soothing, to settle our spirits and ease our daughter-sister in her healing."

The drums stayed silent, but the flautists and harpists began a series of rippling chords as the crowd began to clear the floor. Slow, though, for most glanced often at the growing cluster of healers. Cries of pain escaped the injured princess until one of the healers laid a hand over her brow. Then the four strongest carried a limp body from the chamber. The Terparchon's children followed, and other princesses and their partners as well.

Stevan made a bow, but before he could leave with the crowd his hand clenched around something hard. He held the fallen princess's circlet, and needed to find someone suitable to whom to entrust it first.

The Terparchon's hand wrapped too firm around his arm for him to shake her off even had he the nerve.

"Accompany me." She jerked her head in the same direction the healers had gone. "Amara, you are needed as well."

Thus instead of fleeing, he found himself escorting the woman into a nearby antechamber. Cool air dried the sweat on his skin, though his tunic and mantle still clung unpleasantly close. The chamber itself was long and thin, with pale green walls and a rendition of a summer picnic painted on the ceiling. The floor was simple black and white squares of some material that made a swishing sound when trod on by sandals. Only a few pieces of furniture lined the walls: chairs along the length and a desk at the far end.

The Terparchon's earlier attendant reappeared at her side, as reticent and withdrawn as before despite bearing an ancient name and the ruler's trust. Head tilted downward, she played with the ends of her braid.

The ruler's guards moved to block the door and keep any others from following them.

The Terparchon marched to the far end of the chamber. Stevan followed, in step with the other woman. His hands twitched. When the ruler whirled around to face them, only an arm's length away, he extended the circlet.

She stared at it for a long moment then took it from him, leaving his fingers still warm where he'd held it.

"A bad sign. A bad break, too. She'll be months in healing, before she can even think of dancing again." A thin sheen of tears damped her eyes, although none rolled down her cheeks.

"Already there are rumors she was tripped." Amara had a low, pleasant voice as musical as the Terparchon although nowhere as commanding of attention.

"There will always be rumors. Maybe they are right, maybe not. We will see. If someone did this on purpose, they will pay." Teeth flashed as the Terparchon drew back her lips, then shook her head. "But in either case the end is the same. She cannot dance. Which leaves us only eleven, since Felipa is near bursting with child. Even if the birth goes well, she may not return for weeks or months, and we cannot be so long without twelve princesses. The security and welfare of the realm demand it."

Amara nodded, steepling her fingers under her chin. "There's the candidate near the winter palace—"

"Too far." The Terparchon grunted. "No, I stumbled on one a few weeks ago by chance. In some village nearby. Fillie . . . no Fo . . . Foleilion."

"Never heard of it." Amara said.

Both women glanced Stevan's way. He shook his head, no more familiar than they.

"It matters not. You two must go with all speed there and do whatever you must to bring her here. I'll give you a writ of empowerment." The Terparchon laid the circlet on the desk and yanked on a drawer. Wood screeched as it opened, at an angle, and caught.

A moment later, Amara eased herself between the Terparchon and desk. With deft movements, she laid out paper, pen, and ink, and shifted a chair to just the right spot for the Terparchon to sit as she wrote.

Then effaced herself back to Stevan's side.

He hadn't moved. Why did the Terparchon wish him to go on this errand, such as he'd never done before? Surely some more practiced courtier would be the better choice.

He didn't think he'd spoken, but Amara stirred next to him and gave him an encouraging smile.

"You have the potential to be a princess's partner in the Dances. A compeer: able to withstand and channel the power they raise. To match and support their magic. As you're still new and untried, you'll likely be near irresistible to any potential princess." Her soft words reached only as far as his ears, sending a shiver through him. "The prospect of dancing with you may be a lure in itself to convince her to come to court."

"I'm not . . ." He shivered again. He'd danced for years without experiencing . . . whatever had happened on the floor. Which he could have—would have—written off as imagination, except Amara kept smiling at him.

"You may not have been before, but now you are." Eyes dark with worry despite her smile, she gazed over at the busily writing ruler. "I haven't been a princess for many years, but even I can sense that much. Someone sturdy and rooted, a bulwark against the arrows of fate."

"There." The Terparchon waved a piece of paper in the air before extending it to Amara. "Don't promise too much in luring her here. The village is peopled by Escalli, now I recall. Communal. Get the elders on your side, and they'll hand her over to you fast enough. I want her here to begin learning the core Dances within a week."

"Make it two." Amara blew on the paper, then rolled it up although the smell of wet ink lingered. "I can teach her some of the basics, but you must give her time to pack and say her farewells."

The two women stared at each other for a long moment.

Stevan barely dared breathe, calculating the odds of getting out of this without losing his head or other valued appendage. But also twitching from the same energy as on the dance floor. As one of the youngest, but not the baby, of a long, large family, he'd never been noted for much more than trouble—quickly quelled—and a knack for dance. To suddenly have more was wonderful and strange, and he wanted very much to sneak away and spend time in contemplation, to re-root himself in his world, before having to go find a stranger.

"Two weeks if necessary. Make it less if you can." The Terparchon clicked her tongue. "Only for you, my friend, would I bend so far. Gather what you need and be on your way."

With a sharp nod, she headed back toward the dance chamber.

"Er, Excellence?" He said before he could call the words back.

"What?" She stopped and turned, lips tight at his impudence.

"What's her name? The woman, the dancer, we're to find."

A blank look crossed the ruler's face, then she waved a hand at him. "Don't worry about her name. You won't be able to miss her. Or her you."

Again, the emphasis on him as a part of the mission.

Exactly what did she expect him to do?

CHAPTER 3

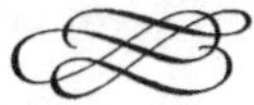

Gisela's back ached from bending too long over a table of wood planks. Dull pain radiated from her spine outward. She laid down her stylus and stretched. Arms up overhead, tunic sleeves falling back halfway to her elbows and the cord at her waist rising, then to the side. Muscles and bones creaked and the pain dwindled to a low throbbing.

Quick tugs at the sleeves, and her corded belt resettled her tunic into proper place. The distant clamor of festival preparations—hammering, yelling, clangs—all blurred together into a single noisy mess that the wooden walls of the village hall partially blocked out. On the other hand, the savory scents of fresh baked bread, fruit pies, and meat deep in the fire pits on the outskirts of the village easily sifted through chinks to reach her. She nibbled on a heel of stale bread, careful not to let crumbs fall on the papers covering the table.

Her summer-weight over-tunic of linen in green and blue stripes cascaded over another backless bench nearby. She'd discarded it earlier, when its warmth made her sweat and think longingly of slipping out of the village to dance in the fields.

Next to the over-tunic lay the thin band of matching cloth she'd used to bind up her hair, leaving the dark strands to cascade around her shoulders and occasionally fall forward to veil her work from her. Given her preference, she'd have put it back on. Alas, earlier in the day she'd had the purple streak re-touched and it had yet to finish drying. Her bare feet rested on the smooth wooden floor, toes curling occasionally as cool drafts snuck in through the door.

Scraps of scraped-down parchment covered the scarred work table. Her wax-covered tablet sat in the middle, half-filled. The abandoned stylus had rolled to a stop at an angle, lying athwart the lists of those Escalli who'd sired or borne children in the village nurseries, and those currently in anticipation of births.

In a brief fit of generosity she'd freed her assistant to go help assemble tables for the feast, and flirt and frolic in the process. After all, her predecessor had done the same for her.

Letters danced before her eyes, forming names and then bouncing to reform into different ones. Nonsensical words. Names of those dead, or aged or vanished . . . any names save those she should write. Those unfortunate individuals who appeared on too many of the parchment scraps as having skipped certain festival duties these past seasons.

Names of people she pitied and envied in equal measure. All those currently suffering polite visits from the council of elders. Earlier in the day, one of the eldest, Ilburna, made her displeasure at the number of people on her list quite clear.

"A disgrace." The old dam had thumped her walking stick against the floor. Her legs might be too weak to walk far without assistance, but her arms remained strong. Dark brown eyes had flashed in a parchment-colored face lined from top to bottom with wrinkles. "Do your siring and bearing when you're young, and blood runs hot. Duty to village first. Fuss with love and life partners after. That's how it was in my day."

No one contradicted her, although at least three were near as old and sharp of memory.

None of the elders would ever knock on Gisela's door or track her down for such an errand.

Although the room was long and wide, well able to hold not

merely the councilors but the small crowds regularly attending their meetings, the walls nevertheless seemed close. The still air, heavy with scents and humidity, turned thick and hard to breathe. Her toes curled against the smooth plank floor and a shudder ripped through her.

Clasping hands grown chill, she massaged her fingers and blew warm air on them. In and out, in and out. Her shoulders slumped, the ache between them returning.

Somewhere in the distance, someone turned the raising of the dance floor and erection of trestle tables for the feast into a matter of music. Hammering became drumming. Over the excited cries from here and there, deep voices and a few higher ones began a chant of thanks to the sun for warmth and light. The walls muffled the words actually sung, but the familiar tune readily brought them to mind.

The muscles in her legs twitched. Randomly, but only for a moment or two. Within a handspan of beats, her legs began to move to the music. Her hips swayed, unable to resist the driving rhythm although she remained planted on the bench.

She hadn't danced in public for quite a while. Not yet long enough for her name to be at risk of appearing on the lists—were she not, sadly, excused—but so much time that the very notion of dancing in public made her shiver. In worry and fear as much as hope and delight. A sad thing for one once known and admired for the figure she cut on the dance floor.

The loss of that admiration cut, deeper than she'd expected. Its absence left her chilled within. But the lack of dance was worse. She could slip out to the fallow fields only so many times without notice.

People would understand her not dancing tonight, of course. Click their tongues and shake their heads. Pat her hand and speak bland phrases that blended together until she wouldn't remember who'd said what.

Was that so much worse than standing up for the measures?

Again, people would know. A glance at her hair—for no one danced with a head scarf—and the sight of the purple streak would no doubt ensure she lacked for partners, or paired only with those who no longer needed to care or had been deemed incapable of siring or bearing. Most purple-marked avoided festival dances for just such reasons.

Quite the come-down for one accustomed to selecting among many. The flirtations set up during festival dances usually comprised a third of the evenings' pleasures.

But not all.

The joy of dance itself remained. The linking of movement and music. Weaving among others to make a dance of many into something bigger than each alone. Finding ways to express deep, sure feelings for which words alone were inadequate and incomplete.

The chant shifted to a new song, also familiar. A list of summer blessings, from the greening of the fields to the arrival of chicks and piglets, calves and kittens. Long summer evenings leading to warm nights.

Again, her legs and hips shifted, muscles tensing and relaxing as she swayed to the music. Even her torso and shoulder began to circle as much to match the beat as to release the last ache in her back.

Even those such as she could join hands with others and participate in communal dances. Some dancing, however limited, was much more appealing than sitting at the tables through the first of the feast, and then fleeing to stuff her fingers in her ears. Suffering through the vain and impossible task of shutting out all the sounds and thrums of the dance merely because she would lack a partner for the ritual mating afterward.

Maybe she'd dance. Her lips curved into a smile and she stretched her arms up and out again. Let her head roll back on her neck, working out the kinks.

For the love of movement and music, she'd join in tonight and stay as long as she had willing partners.

"Pardon me?"

The soft words broke Gisela's reverie. She jerked, head lowering with a crack and arms clenching against her torso. The bench legs squealed against the floor as she pushed back from the table and rose.

She expected one of the elders returned to seek more names for last visitations and "encouragements" before the festival began.

Instead, a stranger stood in the wide space left by the open double doors. Rather a misty apparition, short with light skin tinged with lilac undertones, sheer-white hair in a braid that fell to their waist, and a thin length of foggy gray fabric wrapped around their body over their tunic. Even the dangle of jeweled bells at ears and the metal girdle at waist seemed dull and hazy. In all, a sight completely unsuited to the summer season. Better fitting for the festival turning from winter to spring than spring to summer.

Gisela blinked, but the figure remained. "May I be of assistance?"

"This is the village council chamber, is it not?" The lilting voice slurred their esses, the very words proclaiming strangeness.

With light, graceful steps, the stranger—likely an old dam— entered. She lifted her skirts ankle high, revealing sandals held in place with numerous thin straps of leather all dyed gray or bearing layers of dust. Her footwear alone marked her as not merely a stranger, possibly from a not-too-distant village for the festival, but a traveler from farther distance. None of the villagers owned a pair of sandals so elaborate and fine. Most went barefoot.

The closer the new arrival drew, the finer her apparel appeared. Gray the over cloth might be, but by choice, for it was clean, the weave narrow, and the soft threads touched with hints of silver. Beneath a thin layer of travel dust, her hair likewise had a subtle sheen unlike the duller appearance of many of Gisela's fellow villagers even after multiple applications of oil and vinegar.

"Yes. Is there someone in particular you seek? The first councilors, perhaps?" Gisela buried her hands in the skirts of her tunic. Her fingers twitched toward the over-tunic she'd previously doffed.

Dark eyes in that narrow-featured face flickered in the direction of the cloth, then fixed on Gisela's face. "Are they available?"

"Not at this time, no, but a meeting can be arranged. Tomorrow? It is the midsummer festival tonight, and the elders will be busy ensuring everyone who needs to attend does so." Gisela gave a sharp shake and closed her mouth. So many words where a simple answer would have sufficed.

The flicker of movement at the doorway drew her attention there. For an instant only, yet long enough to register that two soldiers in knee-length tunics and red cloaks stood to either side of the open doors.

"Tomorrow will be well enough." The outsider glanced at the array of papers covering the table, then sank onto the stool on the far side. "Though we will need to spend the night. Will there be room?"

"Lodgings for the night?" Gisela shuffled the papers into a pile and set them at the far end of the table, out of the stranger's reach, all the while considering the possibilities. Within moments, she shook her head, hands trembling as she settled down onto her own stool. "That will be difficult, very much so. You see there already so many here for the festival, although we might be able to find a corner to lay down a pallet or two." This time she nearly bit her lip when she snapped her jaw shut to stop her own babbling.

The outsider laid hands on the rough wood table, weaving long, thin fingers together.

"More than two, I fear." A touch of compassion shone from her face. "There are eight of us. Myself, my companion, four guards, and two servants."

Worse and worse. So many to squeeze in? Already spare beds and pallets in homes were reserved, to say nothing of the guest houses near full to bursting since two nearby villages had opted not to hold their own festivals this year but instead join in Foleilion's—the better to increase the jollity and fertility all-round.

"Eight?"

Across the table, the dam gave an apologetic smile. "And we come from the summer palace."

Gisela snapped her mouth shut.

The court. The Terparchon and Marchon were ensconced, for the first time in several years, at the nearby palace.

Which explained the outsider's fine attire. A second glance at the door, and the two she'd thought to be petitioners waiting their turn resolved into soldiers on guard. Without armor, yet the combination of short tunics and red cloaks should have registered.

Less than fifty years earlier, the ancestors of the current rulers had given the Escalli sanctuary and permission to build among these stone-ridden hills, and thus ended a decade of wandering. Something Ilburna and her compatriots among the elders never let the council forget—that they owed their current fortune to whatever whim had convinced the rulers of Codaros to let them stay.

The stranger bore no arms or scrolls, nor any sign of message. Yet given where she came from, Gisela might already have caused offense.

"My apologies for the poor reception I've offered you. Please, may I bring you food or drink? Some wine perhaps? Or bread or the first berries?" Gisela sprang to her feet, clasping her hands together.

The two courtiers would take the finest rooms of course, in the head councilor's dwelling. Unfortunately, those were already occupied by councilors of other villages. Moving them into the next best chambers might be done, as they had a clear awareness of their importance relative to court representatives. Yet displacing them in turn required doing the same of others, many of whom would take or cause offense. Although all villages and villagers enjoyed equal station, Gisela and the elders had assigned visitor lodgings based on careful considerations of temperament, trade, and likely level of participation in the festivities.

Blood drained from her face. Her fingers dug into the edge of the table as she held on, trying to stay straight. Even the chamber in which they sat already had been allocated as quarters for visitors.

"Child, do not worry so." The stranger leaned forward and laid a warm hand atop Gisela's chilled skin. "I fear I have not been so forthright as I ought. When I asked for room, I meant to set up tents. We have brought our own lodgings with us. You need not redo your arrangements."

Gisela let out a long sigh, all her body releasing tension with the air. She shook her head, then tucked strands of hair back behind her ears.

"On behalf of the council, and most especially myself as their arms and legs, I thank you." Gisela settled back onto the bench.

She ran through a mental list of possible places to pitch tents. Not the banks of the brook, traditionally set aside for trysting couples. Nor the greensward by the bath house, which was likewise favored for liaisons. The greensward near the trail between villages would be filled with other tents. And the village green, of course, would hold the festivities.

"Perhaps you might accept a nearby clearing? It will be much quieter, although at a slight distance from the village."

"It sounds excellent. Let us begin again." The stranger extended a well-shaped hand with neatly trimmed nails and a gold ring on the forefinger. "I am Amara. Once, long ago, I was one of the Dancing Princesses. Now I serve at the pleasure of the Terparchon."

A former princess and a servant of the Terparchon.

"It is an honor to meet you." Gisela laid her ink-stained and callused hand in Amara's. To her surprise, she found the visitor's hand strong and callused along the writing fingers—and heated as though she ran a high fever despite showing no other signs. Lilac-toned skin was bad for betraying high blood and color, but no such marked Amara.

"And you are?"

The stranger's prompt made Gisela's cheeks flush hot instead.

"Gisela." Her name alone did not seem enough. "Ah, scribe and aide. I serve at the pleasure of the Foleilion Council."

"Excellent." Amara turned Gisela's hand over, lightly running fingers over her muscles and sinews, before letting go. "Though I think clerk and aide is not all you are. Something tells me you are a dancer."

"In Foleilion, we all dance." Gisela ran a finger along the stylus, but managed a smile. "You shall see tonight, if you choose, since you are here at the time of the summer festival. I am sure the councilors would be happy for you and your companions to join the festivities."

"On behalf of my companions, I accept." Amara nodded. "Is it permitted for strangers to join the dancing?"

"Some dances are for everyone."

"And others only for those who live in this village?"

"No, no such restrictions based on residence. Rather, age and fertility." Picking up the stylus, Gisela traced a four-step dance pattern on the bare table. "Anyone may dance at the start; indeed all are encouraged to do so, to honor the Powers and express joy in life. Then, as with other times of the year, we recognize and cherish the full variety of humanity. Sire and dam, and those who are both or neither. We do so tonight as well, until the initial dances. Those divide us into two groups."

A remembered surge of excitement washed over her. Standing in the choice lines, scanning over likely partners, those first festivals when she was young. Her nerves had nearly overborne her, setting her toes twitching and body shifting as new and strange urges pulsed in her blood and bones.

"All will have to choose at the start of the music whether to dance as dams or sires. We shall wind betwixt and between, giving ample opportunity to look each other over. First the very young will drop out, though some of them try to stay until the nursery guardians gather them up and sweep them back to the creche. Then elders step back, and those others who have sired or borne as many children as required and no longer wish to sire or bear more—and eventually those who cannot do either as they go without partners."

Dwindling numbers left gaps—made it easier to see who was left. Which pairs had all but declared for each other, dancing with no one else. Or, at the other extreme, who flitted from one to another leaving laughter or tears behind until they made their final choice.

Gisela had never been either type. In her years, she'd never found a lover early to dedicate herself to, nor waited and teased to the last. Her preference was to cast a wide net during the first winding dance where sooner or later all dancers touched hands with each other. Some pair of hands and eyes always managed to catch her fancy, and by the next dance she'd slip into a firm flirtation.

"Some trysting pairs may slip off early."

Also something she'd rarely done, though more than one partner had tried to lure her away. Given the choice, she danced every dance until the last—and then went joyously to do her duty by her people unknowing it was for naught.

"But even they will usually return for the last dance which is only for those pledged to fulfill their duties to ensure continuity and prosperity of the people."

"It should be a most enjoyable evening." Amara nodded, smoothing her hands over her tunic skirt.

Gisela froze, her own words suddenly running back through her mind. All the things she'd let slip. The information was not secret. Could not be, since all Escalli knew—those here and in the kindred towns nearby. Yet equally, rarely was it laid forth so plain before outsiders. Rumors abounded already about their ribald festivals.

And although Gisela was too young by far to remember, in the years when her people had wandered for many years after the loss of their homeland—often other lands accused them of unbridled licentiousness and turned them away when they sought to settle.

"Do not fear me." Amara grasped Gisela's fluttering hands and pressed them together between hers. "I am made of secrets, and so attract ever more to my keeping. I pledge that any you entrust may be safe with me."

"But you serve the Terparchon." Gisela shivered. "What if she cares? And chooses to throw us out onto the road again?"

"I serve not the ruler but *at her pleasure*." The dam stroked Gisela's wrists. "There is a difference. I do not let secrets slip by chance. If ever there is a danger I will need to share yours, I shall give fair warning. But this type of secret the Terparchon is unlikely to care much about. The more so since she wants something from your council. If they agree, your people may be safer and more secure here than ever before."

"I want to believe you."

Amara smiled. "Then do. And be sure to enjoy the festival yourself. May you make memories to keep you warm for years to come."

"Thank you for the good wishes. I hope you appreciate it as well." Gisela nodded and returned the smile. A chill ran up her spine, making her shiver. A foreboding, from nowhere she could discern, warned that if she did not dance and relish this evening, she might never do so again.

CHAPTER 4

Stevan's empty hands ached for a pen with which to write. Sword to slash. Or hammer to hold and nails to set. In short, any physical labor. An excuse to doff the new travel mantle—dark green with a fluttery ribbon trim along the edges—bestowed on him, along with other items of clothing, before leaving the palace. Although cast-offs, they were one and all finer and less worn than anything he'd owned before.

Quite possibly royal cast-offs, for Amara had muttered about his size compared to the Marchon before vanishing and returning with a pile for Stevan to sort through and try on. Even the simple green tunic he wore beneath the mantle seemed stiffer than his former attire. No matter how much someone had worn it before him, the band around his neck made him itch.

His sandals too were new, or at least new-to-him. Although simple by court standards, the straps binding the soles to his feet bore subtle bronze loops and whirls inlaid into the leather. He'd broken the footwear in on the trip, or they had him. From the second through the fifth days, one of the servants accompanying them provided soft slips of sweet-scented lambswool for Stevan to tuck between leather and skin, to cushion his blisters so he walked in relative comfort. He no longer needed the extra padding, but his feet looked different in the decorated sandals than in his old ones.

How quickly fate turned, from embarrassment at old, well-worn hand-me-downs one minute to discomfort in new clothes the next. Especially as his older clothes would have drawn less attention in this particular time and place.

Foleilion bore little resemblance to the village where he'd spent his youth. He'd run and played over high hills covered with long grasses and scrub brush enjoyed by sheep and goats. Stood atop hills pretending to be one of the giants who tamed the winds. Fished in lakes fed by streams running down from the snow-capped mountains beyond the hills. At night, he'd settle into dark corners of stone cottages to listen to tales from the older fisherfolk, who always bore a whiff of fish scales about them, of the latest attempt at the big catch that got away.

No stone buildings whatsoever here. The only stones visible edged the wells. Instead, the Escalli built with wood and topped everything with thick thatched roofs. Rather than clusters of small cottages, they favored long houses more closely resembling soldier's barracks. All the buildings were laid out to trace a series of three large rectangles around the central square.

The hills boasted trees grown high and thick, save for fields kept clear for planting. No sight of a stream or river anywhere, nor had he seen or smelled anything fishy in any way, though the wells evidently provided ample water.

Nevertheless, the village had at least two things in common with his childhood home. The villagers' clothes were well-worn and bore signs of mending and patching—and everyone worked.

Folk engaged in physical labor wore only tunics, no mantles, although a few wore old-fashioned over-tunics. Most favored ankle-length tunics rather than knee-length, but one and all hitched their skirts up around their knees the better to labor at the gargantuan task of assembling dozens of trestle tables to hold a feast and feed a horde of ravenous celebrants. The luscious smell of meat roasting and pies baking made clear he'd be well fed tonight.

If only he could determine what else he was supposed to do and how to go about it.

Or, more particularly, how to go about it in a discreet manner.

He and Amara had plotted their approach on the march from the palace. Rather, she'd done the plotting and he'd nodded his head in agreement. She'd probably something similar often before. Why bother arguing with sense? Too many of his brothers, sometimes even the otherwise sensible Brenn, preferred arguing to accepting others' ideas unless brought to consider them their own.

Such silliness, not that he ever made the mistake of saying as much. If something made sense, did it matter who came up with the idea? Or who received credit? Better to be about and doing than wasting time arguing minor points. The more so since Stevan had spent too much of his youth listening to his suggestions be ignored, overlooked, or credited to others.

Brenn accused Stevan of lacking ambition, not without some justi-fication. Stevan lacked a burning need to clamber atop a mountain, pound his chest, and proclaim a great achievement. He preferred the quiet satisfaction of a job well done.

He might have been better off born to the crafting classes rather than to a father hanging onto aristocratic status with his fingernails.

Stevan's background had little to do with the vicissitudes of fortune that had snatched him out of his comfortable role as scribe into the lofty circles of the princesses whose magic protected and shaped the realm.

It merely imbued him with a sense of honor at odds with his task in the village. He longed for pen or sword or hammer. Or an opportu-nity to get in line hefting planks from one part of the green to another.

Anything to avoid setting himself up as bait.

Amara hadn't used that word, but anyone who'd spent their youth fishing would recognize the principles at work.

Stevan was bait for a princess.

He and Amara had only two tasks to accomplish. Find the dancer whose name the Terparchon had managed to not obtain—something that still puzzled him, since she'd known his readily enough and he hardly ranked as high as a potential princess—and ascertain the payment or other arrangements necessary to ensure she returned with them.

Amara had taken the latter upon herself and assigned the former to him.

He hadn't argued then. Now, if wishes could whisk him back in time, he'd do things differently.

Neither of them had realized that while the court celebrated midsummer on the longest day, the villagers of Foleilion followed a lunar calendar and set their great festivities for the nearest full moon.

Hence the questionable fortune of their arrival. The princess-in-waiting must be here, but she was hidden in a crowd.

The green at the center of the village thronged with people young and old, almost all ready to throw themselves into the festival with their whole hearts and bodies. Here and there were grumpy faces and pouts and the other unpleasantness that managed to show on any occasion, but most bore smiles and bright expressions.

More to the point, there were hundreds of lusty young people looking over each other. Promenading before each other. Flirting and flaunting their bodies.

Many of the women and some men took entirely too much pleasure in studying him. One woman licked her lips, eyes dark and intent. Blew him a kiss. Blood rushed to his face.

Any potential princess would find him irresistible, Amara had assured him.

But there was only one here, surely. The ability to draw and channel power ranked among the rarest of gifts. Therefore finding her should be a simple matter.

Hah.

Why hadn't Amara warned him that so many others might also find him of interest? Be willing to act upon it? Anyone would recognize the signs of people ready to celebrate fertility in every fashion.

Men watching women and other men. Women watching men and

other women. Likely if there were any eleee among them, they watched all likewise.

In short, everyone gazing around and making no bones about who they found attractive.

And many not stopping at watching. Flirting. Surreptitious or open caresses. Kisses.

Some weren't waiting until evening. Unmistakable grunts and cries slipped from the occasional pockets of shade between buildings. The smell of sex mixed with that of the laborers' sweat, so that the sweeter scents of baking and roasting overlaid a musky base.

The same took place at court after all, albeit usually with more discretion. No sooner had he arrived than his brother had alerted him to the types of places to avoid unless he wanted to tryst. He'd figured out others on his own.

Stevan idled at one corner of the green with an excellent view of the organized chaos setting up for the feast—and the council chamber doorway through which Amara had vanished. The Terparchon had insisted on sending guards with them, and two stood watch to either side of the broad opening. The servants who'd accompanied them lurked nearby, one holding the reins of the donkey cart bearing all the supplies the royal logistician considered necessary.

Food stuffs. Gifts of clothing to ensure the new princess made a proper appearance when they returned with her. Large tents for shelter a nice touch although he'd spent many nights sleeping out-of-doors wrapped in a thick cloak against the cold.

The fuss he could live without. The cart, marked with the royal insignia—multiple circles forming a sphere that in this case appeared poised and ready to roll off the side even though painted on—drew attention.

Hence the guards, to keep Amara safe.

And him.

Two lurked near him at all times. From an unobtrusive distance, so that he had room to breathe without hot breath falling on his neck. That same space allowed him to pretend they weren't there so successfully he sometimes turned around and nearly tripped over them.

"Here to dance?" A woman his age, maybe a little older, flitted just out of arms' reach. Long dark-brown hair with a bright pink streak fell over her shoulders, reaching to her narrow waist. Her sun-kissed beige skin shone under a sheen of sweat, as she came from the crew assembling trestle tables. The fabric of her yellowed tunic was worn thin to the point the underlying threads gaped in places. She'd hitched her skirts high, tucking ends under the cord serving as a girdle so that she flashed bare feet, ankles, calves, and knees.

"No. That is, perhaps. But I'm here for other things. Thank you."

"Ah, good, we can use a new sire such as you. I'll look for you later."

He drew in a sharp breath, working through the words she pronounced so different than he was accustomed to until the meaning dawned. Did she consider him a bull brought to leave a herd of cows in calf? Surely not.

Before he had time to do more than frown and shake his head, she headed away from the green—but at such an angle that she slipped behind him in the process.

At which point, her hand pressed against his mantle. Found the curve of his buttock.

Squeezed.

"What in . . ." He stiffened and lurched forward, away from the grabbing fingers. Whirled around. The woman blew him a kiss. Then she toddled off on her merry way.

At court, no one ever groped him. Looked? Yes, on occasion, but touched without permission? No.

Both guards appeared likewise taken aback. The elder turned as if to follow and accost the groper, but Stevan shook his head. It might be a local custom.

Might.

He needed the favor of the village leaders if he and Amara were to leave with the princess.

All the same, no need to leave himself open to further molestation.

With a regretful sigh, Stevan allowed his guards to stick closer. Cover his back and protect his backside. Literally.

Alas, that meant drawing even more attention.

Back stiff, Stevan re-ensconced himself in his former spot with a view of the preparations and council door.

Flowing cloth captured his gaze, as pairs of mature villagers paraded along the assembled trestles. Unlike the younger workers, they wore mantles in bright colors over their tunics. At each table, two unfolded a long yellow-and-red striped cloth to cover the wood. Behind them, their fellows with baskets efficiently laid out flats of bread to serve as edible plates. Rather than simple roundels in golden brown, each had a medallion of color at the center. Reds, blues, and greens predominated, with the occasional purple and orange.

Although the fittings and fixings were simple—rough boards, unleavened bread, and tunics and mantles with few ribbons or other pieces of decoration—the village boasted an astonishing array of color. Far more than the almost-equally poor manor in which he'd grown up.

Even the people bore color—every one had a streak of some contrasting shade in their hair. The older favored greens and blues, while the younger boasted shades of pink and red with the occasional flash of purple.

A slight cough from close behind had him whirling around, hands reflexively slipping down his back to protect his buttocks from another attack. He snatched them away to dangle stiff at his side as Amara moved closer. Her guards melded with his. In whispered phrases, the latter updated the former as to the earlier incident.

His ears burned hot. He sighed as the villagers shifted to make more space around them.

"Any news to share?" Amara tilted her head to the side in a birdlike gesture.

No twinkle lurked in her eyes or twitched at the edge of her lips. "No."

She nodded, turning to view the scene and smile at the cooks beginning to march immense platters heaped with meats and grilled vegetables around the green. Cheers followed the procession, the more so as the first to be served were children at the low tables set up for toddlers to those just below the age of consent.

Stevan smiled too, particularly at the youngest trying so hard to imitate their elders and wait for the food even as their eyes and hands betrayed them. The savory smoke rising from the platters made his stomach rumble, and no doubt theirs as well.

"We're to sit with the council at the high table, but before we join them, a piece of news first." An even broader smile stretched her lips wide and her eyes were alight. "I think I may have found our princess."

"So fast?" His neck ached as he whipped his head around as though he, too, might spot her in a moment. None of the many women caught his attention in particular. "Then when may we leave?"

"You're not fond of this place?"

"It's no worse than where I grew up, but . . ." His backside still felt the imprint of unwelcome fingers. "Very different."

"Indeed." Amara steepled her fingers together and rested her chin upon them. "I forgot Foleilion is an Escalli village, or I might have delayed us on the road rather than push for speed."

"That makes a difference how?"

"Have you never heard of the Escalli?" she asked.

"Not that I can recall."

"Ah, yes, you're from Silver Hills. Far enough away to pay less attention to the doings in the deep valleys. Permit me to illuminate you inasmuch as I can, as certain topics are best avoided."

"Please." He nodded.

"In the time of, oh, most likely your grandfather, the Escalli controlled a small territory." Amara shifted to face the east and rising moon, her back to the slowly setting sun. Gazed over Stevan's shoulder into the distance.

"A lovely, fertile spit of land circled on three sides by the Omirisi River just before it emptied into the sea. Unfortunately for them, a series of earthquakes shook the land. Destroyed their homes completely and left the earth in such ruins that rebuilding was impossible. They tried, but the first buildings they raised lasted only days.

The second attempt at rebuilding turned to ruins in even less time. Everywhere Escalli set foot, the land shook until the survivors were forced to flee. They had a certain reputation for licentiousness, or so folks said. Rumors flew that this had drawn the earth's rage upon them and their destruction was a warning to all. Hence few rulers were willing to let them settle in their territories. At length, the Terparchon and Marchon offered the Escalli these lands here—largely overgrown and untenanted then—on condition that they pledge never to roam, and adapt their laws and customs to abide with ours."

"And they agreed?" he asked.

The shadows in Amara's eyes suggested she didn't consider the bargain fair.

"They had little choice." She shook her head, white braid snapping back and forth. "And they valued their people above their land."

"That speaks well of them."

"Yes, though, you should know they value the good of the many— at least of their own kind—above the interest of any one person." She pointed her chin at caressing couples among the masses gathering for the feast. "Their reputation for licentiousness derives in no small part from their insistence that all sire or bear at least two or three children to be raised in general for the common good."

"Interesting." Stevan took a second look. Many kissed and touched with affection, so far as he could tell. Yet at least two men and one women showed signs of tolerating rather than welcoming the caresses. Perhaps they were driven by the need to contribute offspring instead of delight in their partners. Beneath his robes his toes twitched and he swallowed in an attempt to dispel the small lump forming in his throat.

"They do not believe in marriage between individuals, although they accept and respect those people among them who prefer limited partnerships. Or who prefer couplings guaranteed never to produce offspring. Except on their quarterly festival nights, when anyone not yet known to have done their part in ensuring the people continue is expected to find someone by the last dance and go off to attempt their duty."

Her meaning hit him with all the subtlety of a hammer. The woman who'd groped him had indeed considered him in the same manner as she would a sire—available for breeding. No care for forming a connection with him. Merely a transactional desire to engage in impregnation and have him depart.

"But you have located the princess already. So we can retire to the tents and return tomorrow to ask her to go with us?" He pasted a polite smile on his face. The neckline of his tunic seemed suddenly too tight.

"You do not want to stay for the dances?" The light in Amara's eyes and tilt of her head suggested she teased.

"The dances, yes. Not necessarily what follows. If I am going to sire offspring, it will not be until and unless I can maintain them and take part in raising them. I would not leave a child behind, perhaps to be neglected." He snapped his jaw shut. An urge welled up within him to let more words spill until she understood in full how little the prospect of siring and walking away appealed. Holding his breath, he counted to ten—a way to resist the tendency to share with her more than he should. Beads of sweat rolled down the sides of his face, despite the slight cooling breeze rising as the sun fled the sky.

"That may disappoint many here." Amara tapped his arm, a gentle touch that eased the urge to share more.

"I am sure others will be happy to save anyone from suffering loneliness for long." He crossed his arms over his chest, mimicking her earlier actions and gesturing with his chin at the many eager young men among the festival goers.

"Though you may dance without moving on to mating after."

"I may?" As though he needed her permission. Senior to him in age and rank though she was, there were some things no one could command. Then his eyes lit on a young man, little more than a boy. A woman whispered in his ear as she stroked his head, arm, and chest. His shoulders slumped, but he made no move to shake off her touch. Amara could not command Stevan in matters of the heart or groin, yet clearly the elders of the village had no compunctions about mandating the actions of their people.

"I hope you will. Join in the dance, not the mating—unless you so wish—and see which woman most draws your attention and vice-versa." She spread her hands wide. "If it is the same woman I suspect to be our princess, we may be doubly certain we ask for the right person when we bargain with the village elders."

Across the green, a drummer began a steady beat. Soon all the people began clapping to the same. Stamping, too, until the very earth beneath their feet moved to the steady, insistent cadence.

The moon rose fully above the horizon, and a great shout rose. Three runners approached the high table with blazing torches held high. Exchanged bows. Then ran in great loops around the green, lighting torches as they went. Whatever the torches held, it wasn't any wood or kindling Stevan recognized. These burned with a soft white light, miniature versions of the moon, and gave off a musky aroma that set his body thrumming in unexpected ways.

Sometimes, dancing alone satisfied his need to move. On other occasions movements aroused and built desire. This whole night was meant to accomplish that for the villagers, but it had an effect on him as well.

Particularly as a form in the shadows farther down the green caught his eye. Even with the bright moonlight and mirrored torch-light, he couldn't make out her features. Nevertheless, something in her way of moving summoned an urge to dance. To meet and twine hands. Her hesitant steps gave an impression of grace, sorrow, and a seed of hope.

"Good. I'm glad you've agreed." Amara clapped a hand on his shoulder. "But first, come and meet the council and eat. You'll need fuel to dance."

The woman had vanished back into the shadows. Stevan followed Amara, the guards in turn behind them, but he kept glancing over to seek her in the darkness. If he couldn't find her there, though, surely he would in the dance.

CHAPTER 5

Gisela waited for the drums to start. Her heart pounded in her chest, hot blood running in her veins. Bright moonlight and dark shadows reduced most color except the blazing orange and red flames of the bonfires burning in each corner of the square. Smoke from the fires spiced the air with a golden scent reminiscent of fall's splendor. Of the season of bearing fruit—but this was not autumn. Rather, summer still lay ahead, during which all that bloomed in spring might dream of ripening into autumn. None yet knew which fields and crops would flourish, and which wither and die.

Grim thoughts with which to begin the celebration, but apt nonetheless. Among the last to arrive, she'd barely tasted the feast. Didn't even know for certain what she'd consumed, save that the last sweet had been drenched in honey. Drops still lingered on her lips. The air was redolent with smells, from the foods laid out to the scents with which some adorned themselves, to the more basic element of sweat —it all mixed into a giddy, dizzying whole that she associated only with well-attended festival nights.

A simple unbleached tunic hung from her shoulders, gathered at the waist with a braided cord. A similar cord at the nape of her neck bound her hair back so it became a tumbled fall rather than cascading around her. No other adornments, not even an over-tunic. Nothing save a thin layer of cloth covering her skin. She rubbed the goose bumps lining her bare arms as the sun slipped from the sky. Delicately stretched her legs and ankles. Ss soon as the dancing started, she would warm up.

For however long she managed to dance.

At least the earth remained warm beneath her bare feet.

The cords binding her waist and hair matched the streak dyed into her hair.

Four others so marked had risen for the dances as well. They clustered together, well behind the more forward array of people who danced as potential dams of children and opposite the line of those who danced as potential sires. Under the full moon its light multiplied dozens of times over by moon-touched torches burning atop wooden poles, the purple cords had the glitter of a brook or river coursing down to the sea.

On most nights when Escalli danced, those who participated did not break into distinct groups. Rather, everyone formed a single joyous mass tackling whichever dances they preferred or could convince the musicians to play. Anyone might lead who chose to, or follow. What mattered most was joy and music.

But tonight had multiple purposes.

To render honor to the moon.

To farewell spring and welcome summer.

And to ensure the strength of the people through conception of future generations.

Honor, farewell, and welcome came first, as was proper. Sire or dam or both or neither, old or young or in-between, the first dances were meant for all.

Nevertheless, people were forced to sort themselves into two categories for the dances tonight. Any incapable of bearing or siring children might pick a line, but must take the last places.

Across the green, those who danced as sires this night gathered into a long, twisting line. The order of dances was fixed and would not vary, not for a festival night. A chain dance to start, to let the dancers view each other. Each succeeding set would split dancers into ever smaller groups until all who wished found their match.

Gisela braced herself to be cut out partnerless by the last set.

Nevertheless, the sires opposite compelled her gaze. She could pretend, after all, that the last year had never happened and she still danced with her hair streak dyed pink. Imagine anyone opposite was still a possible partner. Even search for the red streaks in sires' hair that denoted proven ability and acknowledged offspring as though that still mattered to her. Fancy taking a chance on an unmarked sire in hopes he proved a good dancer and virile to boot.

In the end, what she wanted most this night was a good dancer. Grace, movement, and the alignment of bodies to music.

The pink- and red-streaked fertile dams whispered and giggled. Their gazes lingered on their equivalents among the sires.

Gisela skipped signs of fertility and searched instead for sires who moved even though the music had yet to start. Those who lived with an internal beat, or heard the earth's heart moving far below them.

In the back stood several who shifted to music they alone heard. The blaze of moon-torches behind them cast their faces in darkness, but she marked their attire—one in an undyed tunic, one in orange, and a last in green.

Then the drums began. A deep thrum, doubled, tripled, all in a steady progression that quickened. Slow to fast to faster to a cacophony as the drummers deliberately lost the shared beat and each went at their own measure.

Utter silence when it ended, save for a babe in arms crying somewhere and quickly hushed.

The council of elders, all eleven of them, formed a procession onto the green. Linked hands in a circle as they gazed outward. Their heads swiveled this way and that as they sought to make eye contact with each and everyone within their field of view.

Gisela jerked as one, two, three stared directly at her. Dampness formed at the corners of her eyes, quickly blinked back. She would not weep. They had not seen her, not truly; it was an illusion. A set action performed at the start of every festival, to ensure all felt known and included.

"We gather." The elders spoke as one.

"We are gathered." Gisela whispered the response with the others. To either side, hands slipped into hers. Warm, living flesh joined into one mass greater than the component parts.

The ritual words flowed over her. Closing her eyes she tilted her head back the better to let the full moon's light likewise wash her clean.

Take our sorrow, share our grief.
Take all bitterness, the better to breathe.
And sure as full moon follows new,
Fill us yet with what you choose.

Mere words, and yet Gisela swayed. Needed the hands holding hers to remain upright, even as she helped her close companions stay on their feet as well. A knot of bitterness remained, tucked in her heart. All the same, she drew a deeper breath, filled her lungs with more air than she had in weeks.

"Now for the dances," the first elder spun off and away from the others. Turned tipsy circles until she ended at the far side of the dams' line and settled into a seat.

"For the strength of the people," the next oldest followed suit, although he wound up crashing into the musician's platform.

One by one, the others took their turn until the square was empty of all save the most recent to rise to the council. They stretched out their arms to either side and whirled in place.

"Let the chain dance begin!"

The drums began a steady beat.

Dams and sires formed two separate lines, members linked hand to hand as they promenaded onto the green until they met right before the musicians' platform. There, the leading sire and dam took hands and pulled each other past—to face the next in line. Extending the other hand, they did the same until the leaders reached the third dam and sire. These they whirled around twice in succession.

Then on.

Shake.

Shake.

Whirl. Not always the third, but randomly whenever the drums gave an extra flourish.

On and on, as all dancers joined and formed two intertwining circles.

The beat would continue until some random point after the leaders met up for the third time. This meant those towards the end, such as Gisela and her fellow purple-streaked, would make only two rounds of the other line—assuming the lines were of similar length.

She absorbed the vibrations of drums and footsteps against the earth through her bare feet. Watched the sires making their progression and enjoyed, just for this one dance, the illusion that any of them she chose might pair with her after.

A bitter residue in her mouth warned that disillusion and pain would follow, but the dream nevertheless lured her in.

"Do you see the one in green?" A whistled breath escaped the former dam behind Gisela, the very last in line.

Easy to guess which sire she meant. Tall and well-built, with wide shoulders suited for hefting heavy loads. Long dark-brown hair pulled back in a braid to show a broad face with a tip-turned nose and warm-hued skin begging to be kissed and caressed. No streak in his hair to proclaim fertility, but neither was it needed to draw the eye. He moved with comfort. Solid and assured, as though certain he'd never trip or fall or let his partner do so either. Unless the dance called for it. Fanciful though the notion was, he seemed to her a well-grown tree whose branches moved with the wind while his roots went deep.

In all, a most desirable partner. Quite apart from the elegance of his tunic, which clung to his chest, revealing a wealth of muscles, and rippled around his legs.

"From the court." His clothes alone proclaimed his difference. Impossible to mistake the splendor of his clothing.

"Of course." The other former dam chuckled. "We'll not have a chance at him later, but there is no ban on gazing. And who knows, one of us may whirl with him in the early dances. May it be me or even the both of us."

Gisela laid aside thought of him as the tail end of the dams' line finally began to step onto the greensward.

Smiling at every sire whose hand she took, she wove through their line in the winding circle.

Laughed once or twice as she linked arms when the drums signaled times to whirl.

Each sire's eyes flicked to the streak in her hair. Their expressions altered, however minutely. Easy to guess who wouldn't seek her out after the first dance.

Yet always, *always*, some thread of her awareness tracked the sire in green. Counted down the hands and whirls as he drew nearer. Three away. Two. One.

Then there they stood, face to face.

Only a heartbeat, yet every element of their meeting imprinted upon her as though they existed apart from time for that one, long breath.

He stood a head taller than her. She tilted her head back. A light sheen of sweat dewed his skin, mirroring that on hers. The bright, silvery moonlight leached color from his skin, rendering him in tones of gray. Somehow his eyes retained a glint of color, rich amber that warmed her as they exchanged gazes.

Her chest rose and fell as she dragged in air. His gaze skipped from her eyes to her lips, down to her breasts and the thin linen covering them, and then back up to mesh with hers. She didn't look away from his face at all. Her hand stretched out to wrap around his.

Instead of meeting hand-to-hand, he reached further. Gave an older form of greeting as he cupped her elbow in his hand and supported her arm with his. His tunic sleeve had fallen back. So too did hers as she shifted to match his lead and wrap her hand around his upper arm for the time needed to pass him by.

Skin to skin, hand to hand, arm to arm. Bright warmth bloomed in her, rushing from head to toe and back again. A shock that made her start. His fingers tightened, giving support. Their heads turned in unison, maintaining eye contact as their bodies passed. Shoulders brushed.

A second shudder rippled through her, cold and unwelcome, as they had to let go to continue the dance.

Her breath came in pants, shallow and ill-matched with the beat of the drums as she took the hand of the next in line. Equally tall and well-made, if not so well-dressed, nothing about him stirred her blood—particularly when his glance stopped at the streak in her hair and proceeded no further.

Without making eye contact of any kind, their hands nearly missed the shake. Skin brushed skin, callous and passing, and then they both moved on to others without caring who they'd left behind.

She waited until the circle progressed at least a third of the way further before daring to rip a second's focus away from those ahead to glance across.

Discovered him glancing back at that same instant.

Eyes met.

A spark, unseen, passed between them. Set her blood ablaze with rippling energy.

Gisela turned away first, heart thudding fast and hard in her chest. She'd have one more chance to touch him—clasp arms or whirl— before the two line leaders met and the dance ended.

The others who passed between them as she circled her way back towards him became a blur.

Each time the drums played the extra flourish and she whirled around whomever faced her, her gaze darted off into the distance to find him watching her.

She counted the moments in breaths, heartbeats, and footsteps until they faced each other again.

No extra flourish of the drums. No whirl this time.

Once again, though, instead of hands to hands they matched arm to arm. Watched each other's face the while. Witnessed the catch in two sets of lungs as skin touched skin, warm and soft.

Then wrenched away into cold as the dance forced them on.

When it ended, they both remained on the greensward for the

next. The dancers split into three equal groups for this, each one taking a third of those dancing as dams and those as sires. Chance divided them into separate groups.

His brow wrinkled as he stood in the midst of the sires and dams taking new places for a circle dance requiring smaller numbers.

By custom she should remain with the third into which she'd been divided. But some shifts always took place, as sires chased dams and dams sires, and those caught in lust ensured they were in position to pursue the objects of their affection.

She took advantage of one such, making her move with discretion and efficiency. An instant before the music struck up again—this time a flute and fiddle joining the drums—she slipped from her previous group into his. Few noticed, or cared. They'd written her off already as object of interest or competition. Fair enough. She knew her place.

But she could enjoy his company, presence, and the chance to link arms for another dance or two.

He was a quick study. When the next dance required division into groups of nineteen, it was he who made the move to remain in proximity to her.

A still, small, frightened voice within warned that he might be intrigued by someone else and his continued closeness to her mere chance.

She squashed it, refused to listen. They had made a connection given the way his mere gaze saw and knew her in some deep way. Tremors rippling through her body and blood heated her cheeks. The fancy struck her of being a bird free to flutter and dance on the wind, yet always returning to rest in the branches of his tree as he gave her roots and a firm foundation.

Under the bright light of day, such a fantasy would dissipate as quick as steam escaped a boiling pot—but the full moon bred dreams and nightmares. She'd lived enough of the latter to allow herself to enjoy the dream this once.

She laid her hand in his again, and again, and again as they twined through intricate figures. He stumbled a few times at the start, the forms of this dance being strange to him, but he picked them up with speed albeit less grace than before.

Gave her a smile as he caught a misstep half-made and corrected it.

For that moment of brightness and as many more as she might drink, no matter how short it lasted, she would not refuse or deny.

Not when the dancers rearranged into groups of seventeen, thirteen, eleven, seven, and five.

Nor even when he and she, as part of a group of three, wound their way among other such groups. Him gathering all manner of attention, of course, at the center of their trio. A dam with pink hair clutched at his far side, alternately gazing adoringly up at him and smirking at others as they paraded about.

He returned only small smiles to the other dams, and none to Gisela—but the heat in his eyes kept her warm no matter how many times someone trod on her toes or bumped her side, whether in jealousy or simple uncaring.

Or sheer exuberance. This was no time to be holding grudges instead of dreams.

Yet when that dance ended, she let go her illusions.

The musicians called for a break, to rest, while the dancers settled on partners for the last set. Partners of two, one potential sire and one willing dam.

Not her.

Other dams with hair streaked in pink and red hovered around him. Cooed, oohed, and ahhed. She dropped her gaze away rather than continue to stare. They did no more than she might have, as little as a year earlier.

Indeed, she'd enjoyed the hunt before. Surveying available partners, taking charge of finding who she liked, and asking them to dance with her, to music or to the beat of their hearts.

The bitter taste blossomed again in her mouth, but she refused to let her disappointments sour her to the point she frowned on others following the whims of their hearts and loins. Made a silent wish to the moon and earth—powers above and below—that he find a partner truly worthy of him.

She turned away so as not to watch. Took all of eleven steps away from him, whose name she still did not know, toward the tables bearing the remnant of the feast. A slice of honey cake or goblet of wine would help counter the bitter flavor.

Except footsteps against the earth—not hers, someone else's at a swifter pace—reverberated through her. Her heart sped up to match the beat.

Someone tapped her shoulder.

"Excuse me."

No matter that she'd never heard his voice before, she recognized it anyway. Deep and resonant, fit for a sire of his height and breadth.

"Permit me to introduce myself." He laid a hand over his heart and bowed. "I'm Stevan."

"Gisela." She mirrored him, tilting her head back to meet his deep gaze. "How may I be of assistance?"

"You do not wish to dance again?" Stevan stretched his hands out to either side.

"Wish, yes, but you see my hair." She gestured at the streak, without touching the dyed strands.

"I don't dance with hair, but with people."

"Has no one told you what it means?" Any number of red-streaked dams watched them with tightened lips. Some shrugged and went on to pursue other partners. A few lingered, although none quite dared venture into the circle of space surrounding Gisela and Stevan.

"If it marks you as off-limits, then say the word and I will apologize for my intrusion." He planted his feet firm on the ground, almost palpable warmth emanating from him. A faint musk tinged the air, making it almost sweet to taste.

"It doesn't." She drew in a deep breath. "But—"

"Then will you dance with me?" He extended a shaking hand toward her.

Her palm itched to match his. Gritting her teeth, she tried to do her duty. This once, at least.

"You should go with one of the other dams. Any would be happy to bear a child of you."

"That's not why I'm here." He bent close, voice dropping yet every word falling clear into her ears. "It's chance we arrived in time to attend your festival. Or fate, perhaps, though they're a tricky force to decipher. You're the one who caught my eye in the dance. The touch of whose hand made every nerve stand on end. The only one who looks at me and sees more than a means for conception."

"I'm sure the others see you as more than that."

He raised an eyebrow, lips quirking to the side.

"Some, at least." She chuckled.

"If they do, they are going about showing it the wrong way." He laughed as well, though his eyes remained fixed on her. His hand outstretched, still trembling. His head ducked and shoulders rose nearly to his ears. "All I ask for now is someone with whom to dance this evening. Yes or no?"

She should say no. Should send him back to see if another one of the dams could catch him even though he had not expressed a desire to sire offspring. Then again, he said that wasn't his purpose and she believed him.

And she wanted to join as much of the festivities as possible. To feast, but more to let music move through her body and be a part of the great mass of celebrants. No matter the consequences, she would take what he offered. For this one night, let desire take her where it would.

Another spark jumped between them as she laid her hand in his.

CHAPTER 6

*H*ow could an innocent dance seem at once so right and so wrong?

Then again, innocent was probably the wrong description. Stevan's tunic swirled around him as gusts of night air failed to cool his heated skin. Although vigorous, the pace of dancing eased. Instead of twisting back and forth across the green, he promenaded alongside his partner as they wove through and around other couples. The movements required little exertion, so his body should be easy and fluid. Instead, he remained tense and alert.

Blood pounded in his veins. His breath came heavy and deep, thanks to his exertions.

He wiped sweaty palms on his mantle and hoped they left no marks on the soft linen. Though if it stained, better the cloth than risk his hand slip when taking a turn with one woman or another.

Particularly with one. Even when she wasn't close, he knew where she moved in relation to him. Was she the one they sought?

The Terparchon hadn't described the new princess. Nor had Amara offered any details about whom she suspected. He'd formed no mental image in specific. Impossible to imagine who they'd find, given how little the princesses had in common. Short and tall. Slender and full-figured. Of all complexions and demeanors, ages and genders.

All he could assume was that they sought a woman given that the Terparchon had referred to the unknown as "her." Although even that was relatively little help. The Terparchon might have mistaken an eleee for a woman. Eleees comprised a vast variety including male, female, both, and neither. Some were reputedly able to change their bodies: height, breadth, frame, and sex organs. Nevertheless, it was all he had to work with as of yet. On that basis alone, he joined the line of those dancing as men, or sires in the local parlance, in hopes the Terparchon had the "her" right.

Then he'd seen *her*. The princess? Whether or not this woman was the one they sought, everything faded, dwindled, lessened—except for a wary woman carrying an edge of sorrow. Dark of hair save for the bright purple streak running through it from one temple. Shadowed of eye. Light brown of skin. Made of curves that the delicate material of her tunic alternately concealed and revealed.

The touch of her skin against him, when he slid his arm forward to take hers, had set every hair on his body on end.

Gisela. A lovely name, with a hint of mournfulness which suited her, though he hadn't learned her name until after the first dances.

Ripples of pleasure shot through him every time they touched, even so little as a brush of fingers.

The fiddle and flutes overrode the drums now, melding into a light melody and counterpoint—albeit one with a sensuous edge. Or perhaps that came only because the tune paired with dance steps that teased, taunted, and tempted.

Forward and back; now a brush of hands, then apart.

Right and left; gaze deep into eyes then turn away.

Tap toes against the ground, then swap places with the couple promenading the opposite way.

At least for the grand promenade, couples marched together. He wrapped one hand around Gisela's, high in the air, and laid the other at her waist. Her free hand rested over his. His fingers felt no chill, not under her touch and so close to her breast and hip. Only thin, gauzy layers of linen separated skin from skin.

A sweet flowery perfume wafted from her hair, sending bubbles of delight through him as though he'd drunk too fast and too deep of the most effervescent wine ever fermented though all he'd imbibed earlier was watered wine.

One of the elders at the table had muttered something about this being a night where inhibitions might be lowered, but villagers still needed to *choose* to do their duty. Only a few appeared close to getting drunk—and they weren't among the dancers now.

Dozens upon dozens of couples paired off and filled the green in a massive array of twisting lines and swapping places. Mostly men and women, though here and there women embraced women and men men.

Some partners leaned into each other, bodies aligning along legs, torsos, and arms. Others maintained a slim distance, enough for wisps of air to pass between. Though he'd have readily acceded should Gisela lean into him, he made no protest when she kept a degree of distance—except where hands pressed close.

Strange, that he was supposed to be the bait to call the potential princess. The lure she couldn't resist only to become enraptured instead.

Perhaps he'd failed in his mission. Turned it inside out.

Then again, entirely too many women had seemed enthralled with him earlier. They'd oohed and ahhed over his shoulders and arms, torso and legs. Hands had hovered a little too close to certain parts for his comfort.

The grope hadn't been repeated, though it was a near thing on a few occasions.

Yet so many of those women spent their gazes and attention on his body, without lifting their eyes to meet his.

None had asked his name. The whole time he'd spent in the village thus far, only a few of the elders had bothered with that detail.

Even Gisela hadn't enquired.

But she met his eyes. Watched him. Responded to him, seeming as bemused and light-of-head as he.

And then, with a sorrowful cast to her face, tried to slip away.

Leaving him to pursue, which he had.

And she'd said yes.

The question remained, was she the one for whom they searched?

A faint aura of energy surrounded them as they danced. Barely there, manifesting as little more than a distant haze—and that only glimpsed out of the corner of the eye. Likewise, each time he touched her anew, a jolt of connection rattled him from teeth to toes. The very air took on a giddy zest.

In all, an experience quite reminiscent of dancing with the Terparchon save for two major differences.

He didn't worry displeasing Gisela would result in threat of torture or dismissal.

And, more pleasantly, his body responded to her closeness with eagerness. A development as welcome with her as it would have been unwelcome with his ruler. Though he wished his flesh less active on the dance floor. The appearance didn't matter; he was hardly the only man in this position. All the same, certain types of movement made the loincloth under his tunic chafe in unpleasant ways.

Unfortunately, his very response to Gisela raised concern he was allowing himself to be led by his lesser head rather than his greater.

Such a torment, sliding this way. Deciding he had guessed the princess right, then doubting himself, and back and forth.

Until the moment he turned in the dance and spotted Amara, seated on a bench, with her back resting against the edge of a table. Hands tucked in her lap as her plain gray robe spilled around her. Her shoulders slumped and head tilted down and to the side. Nevertheless, she watched the dancing with heavy-lidded eyes.

Catching his gaze, she smiled. Lifted her hands, palm to palm, and kissed the tips of her fingers. A simple thing, soft and radiant as a beam of moonlight.

Amara approved, had identified the same woman. His judgment he might doubt, this being his first time on such an errand, but not hers.

Freedom from worry allowed him to luxuriate in the remaining dances. Each brought couples closer, and involved less contact with others. From winding up and down long aisles of other couples, they dwindled to a group of eight dancers forming a square.

Then two couples opposite each other. Making slow exchanges of partners, with ample opportunities to glance over one's shoulder and stare into one's original partner's deep brown eyes.

The music slowed, all but one of the drummers dropping out. The remaining beat became less audible and more felt in the pulsing of blood in veins.

At the last, only the two of them existed. Dancing alone, even as every other couple moved apart. Arms entwined. Bodies aligned so that they constantly brushed each other without lingering anywhere long. Yet they barely moved, their dancing restricted to a small oval.

She turned her head, hair flipping and spilling over his hand where it grasped her shoulder. A few steps later, her hand slipped behind his back and brushed his braid. Her shiver made him do the same.

Hands brushed.

Her breasts swayed against his chest.

A brief, promising sweep of her hips pressed against his, only to immediately withdraw.

The next he knew, the music ended.

A luminous, moon-touched fog rolled out of nowhere to cover the green. It parted just enough to curve around them—and left the air open above them for the moonlight to pour down.

A moment out of time, for the two of them.

Under such a light, not even the shadows in her eyes might hide her desire from him. Nor, likely, his from her. Though it was not desire alone rising in him, but something else entwined with it. A connection. A surety that where she went, he would always wish to follow. Or lead, only if he might find her ever by his side.

Surely she felt it, too. She licked her lips, leaving a glossy wetness behind.

"Where would you like to go?"

He fought to keep his hands steady as he held hers, braced her. "Where is there to go?"

"Down by the brook, or over near the bath house. Or my chamber, though it is a very small afterthought. Little more than a cranny tucked into the edge of one of the elders' homes." She laughed and gave a deprecating shrug. "Filled with the bed and all the scrolls that do not remain in the council chamber."

Joy flushed through him, following the beat of his heart along every part of his body. The air between them heated, giving off a sultry scent that seeped into the fog until he inhaled it and found that, too, sent thrills through him.

Pleasure doubled by her quiet interest. The ease with which she pressed herself against him.

This he desired with all his heart, soul, and most especially body.

But his mind declined to let go and become so entranced.

Were he merely a passing stranger, he might have stayed and found some way to woo her.

He wasn't.

All the worry he'd let slip before, about whether or not she was the princess, now raced back. She was or would be a princess.

Any offer she made to him now was on the understanding that he didn't belong here and would leave soon.

Only he and Amara knew that tomorrow, or the first opportunity afterward, they'd bargain with the council and Gisela for the right to take her away from everything she'd ever known, her home, her family, her place.

Drop her in the court as fresh blood.

She'd be alone, except perhaps for Amara and for him who had little influence even though he'd made an unexpected leap to a degree of prominence. Moreover, she'd also endure the cynosure of most eyes as she catapulted into one of the most powerful positions in the country.

A position that the previous occupant left unwillingly, possibly due to malfeasance on someone's part.

Mind over body cooled his lust enough, alas, to continue along that train of thought. Something of his concern must have passed to her, for she took a step back. The movement allowed air between their bodies—chill in comparison to flesh on flesh.

"Do you want to go apart and lie with me?" She asked, head canting downward. A sheaf of hair fell to conceal half of her face.

"More than I can say." He brushed the soft strands back, tucking them behind an ear. "But I fear you may regret it, if not tomorrow then soon after."

"It is more likely you'll regret." She took another step, her shoulders hunching inward and fingers twining with her skirts rather than his hands.

The haze in to the air began to sour, wine turning to vinegar.

"No, I want this." He grabbed one of her hands and laid it against his chest. "But this is not the time or place. I . . . we do not know each other well enough yet." He brushed a finger along her face. It came away wet. "I did not come here by chance, as you will learn soon enough."

"If you regret your choice, that is your right. You are free to make another." She waved at the fog surrounding them. "Leave me to seek and you will find."

"No need to send me elsewhere." He blew out his cheeks and sucked in sour vinegar-flavored air. "You know who I am, surely, or at least from where I came?"

"From the summer palace." Her fingers stroked the fabric of his tunic. "No one from here would have cloth so fine."

"And that is why I must wait, until my business is done. Ask me again when the moon next is full and I'll give a different answer." He pressed her hand between his, willing her to understand. "Say yes so fast your head spins."

"If you're here." A bitter laugh escaped as she turned her head away.

"Wherever you are, there I will be."

She nodded, but, as she slipped away from him, he knew she didn't believe.

CHAPTER 7

Gisela woke cold and alone. Beneath her, layers of grasses stuffed into a woolen mattress cover kept the chill of the earth away. The aroma of sweet herbs still wafted up from the grass, gathered from the first spring harvest. She'd pulled her winter cloak over to keep her warm, and wore her oldest tunic—no longer fit for public—to protect her skin from the coarse wool cloth.

Which somehow had ridden up in the night and left her toes exposed. Cold toes meant cold from toes to nose. Or so one of the nursery guardians used to sing when she was small and still tucked into bed at night. The old dam would bop Gisela on the nose, then run her hands down to Gisela's toes and ensure the cover was securely tucked beneath them. A complicated matter, back then, for younglings in the nursery usually slept four or five to a bed. The guardian preferred to arrange them so the tallest lay at one end and the second tallest at the other. Tuck the covers under their toes, and odds were all the children would make it through the night warm enough. Unless someone tossed and turned too much.

Gisela had tossed and turned last night before slipping into sleep. How right the old guardian was, for little bumps lined her arms and legs and a chill had settled into her bones. Had she a bedfellow this night and morning, particularly a nice warm sire as tall or taller than she, he would have weighted the cloak so it couldn't slip from over her toes. Or, if it had, she could've warmed her feet against him.

If he woke from the chill, well there were things they could do together to ensure both ended warm.

Except, she'd slept alone.

Again.

She hadn't had a bedfellow since dying the streak in her hair purple.

Pride, Ilburna had called it and wagged a finger at Gisela shortly after the change of color. "There's no shame in being unable to bear unless you make it so. All dams reach the point sooner or later if they're lucky enough to live that long. Sires fail in siring too, though they last longer for it takes less out of them. Go find what makes you happy, and tumble any you fancy along the way. Just let them into others' beds if they're fertile and haven't yet done their duty by the village."

Wise words, of course. Ilburna made a point of never being other than wise—albeit heavy handed in sharing her wisdom.

But she'd had time to grow into her fate. It had fallen on Gisela far too early.

Gisela had smiled that day and every other time she received unwanted advice, or at least pulled back her lips and shown her teeth, and been polite to the elder's face. Saved her grumbling about old noses stuck in where they weren't wanted for when off on her own.

When dancing in fallow fields.

Or lying abed—alone.

Except this time she had someone else to grumble over.

Bad enough her choices in bedfellows narrowed down. Worse that she'd done the winnowing. She'd been busy avoiding sires. Preferred the safe route of finding pleasure with the one person who'd never disappointed her in that respect—herself—to the danger of testing the waters with another and then discovering her inability to bear did make a difference.

Understandable enough in the first flush and panic of response, but rejection had become a custom. A habit.

So irritating to have been lured out of that habit.

Tempted.

Enticed.

Only to be declined.

Past experience had taught her how to handle meetings with former and current lovers in all manner of circumstances, from alone one-on-one to in company to encountering along with their other previous and current liaisons. Some might prefer to keep to one bedmate while others dallied as they would, but so long as they were honest about what they had done, were doing, and planned to do, all was well enough. Those who held grudges had less opportunity, and marked themselves as less preferable in the process.

After all, she and her fellow villagers absorbed the same advice from the nursery guardians all through their growing years. Children chanted familiar phrases as they played hop, skip, and jump.

Never promise what you cannot deliver.

Tell the truth whatever it be.

Be angry over a lie, but never over love.

Stevan had promised her nothing with his lips, only with his body and the connection between them.

And *then* declined to follow through.

She'd actually offered and pursued and Stevan had said no.

Oh, he'd made his refusal a matter of poetry. She needed only wait until the moon was full again and he would consent. What good did that do, when they would be far apart? Last night the whole moon had shone down upon them, their blood ran high, yet it all dissolved into nothingness.

How did one greet a potential lover who had disdained one the morning after?

Perhaps by appearing serene and content regardless of the state of her innards and nerves.

As a first step, she rose. Stood in the small free space on the floor in the minuscule chamber to dig through the shelf holding her clothes for the cleanest of her tunics. Her fingers scratched against the smooth board attached to the walls as she extracted a thin, wispy rectangle of gauze. She'd embroidered the neckline during the spring festival with forest green vines, leaves, and deep purple flowers that stood out against the pale lilac cloth. The colors chosen not by chance, though she'd lacked the courage to wear it the previous night.

Then she added a cream-colored over-tunic likewise decorated with vines and flowers although in this case the blooms were of deepest red. It, too, was made of thin fabric. With the council gathered to hear the royal envoys, she could not afford the previous day's laxity in attire.

Sunlight shone through the window in her chamber. Although the air remained cool within, thanks to thick walls, the strong quality of the light hinted that the day would be hot. Already it had dried dew from the grass around the well. Only a bare hint of a breeze trickled through, carrying the scents of oatcakes baking, and burning, in the oven.

With a tinge of regret, she pinned up her hair with a sharp metal pin to keep the curls from bouncing free. Pulling out a nearly transparent length of lilac gauze, she bound it over her hair. Patted her head to be certain no unruly strands had escaped.

In the normal course of events, she almost never wore sandals in summer. But the dam envoy's elegance the day before prompted Gisela to drag out a pair with narrow straps. Sitting on the bed, she bound them around her feet and ankles. As an honor and reflection of the importance of the visitation.

An upthrust of bile filled her mouth, and she stopped with ties dangling from her numb fingers.

How could she have lost herself so thoroughly the day before? Amara had been so kind and gentle even as she drew Gisela's secrets from her—but spilled none of her own. Perhaps the councilors had pressed her during the feast, but Gisela had had the best chance to discover in advance why the rulers had bothered to remember their existence.

And she'd failed.

Only two envoys and four guards, so surely they had not come to take back the village and the land? Perhaps to extract further taxes. Bundles of tally sticks rested in a trunk at the foot of her bed. Tied up with scraps of twine and ribbon, they documented the village's increasing prosperity and growing population.

Why else they might have come?

Maybe the royal guards needed more soldiers and sought to take a human tithe alongside the coins and goods that covered taxes. Though why send courtiers to choose fighters?

Moreover, Amara had said she served at the pleasure of the *Terparchon*, not the Marchon. And war was most definitely the province of the latter.

Then again, Stevan had not said at whose pleasure *he* served. His grace in the dance, and quickness at picking up steps of those dances unfamiliar to him, suggested the Terparchon.

With a deep breath, Gisela turned on her heel. Winced at the unfamiliar bite of the sandals against the sides of her feet. Then scurried out to ensure all was in readiness for the council and their visitors.

She bustled about making arrangements in the first burst of the day, until her feet grew tired.

Turning to head to the council chamber, Gisela had to throw out a hand to brace herself against the side of the cookhouse, to keep from barreling into Ilburna

The older dam also braced against the building with one hand flat on the wide planks. The other wrapped tight around the head of her cane. She'd pulled three over-tunics over the first layer, all in bright shades. Red. Dark green. Yellow. The uneven layers of cloth left corners untucked here and there, and gave her the look of a fennel complete with fronds of white hair falling loose to her waist. A single head cloth, little more than a length of yellow matching the outermost of her tunics, covered her temples and forehead but left the rest of her head exposed to air.

"Ah, good, you are not slugabed." Ilburna lifted her cane. Stretching, she planted it with a thud right next to Gisela. "There's time enough to lay about another day."

"That's not what you said yesterday. Do you not remember?" Gisela retreated, and whirled around to pace the elder. She knew better than to offer assistance unless asked for it, but mimicked Ilburna's tone and delivery. "Sleep well, sleep long, but sleep not alone."

"For the youngest whose blood boils in their veins." The former dam jerked her chin in agreement, then leveled her gaze at Gisela. "But you have reached the temperate age, that of wisdom matched with agility. Enjoy it, and be sure to make the most of it. You worried me some, with your fretting, but, since I saw you join the dance again last night, I have less concern."

"If I am at an age of wisdom, what may be said of you?" Gisela spoke in the most dulcet tone possible.

"I live in ice. Even in high summer, I cannot be warm." Ilburna thumped her cane again as she hobbled forward. "This is the time, in truth, that it is good to have many bedfellows. If only they did not steal my covers!" She paused in her progression and tilted her head to the side. "Perhaps I shall seek out more cats. But that is a matter for another time."

Most of Ilburna's feline friends preferred to bask in the morning and wait until later before mouse hunting. Nevertheless, Gisela flicked her head and searched for any sign of their encroachment—and inevitable demands for attention, amusement, or food, or all at the same time. "More cats."

"Perhaps. But these people from the court, we must hear them this morning." Ilburna shook the hand holding the cane at Gisela. "Go, go, to the cooks and bakers, to the kitchens and store rooms. The freshest and most choice leftovers of last night's feast must be laid out for their morning meal."

"This is being done." Gisela folded her hands before her. A bit of flour yet dusted the edge of her right hand, from when she'd tested the suitability of a day-old bun.

"And those visitors who had permission to lay their bedrolls in the council house, they must be on their way and the chamber swept and aired." Ilburna thumped another step on her way.

"Done and done."

"Fresh flowers placed on the tables?"

"Also underway, to be delivered with the food and drink."

"Truly you are a treasure." Ilburna managed to smile and speak most politely while imbuing her words with a distinct edge of irritation.

Gisela hoped someday to have such control over voice and expression. The elder was her idol in that, if not in temperament.

Although despite her irritation, Ilburna had a distant look to her eye and a flicker of a smile played about her lips regularly. "And what about appointing someone to escort the courtiers from their tents to the council house?"

Stopping short, Gisela stood with her mouth half-open.

"Close." Ilburna tapped a finger on the underside of Gisela's chin, her smile now wide. "No sense trapping flies."

"But . . . they know the way . . ." A gap between two buildings showed the near end of the trail to the clearing Gisela had shown the palace servants the evening before, and left them setting up tents.

"It is a nicety, not to make people find the way even when they know it." The other coughed. "Find someone to do this but do not take it upon yourself, if you don't mind."

"You're in quite a mood this morning." Gisela stepped backward, putting just enough distance to look the other over head to toe. Even wrapped in the multiple tunics and inching her way along, the elder had a lightness to her steps. "Is the news from the courtiers so good?"

"Nothing was spoken out of turn last night." Ilburna laid a finger aside her nose and gave a slight nod. "But Amara let me know, roundabout as it were, that they come here for no ill purpose. Their desire is to conduct a trade of sorts. To take from us something that we appreciate but cannot make use of at its full worth and give ample recompense."

"That's wonderful." Gisela's empty stomach gave a lurch and a sour taste bloomed in her mouth.

Doubt must have shown in her voice or on her face, for Ilburna gave her a sharp look. "You think I would lie? Or mistake?"

"No, never, not you." Gisela shook her head, hard enough her head cloth nearly came loose. "But what could the village have that they would want?"

"Ah, not what my dear, but who."

Pressing a finger against her lips, the elder refused to say more.

Cruel of her. She hobbled off, leaving Gisela ill-at-ease. She should be delighted Ilburna had extracted useful information. A heavy lump formed in Gisela's belly instead. The riddle perplexed her, nagged at her, would not leave her mind as she continued about her errands.

The palace representatives wanted to take someone away with them. For what purpose? Yet that concern came secondary to the question of who.

Had Ilburna shared the news as a courtesy—or a warning?

CHAPTER 8

An ill-night's sleep made for a grumpy Stevan.

How dare the birds sing and wake him so early? Several evidently nested in trees nearby and insisted on calling to each other in light, lilting songs much better suited to full day than early dawn. Their high voices pierced his ears, even when he pulled the wool blanket over his head. This did little enough muffle them, and too much stifled him, so he let the cover slip back under his chin.

His body ached from the previous night's exertions, but it was a minor thing. All told, almost a pleasant sensation wherein he noticed each and every muscle he'd tired in the dance, but none bore more than stiffness. No true pains plagued him anywhere, as in times past when he'd overexerted previously underused muscles.

Though he would ache more if he didn't move with care and ensure his muscles warmed and woke to the day.

He lay on the pallet nude. The soft blue-and-white striped blanket covered him from toe to neck without a single itch or rough spot in the weave. Were he to stretch his arms wide, there was enough fabric to reach from fingertip to fingertip. In a similar unanticipated luxury, a matching cloth covered the pallet below him. Whatever it was made of lifted him sufficiently high off the ground that he didn't feel a single pebble or hard spot below. He hadn't peeked and risked disturbing the careful arrangement, and nor had he asked lest he seem ungrateful, so he didn't actually know what he had lain on. Whatever it was had savory herbs mixed in that discouraged creeping, crawling insects.

Alas, it was also over-soft, even overstuffed—likely to smother him if he rolled over onto his stomach, his preferred sleeping position, so he'd spent the night on his back apart from occasional shifts to right or left.

Lying on his back gave him a too clear view of the slanted tent sides and the line where they met overhead. Much appreciated for the way the expensive layered canvas protected against the dew and wind, yet not made for one Stevan's height. He could not stand up without crouching in some way and mostly had to kneel and crawl about when it was time to enter or leave.

In truth, that discomfort—although unfamiliar—would have made him much more at ease with the whole situation were the tent not covered with ornate decorations. Someone had invested time or money ensuring the sides of the tent bore immense replicas of the owner's family seal both inside and out and thus quadruple embroidered.

Stevan was no mean needle man, able not only repair his clothes but make basic tunics. However much the Minister of Fields and Forests had spent on the tent, Stevan hoped the makers had been adequately paid for their hours of work.

Nevertheless, the very fixings intended to make Stevan comfortable instead left him irritable.

The worst and most aggravating matter of all was his having slept by himself. Completely alone, as opposed to sharing a room, sometimes even a bed, with his brothers when he was a growing child. Then with fellow clerks as he rose in the world. Even when he'd achieved his most recent position, he had to share a room half the time depending on how large the palace in which the court resided.

The tent and pallet were made for two, hence their width and the amplitude of the blanket.

But there was no Gisela with him. He banished fantasies about all the pleasures given up the night before. Shoved away memories of her eyes flashing in delight as he picked up dance moves from her and managed to repeat them in reverse. Refused to ponder how their easy alignment in the dance could have translated into a similar rapport while skin to skin.

The joys of the hand didn't make up for the loss of her beside him. Not even when his conscience turned smug at his moral fortitude, something his stepmother might not have thought possible. But he refused to think about her either, especially not in the same moment as remembering Gisela.

Rolling over, he punched the pillow under his head then slumped against the pallet. The distant clatter outside the tent—footsteps, metal clanging, muffled voices—suggested the servants and guards were preparing for the day. A faint whiff of smoke blew through, carrying as well a hint of tea and fruity sweets baking.

His stomach rumbled. The physical appetite, at least, he could satisfy without morals getting in the way.

From his sideways position, he had a clear view of a small trunk sitting at the far side of the tent. It held the new wardrobe which he'd been gifted, almost all overly ornate and luxurious, if not to the extent of the tent.

Someone had laid out clothing, one of the servants giving him a subtle suggestion of what would be suitable to wear. A blue tunic, almost twin to the green he'd worn yesterday, and a matching mantle embroidered with waves and ocean fishes. A leather belt dyed blue bearing a fish-shaped buckle. Two loincloths topped the other clothes, one in pale blue and the other undyed.

Such luxury, but alas he wasn't suited for this kind of life. In his previous position, he'd had to count his coins and carefully consider before embarking on any expenditure. Still, at least he'd known what niceties came with his position and what he was expected to pay extra for or do himself. He'd even laundered his own loincloths and tunics in his early days of service, when he lacked the means to trade to have someone do it for him.

Now he had risen to the point a servant reviewed and recommended his attire, guaranteed to be clean, and had many options to select from.

So many changes in such a short time, all bringing fears, for the higher he rose the faster he could fall.

Gisela would face these changes—and fears—too. Likely find her new life as strange or more so than he. Would she be willing to let him help as he could? He might not be able to offer much, as he was still learning his new role.

But others could—and more. Princesses possessed power, magical and influential, and were highly sought after as mates and consorts. Whether or not she accepted his assistance, she'd have many people with power of their own eager to help and form alliances. To woo her.

Not so him. Insofar as he was aware, few knew or cared who partnered princesses in their magical dances. Only who they paired or trioed with at the court dances, where all played games of power.

A rustle came from the tent flap, followed by a polite cough.

"Are you awake, sir?"

"Yes." He sat up, letting the blanket pool around his waist. Then flinched as his head approached the slanted tent wall. The air seemed the thicken about him and the tent grow smaller. He hunched his shoulders and shifted closer to the center.

Rik opened the tent flap just enough to slip through sideways. Although a head shorter than Stevan, the eleee entered on their knees so as not to brush their head against the canvas. They'd pulled their hair back in a short, stubby braid of mixed white, green, and brown strands that formed a dramatic frame for their round face.

Selected to accompany the expedition from among the Terparchon's personal entourage, they wore a loose tunic of bright yellow from neck to knee. The color complemented the ochre undertone of their otherwise tawny skin. Intricate embroidery of twining green vines bearing blue and purple flowers covered all edges of the tunic, even the dusty hem, so that it matched and even exceeded most of Stevan's wardrobe from before his elevation.

Being well-mannered and matter-of-fact, Rik had not protested being assigned to care for Stevan. Or Amara, but she'd enjoyed her rank much longer and knew how to handle it, and most assuredly deserved good service inasmuch as she rendered the same to the Terparchon. For his part, Stevan appreciated Rik's quiet guidance— and that they were not of the type to take much advantage of an inexperienced master. Indeed, they waited patiently when it was quite clear Stevan had no idea what orders he should be giving.

This morning, they carried a small tray which they settled within arm's reach of Stevan. It held mug of tea—and a small, shallow bowl of hot water that emitted an astringent-scented steam thanks to the cleansing herbs floating on the surface.

Stevan braided his hair and tied the end, then picked up the top cloth from those provided. Dipped it into the water. Wiping his face with care, he removed the morning bristles breaking through the skin along his neck, chin, and upper lip. Then gritted his teeth against the flash of heat that followed.

Then did a second and third pass in certain spots as Rik discreetly indicated he'd missed them on the first go-around.

Done and cleansed, he took the mug of tea provided with the bowl and drained it to the dregs. The unsweetened fluid left him more awake, and ready to respond to the message Rik had brought.

That Amara would meet him shortly for their morning exercises.

This had him leap to his feet, ducking his head and hunch his back at the last so as not to strike against the tent roof. He grabbed the plain loincloth and wrapped it close in a style offering extra support.

He strode out into the circle laid around the fire pit. His and Amara's tents sat across from each other. Awning strung on either side offered lesser shelter to the guards and servants. Their belongings had been rolled into careful balls wound with twine for the day, save for the one guard who'd been on sentry duty at the tail end of the night and lay snoring under a length of red wool bearing the Marchon's emblem in one corner.

Despite his stomach's growl, Stevan made a wide arc around the fire with the various savories steaming and frying. Nodded to the guard standing watch. Then walked past Amara's tent. A series of patches made a jagged stripe along the top, all having faded at different rates. The sides lacked any insignia, but a subtle pattern edged the front tent flaps with an abstract design.

The first time Stevan had glanced at it, his eyes had traced the intertwining lines of green and blue without end. His body swayed as the blue called to him, so strong and straight no matter how the green swung in loops around.

Amara stretched up onto her tiptoes and covered his eyes with her hands. The sudden darkness sent him whirling and he wound up on the ground in a heap.

Just the memory kept him wary and disinclined to glance too close.

Instead, he looked up and away. If his gaze happened to pass in the direction of the nearby village, so much the better. Distant sounds and smells indicated the villagers woke late to the day even as the camp did. The sun still hung low in the sky, not too warm yet. Although goose bumps formed along his arms, shoulders, and legs, he waited a moment or two.

Long enough to spot the gap between trees where the trail led over to the village. Perhaps Gisela slept still. Alone, or had she sought someone else after he declined?

A light touch on his back broke his reverie.

"That will wait. First let us wake to the day and place." She jerked her head toward the open area behind her tent. Where he wore only a loincloth, she'd covered her body with a plain, unbound tunic that fell to mid-calf and halfway down her forearms. Even so, she shivered. Her limbs seemed little more than bone and thin layers of muscles beneath strained lavender skin although he knew, as the day progressed, she'd grow more flush and rosy. As though surviving the night stole from her and the day gave back.

As soon as they reached the cleared space she started on a course of stretches. No words, just movement.

He fell into the patterns a few beats behind her. This represented progress. The first two days, she'd had to stop between exercises so that he could catch up.

Now the routine had begun to seep into his bones. Starting slow then speeding up and back down.

Feet on the ground, reach high. Arms out, wide, as the branches of the tree. Reach, reach for the sky.

Trace the paths of moon and sun, leaning to the east then the west.

Turn in a circle. Become a bird, with arms rising, rippling. Feel the burn in the muscles as shoulders and back, chest and arms all engage.

Sink low and adore the earth. Belly down, arms and legs up. Roll and ripple again, lifting chest lifting legs. Raise a leg, lower it over the other then back. Same on the other side.

More variations. Lift and stretch. Contract and release.

Sweat covered him, as his exertions warmed the air near as much as the sun rising above. His body became an extension of the earth, all appendages. From easy breathing, he passed to dragging in deep breaths and feeling the muscles of his belly expand to take in a greater capacity of air.

At which point, movement left and he lay prone on the earth his feet and exertion had worn bare. Let a different warmth seep up into him.

A stillness.

Darkness, as his eyes closed. Yet new awareness filled him. Bit by bit, portions of the world impinged upon him. Made him aware of their stillness and movement.

Bees. Flies. Ants.

Birds.

Cats in the woods, hunting.

Dogs in the village.

Humans, many many humans. Footsteps on the earth. Hard here, heavy there, and . . .

Oh, warm and light. Bouncing, yet with a connection to the element below in every press of heel and toe.

Gisela, rising. No sense of anyone near. Just her.

A stiff finger rapped his head.

He jolted, all connection with the earth lost. Rubbing the sore spot with the back of a hand, he rose to his knees. His breath came in uneven heaves. All his earlier grouchiness returned, body suddenly chill with the absence of the earth and the brush of air along his sweaty skin.

"What'd you do that for?"

"You're learning an awareness of the world, that's wonderful." She dropped to kneel opposite him, tunic hem fluttering against the dirt. Only a few glimmers of moisture shone on her forehead. A few strands of white hair had escaped her braid, but otherwise she remained much as she always was. "But it's important never to go so far as to completely give up sense of self as well. Spirits cannot live on wind alone."

Stevan shook his head, her words so at odds with his experience. "That wasn't what I was doing."

"No? You didn't seep deep into earth?" She patted the ground.

"Not deep." A faint ache settled between his shoulders, so he rolled them to keep his muscles loose.

"Then what were you doing?"

"Checking on the future princess."

"Very well." Amara tilted her head to the side and gave a half smile. "You could have stayed with her last night, or brought her to the tent here. I would have turned a blind eye."

"No, it would've been wrong." He pulled back, stretching his arms behind and clasping his wrists. To further exercise his shoulders, true, but also to resist the sudden wish to leap back in time and change his actions. "Not when I knew things about her that she didn't and had no chance of learning until after."

Amara startled. Her mouth open and shut once, twice, three times. Eyes big, she swallowed so hard a big lump passed down her throat. Her head drooped, neck extending and shoulders rolling down.

"I hadn't . . ." Her voice lowered, to a mere whisper. Shaking herself, she returned to her former posture—but with a hint of moisture in her eyes. "Hold that kind of thought when we return to the palace, for there are too few who would agree with you. Even I have lost so much that I did not think as you at first."

"She is the princess, is she not?" Sudden fear rose in his mind, that he'd jumped to the wrong conclusion and Amara had her eye on someone else. That would mean he'd pulled back for nothing. More, he would have to escort the other woman to the palace, and then rush back by the full moon to give Gisela a chance to offer again or offer himself.

One night, nothing more than a set of dances, yet the way they'd matched each other mattered as much or more than the reason he'd come here. Hardly anything he'd have imagined might strike him, but so it had.

"Oh yes, she is a princess." Amara gave a sharp nod, smile kind. "At least, she will be when she agrees."

Stevan hadn't wasted his moral qualms. He would have opportunities along the return trip to court her. By the next full moon—or possibly the one after—she might be ready to offer him a second chance.

CHAPTER 9

$\mathcal{A}$ small gray tom with a demanding miaou insisted Gisela stop and pet him just outside the council house. The general chatter passing over her assured her the meeting had yet to begin. The sun beat down. Other villagers, whether newly awakened or well into their days, rushed by this way and that, raising low breezes and causing dust to eddy around, so she wound up with clothes less clean than before regardless. Still, she was but the council scribe—the attention during the meeting would be upon the councilors, not her.

A trio of other cats pelted from the council chamber with squawks and miaous. As soon as they passed through the doorway, their swift movements slowed to a saunter. The gray abandoned her to join them in a twisting mass of feline irritation.

Gisela stood and let her skirts fall. Brushed at the hairs and dust, then gave up. She grasped the basket handle and slipped into the council chamber. Head down and shoulders hunched, she made her way around the edges to her usual seat. Set her basket down and settled in, then glanced up and saw at a glance one potential cause for the cats' displeasure: there were too many human equivalents to cats in the room for the true cats to have room to pose.

Most council members had much in common with cats. Firstly,

being curious and apt to stick their noses in anywhere. Secondly, enjoying playing with their food or victims. Thirdly and most evident this morning: difficult to herd into place for collective consideration and action.

Gisela had an excellent view of the situation from her place at the side of the chamber. She tucked a blue, down-filled cushion on the hard bench before taking her seat and didn't dare rise again. The cushion cover had worn so thin that every time she rose, additional pieces of down escaped. It offered little protection compared with the thicker pillows set out for the councilors, but was better than sitting the whole meeting on the hard wooden seat.

Her tunics offered little cushioning, but draped well. Her arms rested lightly on the small table. Close at hand sat several tablets covered in thin layers of wax on which to take notes with a stylus. A small pile of documents covered half of the table—tax tallies, yearly balance notations, and, in case there was time after the royal representatives presented their business, scribbled notes of who had and hadn't shown up for the dancing and mating at the feast.

Gisela was not thinking about that last, not a bit. Even when the courtiers in their lovely robes with elegant trim passed through the doorway—the one tall and bright and casting all others into shadow—she was not remembering the night before at all.

Though she might peep over at Stevan as he and Amara greeted the councilors individually and accepted some of the food pressed upon them. Perhaps a ripple of energy stroked up her spine at the sound of his deep voice. Or the hairs along her arms and at the back of her neck stood up when he passed near and nodded in greeting.

That was all. They did not speak.

Instead of glancing his way, she tracked the progress of the eleven councilors who had yet to assemble for business.

Only four of the councilors sat at the table at any given moment —*which* four changing several times. The rest meandered around the room, nibbling on delicacies and scattering crumbs, and talking to whomever they encountered. For they followed the unwritten but often invoked rule of food before business except in the most serious of matters.

Individually, Gisela loved each and every councilor to some degree and found some measure of joy in working with them. Several had served among the nursery guardians when she was young. Two others nurtured her during her blooming years, and dear Fissil taken her as apprentice scribe several years before his wrists and knuckles began to swell with the damp and make writing so difficult and painful he had to give his position over to her.

But even she acknowledged that when they gathered—or worse, one was faced with attempting to assemble them together—they were a thorough pain.

At least Gisela didn't have the task of coaxing them into some semblance of order. That was the right and privilege of the youngest of them, whomever he, she, or they were at any given time. The intent behind the design, according to the nursery guardians who'd raised her, was that all councilors pass through leadership of the council before stepping back to form part of the whole and thus have mercy upon each other.

The idea failed miserably more often than it succeeded. A person had to have a very strong will to make the older councilors bend in line even so far as to sit down and allow the council begin work in a timely manner.

The council as a whole drew only from those who'd passed a minimum of fifty years in life, except during those times when disease or famine or war harrowed the elders.

The four oldest village members still capable of making their way to the council chamber and acknowledging their names claimed seats by right of seniority. Whether or not they required assistance to reach the chamber did not matter, although they did have to speak or sign in their own right when their names were read.

The other seven councilors were chosen for three-year terms, two or three each year, from among all eligible persons by lot. The process always featured grumbling over the result both from those who wanted to be selected and never were and those whose numbers kept coming up whether or not they wished it. Ilburna had the reputation, and record, of spending only one year off the council since turning fifty, even before she received a guaranteed seat by virtue of her age as the third eldest.

Only when all councilors had greeted each other individually and eaten their fill, did the head councilor succeed at convincing them to take their places behind the long council table. Stevan and Amara accepted seats on mismatched cushioned chairs hastily brought from two of the councilors' rooms nearby. Their guards stood watch along the wall.

Villagers and visitors who chose to attend the session sat scattered over long, uncushioned benches and maintained a low level of noise through the scrape of sandals against the wood floor and their eager consumption of the remaining food. Even with the lure of the courtiers and food, the audience ranks were thin. This spoke to a good festival night, leaving many exhausted from their fevered exertions.

But Gisela wasn't thinking about that either, as she refused to dwell on what others did that she did not.

"We gather." The head councilor, Alvi, who also oversaw the mill, wiped sweat from their brow.

"We are gathered."

"Surely every thing's as good as settled, and we've no need to waste dust on it." Dur, the fourth eldest and most crotchety of the councilors leaned against the table, head on his hands. "We can forgo the formalities this once."

All the other councilors began debating the matter until Ilburna thumped her cane hard three times.

"No, we cannot skip the formalities." She glared the others down. "All must be heard through and deliberated with care."

"And then we can vote yes." Dur waved a hand at Ilburna from the far end of the table.

"And then, if you are still of a mind, you may vote yes," Alvi said, before Ilburna could continue.

Their mouth moved without making additional noises, a keen and practiced gesture. The councilors leaned in, as they couldn't read Alvi's lips from where they sat—just as well for Alvi muttered, for the umpteenth time, about looking forward to stepping off the council at the fall drawing of lots.

Still standing, Alvi picked up a small covered bowl from the table and elevated it with both hands. One of the few artifacts surviving from the villagers' prior home, it was plain and unmarked. Nevertheless, it drew the eyes even against the backdrop of Alvi's best over-tunic—a thick purple wool trimmed with black ribbon that partially explained the sweat still beading their brow. The room had already begun to grow warm and close. Gisela patted at the unexpected moisture on her forehead.

"Let us remember and cherish that which we have, for the moment that we have it." Lifting the cover of the bowl, Alvi blew lightly. Several glittering motes of dust flew out to dance in the air. "We meet."

"We are met." The councilors nodded.

"This morn we consider and deliberate with care upon a proposal from the Terparchon. Shall we permit her representatives to speak for her?"

Amara rose and moved forward to stand before the council. Stylus stiff within her grasp and tablet steady, Gisela prepared to take notes.

"I come to you from the Court of the Terparchon and the Marchon, under whose care you live." Amara turned in a graceful circle, her arm gestures encompassing all in the room. "Who in their wisdom oversee all that lies between the eastern hills and the western river, the northern fastness and the southern sea. Their care encompasses this village along with very many others, great and small."

Even as she worked her stylus into the wax, Gisela rocked to the rhythm of Amara's formal declarations.

"Now, as all may know, the land has enjoyed immeasurable peace and prosperity these many generations. This is due, of course, to the wise guidance and leadership of our rulers—but also to those who serve them and in particular to the twelve Dancing Princesses."

Amara lifted her hands over her head and clapped once. Lifted a sandaled foot and pointed off to the west.

The pose sent a quick chill through Gisela.

"No doubt you have heard of them, but I come here to say to you that whatever you have heard, good or ill, is but a shadow of their import. For it is they who, under the leadership of the Terparchon, mediate between land and people. Who gentle the fury of storms."

A flicker of darkness and rumble of thunder passed over the chamber, and was gone.

"Coax sufficient water to survive the harshest of droughts."

Thick humidity infused the air for a moment, before dissolving into warm dryness.

"Calm the mightiest of fires."

Flames crackled and a haze of smoke filled the room. Two or three councilors coughed, and Gisela's throat ached, but a light breeze whisked the smoke away.

"And in all ways make the lives of those who live in this land far easier and more pleasant than otherwise."

Amara lowered her hands and foot. Although she paused take in a deep breath, no one interrupted her.

"They do this through deep connections with the primal forces around us—connections which they shape with unparalleled grace through the medium of movement. Through Dance."

Once again, the dam posed. This time, her body mimicked the stance taken by the leaders of the first circle dance the night before. Flashes of the night before tugged at Gisela—the beat of the drums, meeting Stevan's eyes across the circle, the shock of their first touch. She shook her head hard. Gritted her teeth and dug her fingers into the tablet as she held it steady.

"No matter the means and manner of their birth, their age or breeding, they are royal by virtue of that connection to which many aspire but few are granted. Rarely more than thirteen, seventeen, or nineteen possess the gift at any time, insofar as the Terparchon and her predecessors have been able to determine. In every generation some receive the gift of dance magic, though alas we do not know why they are chosen while others not."

"As bad as lots."

Gisela couldn't determine who'd given voice to the muttered words.

"It is well-documented that there must be twelve." Amara inclined her head but did not respond to the aside. "With their attendant partners to ground them, to accomplish any but the most minor and local of magics."

"Twelve's not a prime number." Dur's head shot up. The creak of his back straightening rang out alongside his words. "It can be divided several times over. All I ever heard of the Terparchon and Marchon said they knew the power of numbers. Why is twelve magic for the dancers when it's never magic anywhere else? Even we gather only as seven or eleven."

"Perhaps the Terparchon does not recognize or consider the power of prime numbers." Fissil waved a hand at Dur. Gisela winced to see how swollen his fingers were, and stopped to massage her own in sympathy. The old sire cast her a warm glance before turning back to the courtier.

"Ah, but she does." Amara spread her hands wide, lips twisted in a half smile. "For when the Dancing Princesses are gathered, she moves among them as the thirteenth."

"That enough for you?" Ilburna leaned forward to shoot Dur a glare.

The elder gave a grunt, and no other answer or objection.

"So, the Terparchon and her twelve princesses protect us. Why does that bring you here?" Ilburna raised her chin at Amara, who nodded back.

"Misfortunately, one of the princesses was injured recently and cannot dance." Amara gestured at Dur. "This leaves us with only eleven. That will hardly serve to protect the realm, not with countries to the east drooling over our borders in hopes to pry away some of our rich farming lands. Or, of equal concern, the rapid approach of summer storms from the sea."

Gisela dropped her stylus as a sharp pain ripped through her leg. She rubbed the muscles. The ache faded as quick as it had passed, but left her nerves jangled.

"We need a full complement of thirteen." The older dam shrugged a shoulder, her body all at once settling into a loose slump with no grace whatsoever. "Dances have been tried with eleven, and with seven and other prime numbers, but only thirteen has proven strong enough to grant us protection with ease."

"That's all well and good, but what has it to do with us?" Fissil shook his head. "What do you want of us? Monies to find another dancer?"

"Don't bother us." Dur wrinkled his nose. "We render our due to the Terparchon and Marchon, and never has there been anything but a request for more monies. I tell you, we cannot pay and pay and pay."

"Nor do I ask that of you." Amara tilted her head in his direction. "Instead, I offer you the chance to pay less."

Every single councilor sat at attention.

"How much less?" Alvi leaned their chin atop their entwined fingers.

Amara bent her head and stepped back.

In her place, Stevan brought forward short, slim scrolls that he passed around. Three for the councilors to share, and one to Gisela for the records. The parchment was still warm and slightly damp from his hold.

When unrolled, the scroll bore a beautifully scribed list of the taxes paid over the last decade. Contrary to Dur's earlier assertion, the number had risen only once over the years. Nevertheless, it represented a sizable proportion of the Escalli's profits.

Below this was written a number far smaller. Gisela couldn't make the calculation in her head, although given the twitching fingers of a few councilors—Ilburna, Alvi—they were busy figuring it as a percentage of the others.

"We are empowered to offer forgiveness of as much as one-fifth of the amount currently owed, for an undetermined span of time." Stevan nodded to each councilor in turn.

Silence fell on the room, broken only by irregular breathing. Stevan's face remained calm and serene, despite the almost comical expressions on the councilors' faces as a whole—many jaws, including Dur's, gaped wide open.

"What are we asked to yield in return?" Fissil snapped his jaw shut. His eyes narrowed as he watched Stevan.

"The forgiveness is conditional. For each year that one among your villagers joins the court to dance with the princesses, so too will your taxes decrease."

Again, silence fell. Distant sounds of life barely registered on Gisela. A villager, an Escalli to join the princesses. Dance with them. Be one?

What would it be like to move among people dedicated to dance? Who had magic flowing through them alongside music? A small sigh escaped her, and she straightened hastily. Positioned her stylus over the tablet. Then dared glance around to see if any had noted her distraction.

And found three sets of eyes trained on her. Amara, Stevan, and, which Gisela found most concerning, Ilburna.

"But you said few have such a gift at any time." Alvi twisted around to follow Stevan's gaze to Gisela, then shrugged and turned back to face him. "Why would one be among us? We are, as a people, gifted in the dance but have noted none with extra grace or, more importantly, magic."

"Perhaps you have not noticed one such," Stevan said, "but the Terparchon did on the progress to the summer court."

The stylus dropped from Gisela's suddenly nerveless fingers, rolling across the floor until it stopped at Stevan's sandals. The council chamber faded from her awareness, replaced by visceral memory of the Terparchon probing her hands and feet.

Her head whirled and she shivered.

When she returned to herself, she'd lost time. Everyone in the chamber stood except for her, even the frailest councilors propping themselves on their canes and chairs. All eyes fixed on her with avarice, pity, hope, other things she couldn't or wouldn't name.

"Will you become one of the Dancing Princesses?" Stevan stood before her, holding out his hands.

Amara smiled encouragement from beside him.

The Dancing Princesses. Leave. Escape from the constant presence of so many people who knew what she could and couldn't do. Voyage off to new places—with all she knew and loved far behind. Out of sight, of reach. Amidst people who thought and acted in other ways. Who would watch her with lascivious or judging eyes when they learned from whence she came. As their ancestors had suffered until they found this haven.

Gisela's voice failed her, not that she knew what she would say. For every lump she swallowed, another formed in her throat directly. Her hands and feet ached from the remembered pressure of fingers.

"You are Escalli. We are one, we are many. What we do as one we do for the many." Ilburna clumped her cane against the floor. "You have always sought to do your duty, at all costs, Gisela, for which we thank you. For some years now, you have served as council scribe. Will you lay aside this duty to render the village greater rewards by taking a place at court and dancing for us and the realm?"

Whether Gisela wanted to go or not—and she didn't know, it was too soon and to strange and unexpected an opportunity—she would. Ilburna's words left her no choice. To insist on remaining here, serving the village only as scribe, would mean putting her desires before the welfare of her people. She could serve better by leaving to go elsewhere.

What would she leave behind, except all she knew. All she loved . . . and all she had failed in one of the most basic services asked of every villager. She did not desire to leave, yet at the same time lightness filled her. For perhaps, by going away and dancing for her people elsewhere she could make up for what she'd been unable to offer here.

In the end, though, her worries and fears and hopes meant nothing.

She'd been asked. Ordered. Guilted.

"I will go."

CHAPTER 10

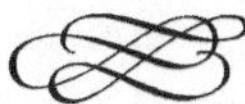

Three words turned Gisela's world dreamlike, a fragile bubble of unreality that she couldn't escape no matter where and how she looked. Better, easier, that way than facing the reality of leaving everything she knew.

An old cloth with the ends tucked under covered her loins. An equally aged breast band wrapped around her upper chest. Both were clean, but simple. Two people more finely dressed than her, in similar yellow tunics, whisked around her. They whipped away her overtunic and tunic, with no word as to whether she'd ever see either again as she was stripped down to her underthings. Little bumps lined her arms and legs and she shivered despite warm air redolent with the smell of rosemary and other herbs known to discourage insects.

Lengths of tarp hung only a hand's breadth above her head. The closeness made it hard to breathe, even though she stood at the center of a tent the equal in size of her chamber. No, bigger, for it held three people besides her and an array of trunks that exceeded the chests of scrolls and bookshelves surrounding her bed.

But here, it wasn't scrolls and books and wax tablets that proliferated and filled space.

Clothes, clothes, clothes. Tunics of fine linen in a rainbow array of colors, all bearing some embroidery or ribbon at the neckline or hem. Even the simplest and plainest had vines and flowers decorating the edges. Likewise the pile of loincloths and breast bands set at one side had bits of ribbon or color decorating them in some way. Then there were the mantles in place of over-tunics. Long lengths, that stretched taller than Gisela, made to be wrapped around the body in various patterns and held in place with pins and belts.

One whole trunk held more sandals than Gisela had ever seen in her life, even when traders came through and offered wares for sale. Those sandals were simple, flat layers of leather or compressed straw to protect feet from the cold of earth in winter. Sometimes the traders pulled out more decorative footwear, but rarely. No one in the village ever bought such. Not even the elders, although they were the most likely to wear sandals along with thick, knitted socks to keep their feet warm and dry.

Her toes curled against the soft, woven rug underfoot.

She'd walked such a short way from the village, yet already entered another world. A place of plenty, where her usual clothes would not pass muster. Indeed, the two servants twittering around her made it quite clear the items they'd taken from her were not acceptable for those who served the royal family and their courtiers.

Service she understood. The younger aided the older. Those who could do a task did so for those who could not, who in turn took on other responsibilities in an endless cycle of helping others and being helped, all for the good of the village and the people.

But this? She had arms and legs. She should be able to dress and undress herself. True, she might need assistance from another in identifying where to take up or let down a hem—but that was a task one turned around and helped the other with.

The two buzzing around her would not allow her to so much as fold and lay away a mantle rejected as displeasing for her coloring. All the while, Amara stood back and watched and smiled and nodded.

That Amara did not take an active role in undressing and dressing Gisela made sense. The other was older, if not quite an elder—Gisela could not determine her age. But one of the two . . . servants . . .

appeared of an age with Amara. Rik had introduced themselves as an eleee in service to the Terparchon and delegated to assist in fitting Gisela for presentation at court.

Both Rik and the other servant, a dam named Emmi, were about Gisela's height and size. Rik made sharp, efficient gestures which made their short, stubby braid roll back and forth along their neck. Emmi had a full, rounded face and twinkling eyes as she pulled and prodded Gisela.

Rik and Emmi in turn dictated Gisella's movements and proved adroit at guilting her into doing what they wanted.

Standing still so they could mark hems for adjustment.

Undoing her hair and letting them comb a cleansing scrub through it.

Wearing what they declared looked good on her.

Why could her new life not wait until she'd left the old to begin?

After untold ages suffering this torture, Gisela put her foot down, literally stamping, when they wanted her to leave the tent in a fine linen tunic and elaborate mantle.

"No. Not this." She ducked as Emmi tried to wrap the light but thickly embroidered purple mantle around her body. "Not yet."

"It is the fashion. You must be ready when you arrive, for many eyes will turn to you and not all friendly." Emmi clucked her tongue and tilted her head.

"But we are not at court here. Give me the simplest for now. The most comfortable. When I get to the palace, I will wear what you decree, but not here."

Emmi looked at Rik, who turned to Amara. The older dam scrutinized Gisela up and down, then nodded.

"For now, yes, except your feet." She pointed at Gisela's bare toes. "The princesses dance in sandals, even when they wear through the soles in a single evening. You will need time to adjust."

That was that. A half-full mug was better than none at all.

Thus Gisela spent her last days in the village wearing much finer clothing. Her tunics had no carefully mended rents. Although little more than a simple fall of linen, each and every one had a strip of ribbon at the neckline, and these were the worst of those passed over to her while simultaneously being nicer than almost any she had owned before. One in a lovely shade of pink lacked any sign someone had owned it before, except for creases where it had been folded into a square and lain at the bottom of some heavy heap so long that even the humid weather had yet to fully remove them.

Then there was the mantle Emmi and Rik deemed simple. Unadorned, yes, but the fabric was almost as delicate and light as a tunic and a strong green far more brightly dyed than anything she'd ever worn before. The launderers in the village had strong opinions about the difficulty of cleaning heavily dyed clothing, and cowed most into favoring pale, easily washed colors.

But so long as Gisela did not wear the mantle to hard labor, or hard dancing, surely it would not need much more than a regular brushing even after she left the village. In truth, she enjoyed the way it flowed about her and allowed cool breezes to sneak under and ease heated skin. Nor did the look of admiration in Stevan's eyes hurt the first time he viewed her.

The easy sway of tunic and mantle alone might have allowed her to continue in a dreamlike state, and overlook the cautious and curious glances sent her way.

After all, she had ducked away from the watchful eyes of her fellow villagers often over the last year. Her failures had inured her to being the subject of caution and gossip. More than once she'd endured nightmares of moving through the village with everyone laughing and pointing at her: nude with all the hairs on her body dyed purple, not just the streak in her hair.

At least when she walked about the village in her new attire she was fully clothed.

No, the clothes were not the change that made the difference—except for the sandals. They, above all else, dispelled the illusion that at some point she'd wake to her old life.

The first hours she wore them she couldn't keep from lifting the hems of her tunic and mantle or kicking up or to the side, just to see her feet, which didn't look like hers but seemed narrower and longer.

Decorations adorned the straps binding the soles against her feet: green vines and leaves, and purple flowers.

After the first hours, however, her feet hurt nearly everywhere the sandals pressed against her skin. The sores the sandals left lingered. Emmi produced soft squares of sweet-scented lambswool to cushion Gisela's skin as she—and the shoes—adapted to each other.

Her feet still hurt.

And she missed the connection with the earth. Only when walking in shoes did Gisela realize how much she'd become accustomed to feeling a distant beat from the earth beneath her. The leather muffled it. Made it harder to sense, to the point she sometimes bent down and laid a hand on the ground to be sure the beat still resided there. The earth always responded to the touch of her bare skin, but when she pulled her hand away, the beat reduced to a distant memory through the leather.

How she walked slowed and shifted as she wore sandals—as much because she stopped at nearly every tree and bush to touch and feel that which no longer seeped up into her.

"Do the princesses really dance in these?" Gisela asked Amara, as Emmi removed a stained square of lambswool and replaced it with a new, unmarked one.

"Oh yes." The older dam nodded and patted Gisela's shoulder. "You will understand when you see the floors upon which they dance."

After which she said no more.

In contrast, Emmi provided word-pictures of floors made of cut stones in all colors, shaped into intricate patterns. Most were laid straight, the tiles embedded in special muds upon the earth or foundation stones, or layers of adhesive atop wood, so that one walked across a smooth, even surface. Sometimes, though, the earth moved, or things shifted so that sharp edges jutted up ready to scrape the unwary.

Specially trained floor wards tried to keep this from happening, or at least fix such instances before anyone might be badly hurt, but they did not always succeed.

And this was where Gisela was headed? She already missed walking barefoot.

In counter-balance, something else throbbed in her blood and bones: growing awareness of how little time remained until the courtiers would leave and carry her away with them.

All the while everyone knew, and watched her with different eyes. As one who would leave.

Nor did it help that, although permitted to sleep in her own bed, Emmi woke Gisela early in the morning. Gisela refused assistance in donning underthings and the plainest of her new tunics, a pale yellow that fell to just below her knees. She sat on her bed and sucked in her breath as the dam rubbed lotion on her feet. Her sores had eased in the night, and the lotion reduced the lingering ache, but the sharp tang drove every vestige of sleep from her head. It also rendered her stomach unwilling to take anything Emmi offered other than a few sips of a tisane.

Then, suitably shod in the simplest of the sandals, Gisela followed Emmi out of the village to the clearing. The sun had barely peeped over the sky, and a light haze lay over the largely somnolent dwellings.

Once in the clearing, Gisela was delighted to discover Amara and Stevan standing on the sunniest side. The warm rays eased the last of dawn's chill from her skin.

Amara wore a white tunic, similar to Gisela.

Stevan had on only a loincloth. The swathe of fabric drew Gisela's attention to the russet brown of his skin, stretched over finely-wrought muscles, sinews, and bones. Dark hair dusted his arms, chest, and legs. Built on tall, solid lines, he carried his weight well. Though she'd danced with him round after round, and kissed him, she'd only grazed his body in passing. The layers of tunics and enveloping cloth concealed too much—he should never wear them again. This was how he was meant to be seen.

She licked her lips to dry them. Wrenching her gaze upward, she watched his smile expand. Pleasure glinted in his eyes. She had not managed to conceal her admiration, but likewise his gaze moved over her in open appreciation and warmed her as much as the sun.

Letting her gaze drift down, she straightened so fast her the bones in her spine crackled.

Stevan's large feet lay flat on the ground, with no layer of leather between skin and earth. Snapping her head to the side, Gisela ascertained Amara, too, was barefoot.

"You may take your sandals off for now." Amara laughed.

"Why did you say princesses wear sandals to dance?"

"They do. But when they choose to exercise outside, most go barefoot. Since we are not at court, or in the dancing chambers, feel free to do as we do."

Without further invitation, Gisela undid the straps, and let loose an immense sigh as her soles pressed against warming dirt.

Amara led her and Stevan through a series of stretches. To Gisela's surprise, after the first fumbling attempts, her body readily followed the dam's lead. The movements were familiar from her childhood, merely done in a different order—and to a greater extent.

The older dam arranged the exercises Gisela remembered as distinct into sequences. Except with more parts and repetitions, pushing her to do more.

The first sequence was solar, tracing the arc of the sun and gently warming her body to work.

Then birdlike, extending arms, torso, and back in ways that left Gisela's muscles with residual aches—but also energized with heightened vitality.

Lastly, an earth-based sequence wherein she lay on the ground and her legs mimicked plants growing and receding. The muscles in her lower body received similar treatment to her upper, and became imbued with the same new-growth energy.

All the while, she was all too aware of Stevan doing the same as her but with more grace. More familiarity. More speed. Where she fumbled and wound a beat behind Amara, he kept pace.

The more so as she had to keep from glancing his way to watch the smooth flow of muscles under skin. The sheen of skin glistening with sweat.

Her skin tingled when he peered at her. No matter that she could not see when he turned to watch her, she knew.

Her breath came in long pants by the end of the sequences, and not merely from the extent to which Amara had made her work.

Trills of desire ran along her arms, her legs. Made her toes twitch. She didn't look at Stevan, even when he chuckled. The deep, resonant sound made her chest tighten.

"That's enough for a first day." Amara handed Gisela a clean cloth to wipe sweat from her brow and limbs. "We'll do this each morning until we leave, then add more along the way."

Gisela escaped the clearing as soon as she could. Did not linger even so long as to break the night's fast there, despite the smell of sweet berry pancakes grilled over the fire.

Better to run back to her home, and hold tight to all that she'd soon have to let go. Even if this meant a meal of stale bread slathered with honey.

Back to the familiar—away from the strange. In particular, as far as she could get from Stevan. He'd turned her down. She didn't want her body to wake to his gaze or touch. For him to note her watching him.

However would she manage to travel with him, being polite and courteous and not betraying how his rejection still stung.

How could she leave?

She would miss so many things. No matter how little she'd appreciated them because they were always there until now they wouldn't be. Or, rather, they would, but she not there to know.

The way the roofs caught the sun.

How a child could start singing a song in the nursery and within a few lines everyone in the village would join in, whether humming or singing.

The frustration on Alvi's face as they herded the counselors to the table.

In place of these familiar sights and sounds, she'd face hordes of people dressed as fine as she or better, even with the new clothes.

Courtiers who knew how to interact with each other. What was expected of them. What they could get away with.

People who talked as Amara and Stevan and Emmi and Rik and the guards and other servants, putting the accents in the wrong places so that Gisela had to listen close to understand.

Anyone in the palace who cared would learn, sooner or later, that she was Escalli—and make assumptions based upon that knowledge. Look down upon her as simple folk, or consider her apt to fall into lewdness at a moment's notice. Perhaps seek liberties. Would they take no for an answer?

Ilburna was the one to give the most open warning, whether or not that was her intent.

The elder arrived without warning in Gisela's room right after the midday meal, at a time when most of the elders, indeed most of the village given the heat of midsummer, tended to nap.

Gisela had planned a last respite in her own bed and her own room, no matter how disarrayed it looked as she'd started packing the items she most cherished into a trunk with her new clothing.

Despite the disorder, Ilburna invited herself in and planted herself upon the foot of the bed. Both gnarled hands wrapped around the head of her cane, she motioned to Gisela to take a seat on her own cot.

"You are welcome, of course, but perhaps we could speak later?" Gisela rubbed her temples. Sweat slicked her skin, from the heat and her exertions.

"Now is best. When there is no one near to hear. It won't take long." Ilburna clicked her tongue. "If I can remain awake, you can as well. Sit."

Gisela dropped onto her cot without grace. The soft layers cushioned her. Easing back, she leaned against the thick wall and waited.

"I make no apology for asking you to go." Ilburna stared at the far wall. Her fingers twitched and shook, raising a soft rattle that underscored her words.

"You certainly gave me little choice."

"There was little choice for anyone." The elder whirled to glare at

Gisela. "What the Terparchon and Marchon want, they get. The only questions are how fast and how much."

"And the answers are fast and for a decrease in taxes, with the exact amount not even specified." Gisela clenched her hands and glared back. "You did not wait a breath to agree."

"Negotiations on the details are proceeding." Ilburna looked away first.

"Then you'll be able to put a price on my compliance."

"That's only part of your value to us, the smaller part." The old dam thumped her cane against the floor.

Gisela crossed her arms over her chest, hands still fisted.

The chamber fell quiet. Distant sounds seeped in. The buzz of insects. The calls of birds overhead. The moans and thumps of those villagers who chose to spend their rest time indulging in the pleasures of the body.

A high cry of exultation rang out from the cottage two over, followed by a second.

Ilburna glanced that direction and shrugged a shoulder, lips twisting in a half smile. She didn't say anything.

This time Gisela broke, her mind empty of what the other might mean. Her contributions to the village lay in her services as scribe, nothing more, until recently.

"What other value do you see in me, then?"

"Consider: you'll be at the palace, at the center of the powers that rule these lands. You, not one of the flibbertigibbets still at the mercy of the heat of their blood." Ilburna pointed her cane in the direction of yet another series of matching cries. "You, who knows how to read and write, who can keep secrets—and perhaps discover them as well."

"What do you want?"

"Truth."

Gisela's jaw dropped as the implications began to dawn. She sucked in a deep breath, then snapped her head up to stare at the other. "Only truth?"

"I dare not ask for vengeance." Ilburna grimaced. "That would cost more than I am willing to pay—especially when I might not be the one who had to pay the price. We live in a world where those who do evil are rarely brought to account for their deeds."

"Escalad." The name hung in the air for a moment. The mere sound carried images, impressions. Even though Gisela had never seen it, and never would—at least not as those who'd fled had—the syllables evoked warmth and a haven.

"Our home." Ilburna closed her eyes and tilted her head back. Moisture trickled down the sides of her face. "Oh, these lands here have taken us in and given us shelter. For you who are young—make no protest, child, for you're too many years the younger for me not to consider you young—these are all you've ever known. But the oldest of us, we remember where we once belonged."

"A spit of land with long views and long sights, from the high, snow-topped mounts to the far sea with its white-capped waves. Where the earth smelled sweet, and nurtured all plants. The sun shone six days out of seven, yet never did the sky withhold needed rain. All virtues sought in a home this had." The words poured easily out of Gisela, although she half-quoted nursery memories and half-paraphrased. The original had held power. Her rendition didn't, but still raised a faint shadow of a series of villages and fields covering a sloping hillside. The high end of the hill jutted out far above a wide river that curved around the land on three sides.

"Those are words to you, all of you. Oh I know you care, but it is different for those who never knew it as it was. Only a few are left." Ilburna tapped her chest with one hand. "We were no great power, but we held our home. Controlled the river for a length, and earned a fair bit of coin by allowing passage across land for those who didn't wish to risk the rapids. Lived there for generations without problem from the earth, our greatest threats the late summer storms that washed the river high . . . and the greed of those who desired the fees paid for passage."

"Who do they pay now?"

"Who do you suppose?" Eyes now dry, Ilburna gave Gisela a level stare.

Gisela grunted, but kept her mouth shut. This was the court Ilburna wished her to join?

"We had one other thing: proximity to one of the Shadows of the Moon. The rulers of Codaros wanted to control them all. Build palaces next to every single Shadow. They don't have them, not yet, but they will. For our land is gone. Shaken and fallen into rubble. I ventured back once, when I was still hale enough for the journey—you would have been a toddler at the time—and there now lies an immense villa close to where our villages once rose from the earth."

"You think the Terparchon and the Marchon destroyed our homeland?" Hardly the first time Gisela had heard such suspicions. She'd never taken the matter much to heart before. Simpler to listen, nod, and curse the court, then go about her daily business.

It was the current Terparchon's parents who Ilburna referred to as having stolen Escalad. If they were anything like the Terparchon the one time Gisela met her, she could believe they'd be that ruthless. Yet how could they shake the earth so much? No one had that much power. Or did they? Amara had said the princesses shaped storms, coaxed water, eased fires. The implication was they protected the land and people, but such powers might be turned in other directions.

Even so, a thread of slow-burning anger lit within Gisela from Ilburna's intensity.

"Someone did." Ilburna leaned forward, voice pitched for Gisela's ears alone. "We never had quakes before and I heard nothing of any after. When I passed by the palace, I questioned the servants who tend the buildings and dwelling places when the rulers and their coterie are away. There've been Escalli before you who went to court to serve, or so they proclaimed, but also to see what they might find. There is one at the winter palace now, though he does not proclaim his origins far and wide. He sends word back as he can. Visit the libraries, and you will find him or he you." She grabbed Gisela's hand, tucking a small piece of paper within.

Gisela opened her fingers long enough to glimpse awkward letters, then closed her hand. Time enough later to study the contents—for Ilburna was not done.

"As a Dancing Princess, you will have access to different secrets than he." The other's grip tightened to the point of pain. "I do not ask you to betray them or to share with me anything you are told to keep secret—but if you can find proof that the Terparchon's ancestors did or did not destroy Escalad, you will ease an old dam's heart."

With that, she thumped her cane again and left.

Gisela didn't move. The thick wall was warm against her back. The paper within her fingers likewise grew warm, edges scratching at her skin. A sharp tang in the air made her nose twitch, then the rain came thundering down. Heavy torrents lashing against roofs and walls.

An apt match for Gisela's mood.

Her head and feet hurt—and her heart as well. So many hopes and expectations placed on her. She'd yet to fully adjust to the year's earlier blow and now . . . They asked her to trade her home for an unknown place where she would likely find a mixed welcome. Arrive with an added secret, an extra load. More to carry. More reason to be wary. More likelihood she'd be watched when she reached the court.

Yet this was something she could do for her people, to make up for her inability in other ways. The memory of which still brought tears to her eyes.

Her cozy chamber had already ceased to be a haven. Her work as scribe slipped from her hands into her successor's. Even the garb she wore was unfamiliar and strange.

She missed home, even though she had yet to leave.

As the rain slowed, the torrent passing, she realized there was one more thing she would miss.

Donning one of her old tunics not yet taken away, she left her new clothes and sandals behind as she darted out into the humid mist that followed the rain.

Walked out the same way she did back in the spring, the day the Terparchon found her.

To dance and bid farewell to the fallow field.

CHAPTER 11

Dancing lured Stevan.

Humid air hissed and steamed around him, courtesy of a late afternoon shower. His tunic, a simple blue save for a thin vine embroidered at the neckline, clung instantly to his skin. His mantle, a lightweight fabric well-suited to summer, absorbed enough moisture that it hung heavy about his torso.

His sandals squelched against damp earth. The soles picked up clods of mud here and there, cast them off a step or two later, keeping him to a slow, steady pace.

The thick vegetation around him, mostly weeds and scraggly trees, gave off strong and not entirely pleasant odors that encouraged him not to stray from the trail. The cleared area was wide enough for a donkey or ox cart to pass through with humans walking on either side. Ample space for one lone man to pick his way as he tried to figure out where he was going.

The *why* he already knew.

He'd spent the storm enclosed within the council chambers reviewing old tax rolls and listening to tales of woe. Several of the oldest councilors pointed to this roll and that as they recounted harvests lost, plagues of weevils, and raids from bandits.

The contract guaranteeing the Escalli's benefit for letting Gisela go had yet to be completely written, much less signed. They had every motive to see if they could raise the consideration from a fifth to a fourth, or more. They wouldn't succeed—their initial joy had been too clear, and both sides knew they'd accept the fifth. Still, they tried.

So he sat with them. Ate and drank with them. Traded his own tales of the evils that plagued his kinfolk at the other side of the realm —lost harvests, weevils, raiders. All while the rains poured down about them. Dripped from the ceiling in a few places. Drops clanked into well-positioned buckets and chipped serving vessels. Such a convenient way to emphasize their claims of trouble and need for more monies that he almost suspected the leaks of being arranged. Except that they'd made clear earlier that the funds were allocated on strict principles of need and worth, and the council chamber did not top that list.

After the rains, the thick air encouraged yawns on the part of many, even all, the councilors. They drifted away, to their beds for naps, and recommended the same course of action to him.

He might even have taken it, had he not caught a glimpse of black curly hair and an old, gray tunic heading out of town.

No suspicion of ill doing seized him, nor any doubt as to who had left.

With all the possible actions before him, he followed her out of the village.

Only to lose sight.

And sound.

Insects buzzed, and birds called in the distance, but otherwise he heard no sounds attributable to a woman out on her own.

Beneath his feet, however, a slow beat began to pulse. More than the stick and plop of mud clinging and releasing his sandals soles. A thrum that found purchase in his toes and heels and from there resounded in his bones.

It came from the left, a little back. When he turned and retraced his steps a short way, scattered small, light footprints in the mud and broken blades of grass revealed a narrow track.

Whomever walked the trail last was shorter and slighter than he. He had to push his way through. Branches pulled back and made way for him, scratching his arms and neck lightly.

Time to find a princess and clarify a few matters. She'd successfully avoided him for too long.

Oh, she had her reasons, ample ones and good for that matter. She spent hours in close consultation with the councilors—always different from those who accosted him—and the apprentice promoted to scribe in her place. Those he certainly couldn't argue with.

She had to decide which of her own belongings to pack even though Amara promised she'd receive a full wardrobe due her station once she arrived. That he found less convincing, although he accepted that she was also needed for measurements as Rik and the other servant adapted the tunics and mantles Amara had brought to Gisela's height.

When she kept slipping away with excuses about seeing to provisions, or farewelling persons he had seen her already speak to, it was not hard to realize Gisela did not wish to speak to him.

Amara was little help. She encouraged Gisela to join their early morning exercises, but then sent Stevan away regularly when his exercises and lesson had finished but Gisela's evidently had not. He'd expressed interest in remaining, but been told in no uncertain terms to leave.

"You have a firm foundation already." Amara had patted his shoulder while giving the impression that, had she been tall enough or he shorter, she'd have patted the top of his head instead. "You need little more but practice."

"Then let me practice here and now, I am ready."

"But Gisela is not."

And that was that. He slunk away, and the relief on Gisela's face at his departure cut.

He did not enjoy being a pursuer. Didn't enjoy hunting at all, for that matter. If he had to contribute to meals, he preferred fishing or helping cultivate kitchen gardens where patience and time worked wonders.

They didn't have time—he didn't have time.

Whatever was between them, they needed some certainty before reaching court. It wasn't finished. Not a gaping wound, but a sore that might fester if they did not address their unfulfilled attraction.

As one of the partners for the princesses in the dances where they wielded power . . . they couldn't avoid each other.

And this much he knew from watching other courtiers: if they returned at odds, it would do neither of them any favors.

So for this, he became the hunter.

The pursuer.

Determined to find and hold and converse with her long enough to ensure she did not feel the need to constantly run away from him at the palace.

Or on the road there, which would be even more difficult. Whether walking or riding in the cart, a rackety, teeth-chattering pace worse than walking, there were only the nine of them headed back. He and Gisela would have to spend some time in proximity.

All these arguments he mustered in his head.

The thoughts drained away when he stepped out of the bushes to the edge of the clearing. No, not a clearing but a field left fallow. The signs were clear, from the broken remnants of a last plowing to the greenery growing uneven within and without the furrows.

Despite the lack of tending and care, here everything blossomed, bloomed, and showed signs of bearing fruit in time. A vine growing along one furrow held berries already gleaming red. A bush farther along bore the glimmer of blue amidst green. Birds of red and blue and gray darted here and there, picking at the berries and flowers. A couple of rabbits nibbled at sprouts further along. Tree rats chittered and raced along tree branches heavy with leaves and unripe fruits.

And in the midst of it all, Gisela danced to the same beat that pulsed up from the ground beneath his feet and through his blood.

He'd only ever seen the princesses dancing at court events, in the same types of dances all enjoyed. Fast or measured. Careful move-ments repeated regularly, or precisely circumscribed random circling. Much the same as the progression of dances at the festival those few nights back. All very enjoyable, but also largely predictable.

This bore little resemblance.

Every movement was freeform.

She'd lost the sash from around her waist. The length of yellow cloth dangled from a tree branch near Stevan. The cloth once covering her hair had come free as well, although this she retained in her hand and let the similarly bright fabric billow out behind her even as her dark locks and tunic belled and rippled in her wake.

One moment she leapt from furrow to furrow. Laughed and raised her face to the sun. Her smile wide and her chest rising and falling with easy motions despite her exertions. A faint aura misted around her, as though the sun shone brighter where she passed. Minute points of light flowed in her wake, so that each movement left a brief after-image behind. These in turn fell onto the ground behind her in a shower of glowing sparks.

Then, abruptly she dropped. Crouched over and around a half-grown plant topped with a tilted, half-broken crown of dying flowers. Embraced it. Stroked the petals as though trying to raise the flower back to its peak.

The brilliant column of light flowing down from the sun to her expanded to encompass the plant. Light, warmth, and healing surged. The petals quivered, their torn ends merging together as the flower regained health and vitality.

Rising, she bent and stroked again. Then took the loose cloth in both hands, wrapping the ends around her fisted fingers, and twirled her way down the furrow.

The free flow of her hair in the wind inspired him to slip off the tie holding his hair. He fastened the cord around his wrist instead. Rather than comb out the braid, he left it to unravel as it would. A breeze wound around him and did the task for him, releasing section after section of hair but always blowing it back and away from his face so he might watch Gisela unimpeded.

The energy emanating from her had a predictable effect upon his body. Slow and sensuous, as though each mote of his being woke to the sunlight shining through her. Much as he desired to reach out, to touch and stroke, he resisted. Far better to remain patient and aware, and stand witness.

Sheer delight shone from her. The air and earth around responded, warming as though she were the sun made flesh and come to dance among the plants.

He'd never seen her so happy. So free.

Shadows had haunted her even that first night, when they'd danced. Something weighing her down, keeping her from this blitheness. Similar cares had lain on her shoulders and face since she'd accepted—at least part unwillingly—the place at court.

Not at this moment. Her every movement echoed the earth's beat —feet tapping or stepping, arms waving, shoulders rising.

Yet something changed. The light around her took on a grayish hue, as her gestures grew broader, wider. Had his presence affected her? She showed no sign of having seen him.

The steady pulse of the earth rippled through him as well as her, but with a different effect. Indeed, leaving the spot where he stood seemed beyond him, as if he'd been planted in the earth. Knees locked, he remained in place although his upper body echoed her movements.

Unable to chase after her and join the dance.

Did the earth fear he would have done so? That he could not recognize this was a private moment that he had interrupted, perhaps even a farewell to the field, birds, and bees?

But it should let him leave, that she have her time alone.

Except . . .

Her aura unbalanced, thickening along her arms and left shoulder while dissipating in a long streak wrapping from the right shoulder around her back and waist to split and stripe her legs. The color shifted from gleaming gold to a sullen, pulsing gray-green. Merely looking at it made his head hurt.

She twirled faster than before. Sped up, bit by bit, so perhaps she didn't realize it. The earth's beat thrummed in him—and she exceeded it. Her elation and happiness rose. She whirled faster and fast. Her arms stretched out, fingers moving as though desperate to grasp and absorb the moment, the memory.

The unpleasant aura seeped into her, speeding her while also making her lurch as though drunk.

Around and around she went. Her circular movements never ceased. Up and down the furrows. She whipped close by, but did not seem to see him. Her eyes had a vacant look that sent a chill down his spine.

The song birds followed her path, hovering around and chirping at her. She smiled at them, but it was an empty thing.

"Let me go to her." Stevan gritted his teeth and tried to pull his feet from the earth's clutches. He failed, his sandals rising not a whit. He bent to undo the straps holding the leather about his feet, but a vine whipped against his knuckles.

He straightened in an instant. Arms pressed tight against his sides and his head ducked to the side. Memory provided the smart of the back of a hand slapping against his cheek, though no true pain followed. A thin red line crossed his fingers but healed as he watched.

"Please."

The earth continued to hold him fast, while Gisela twirled.

Bright light outlined her form. Sparks ran along her body. The stench of burning hair spiraled out from her head.

Overhead, tree rats darted along branches chittering at her.

A rabbit dashed across her path, so close it nearly tripped her. She made no response.

Merely whirled.

Until, as she passed close again, another vine or perhaps the same one lashed out and wrapped around her ankle.

Yanked.

Stevan still couldn't move, yet he was in the right place to catch her as she fell. He braced her upper body, as she sagged against him. Energy flashed through him, as though a dozen bolts of lightning struck his body then condensed into one and drained into the earth.

He eased Gisela down to the ground. Her eyes remained blank and unseeing. Breathing shallow, catching often in her throat.

Until it turned to sobbing.

Then the earth let him lift his feet, so he sank down and held her. Wrapped his arms around and let her cry on his shoulder. Hot tears soaked through the mantle and tunic to dampen his skin. Her chest heaved as sobs racked her body. He cupped the back of her head with one hand, and traced circles across her shoulder blades with the other.

She no longer glowed. Her body exuded heat that subsided moment by moment, sob by sob. A layer of sweat dewed her skin, carrying a not-unpleasant whiff of earth and growing things though a hint of burnt hair remained. Warm air twined around them, breezes wrapping them together and wicking away her tears.

"It'll be all right." He held her close, rubbing her back and letter her bury her head in the crook between his chin and neck. "One way or another, it'll be all right."

"Never." She trembled, burrowing into him. "Never, never, never."

"That's a long time." He stroked her back. "Are you certain?"

Tremors rippled through her, head to toe. Stevan adjusted his strokes to move in the same direction, but slow and steady. He matched the low thrum of the earth below. Bit by bit, the vibrations racking her body lessened and adapted to the same rhythm.

Why her?

Why his body's sudden focus on her and the interest from the moment he'd seen her?

Maybe for this. For her delight in dancing over the earth, her beauty and the magic of her movement.

But also that he could catch her, and brace her fall. Give her ease and comfort. Hold her. Respond to her need. Be needed, and be enough where he never had felt sufficient in himself before.

For how well she fit against him.

And that, strangers though they yet were, still she felt comfortable enough to cry in his arms.

Alas, she drew away. He let his hands slip from around her. His chest and arms cooled quickly, deprived of her warmth. Staying in place, he watched her sway and rub her head.

Then open her eyes. She gazed right into his. Her body straightened, arms clamping tight against her torso as she stared at him with startled—horrified—eyes.

"You!"

CHAPTER 12

$\mathcal{A}$ welcome warmth enfolded Gisela. With the heat and humidity, she should be sticky and uncomfortable. Instead, she rested against a warm, smooth surface. It rose and fell, helping steady her breathing. Wisps of wind blew about, lifting damp coils of hair from her neck. Her tunic stuck to her damp skin, but started to dry in spots. The sweet smell of grain ripening tantalized her nostrils.

She kept her eyes closed, too tired—and sore—to face the world. Every muscle in her body ached, as though she'd run smack into a tree. Quivers of energy shot along her limbs. Irregular, but fast as bolts of lightning.

An even pressure circled her back. Fingers massaged, easing the ache. Her muscles twanged as they released tension. Spiraling out from her back, her body relaxed against the warmth.

She knew who held her, massaged her. Recognized his voice in the reassurances breathed into her ears. The same kind of soft nothings the nursery guardians used to croon when she woke gasping from nightmares as a child.

Yet as long as she did not open her eyes, she could pretend that this was all a dream.

So much easier to lie with her head pillowed on layers of warm cloth without admitting the fabric covered a broad chest.

Preferable to allow hands to continue stroking her back and overlook that they had to belong to someone.

To put off facing the losses and pressures that had sent her out into the field to dance.

Forgo, for a little longer, facing her failure in the field. Without him to catch her, she might have fallen. Worse, in so doing she could have damaged the plants and earth around her.

How long had she willfully ignored the signs of magic around her dancing?

Since meeting the Terparchon, at the least calculation.

Time after time, Gisela had come out to escape the village and all the reminders of what she was and wasn't. To dance and leave behind her cares and woes for however many moments.

On each occasion, she rejoiced in how the field bloomed, the plants flourished, and totted it all up to the cumulative effect of lying fallow enough years to recover from over-use.

Power blossomed in her muscles and veins with every step, every circle, every dance. She moved to the beat of the earth. Let the ground below her dictate the tempo of the dance. Then circled and whirled as she surrendered everything except the pleasure of movement.

Still she'd denied it, but no longer.

At first the dance had gone so well. The ground rejoiced in her return. The earth gave her a bright, sprightly measure to tread. Up and down she'd gone, spiraling and spreading joy.

But unable to surrender fully. An edge of awareness remained that this would be the last dance here for a while, perhaps forever.

She wanted it to last. Desired nothing so much as to grab hold and never let go.

The earth did not understand. She was the conduit: taking energy, transforming and multiplying it, then returning power to the ground and all that sprang from it. This was a cycle, but not an endless one. For every day, there must be a corresponding night. For every dance of power, a matching period of rest, absorption, and recovery.

For her, stopping meant leaving. Facing the unknown future

ahead. The limitations of her body.

All that she had run here to escape.

Increasingly trapped in her longing to remain, she ceased to perform her function, her role in the dance.

Power became trapped within her. Crackled in her veins. Flared in her arms and legs. Even sparked minute fires in her body. Scorched her hair.

Until someone touched her. Braced her. Wrapped his arms around her and all the energy that did not belong to her drained out—carrying away her denials and excuses.

The dam within her heart broke, and tears swept out. All the sorrow she'd pent up, the rage she'd buried deep, and regrets for what would never be.

Her body shook. Lungs heaved. Head sought to burrow into the source of warmth and comfort holding her.

She didn't know how long she wept, only that she did. As the tears eased, her mind cleared. A fog within her seemed to lift, leaving behind a dancer with a newborn respect for the gift she had not asked for, nor recognized when it arrived.

Gisela intended to investigate the powers of Dancing Princesses for Ilburna when she reached the court. Nevertheless, she already knew the part of the answer, half of the truth Ilburna sought.

Had just lived it.

Gisela alone might not be able to cause an earthquake, but the power that flowed in her dancing moved the earth in another way. If all the princesses joined together, she did not doubt they could wreak destruction of the kind that leveled Escalad.

Past princesses surely had.

What might be asked of Gisela? The possibilities Amara described sounded wondrous and worth pursuing—easing storms, droughts, and fires.

Would she be able to say no to doing the reverse? To causing or worsening ill weather? A dilemma worthy of the greatest minds, for in refusing, if she could, she would risk backlash against her people.

All of this presumed she would know what effects her dancing caused upon the world. She'd managed to ignore it quite successfully.

The problems made her head ache.

Pushing back to sit on her haunches, she rubbed her temples. The soothing hands let her go. A breeze flitted around her, chilling her back and face.

Unable to repress a shiver, she opened her eyes.

Stevan sat before her. Back to a tree. Damp spots on his mantle, no doubt from her tears.

The sire who'd rejected her, yet so much kindness and care shone in his eyes.

She startled and jerked back. He grabbed hold of her hands. Braced her. Her head swayed backward, but she didn't fall.

"Better now?"

"Yes." She ran her tongue over dry lips, tasting the salt of her tears. "You?"

"I am not the one who danced all over the field, as a whirlwind." He smiled, fingers wrapped around her cool hands. "I am well. I'm glad you are, too."

Her hands remained within his grasp. Her fingers twitched, yet instead of letting go she slipped them between his. The better to keep warm.

"Is it only you?" She shifted to kneel next to him, their hands still entwined. "No one else saw?"

"I don't think anyone else noticed you leave. I followed you from the village. I would've left when I realized your dance was personal," he said, shrugging, "but the earth didn't let me go."

"It wasn't the earth alone." She glanced away, back at the rows filled with burgeoning growth. "I knew someone was there—you—but it seemed fitting. You meshed so well with the trees and bushes."

"Thank you for letting me watch. It was beautiful." He lifted their hands to his lips and kissed her fingers.

Pleasure swirled through her, heating her cheeks. Nevertheless, a frisson rippled through her. Still more tears leaked from her eyes. Her head swayed as the world blurred around her.

"You were happy for a while." Lifting one hand, her fingers still twined with his, he brushed dampness from her skin.

"For a while." Her chin dropped against her chest. Blinking dispelled the tears. "I am always happiest here where I come to dance, to escape. It's left fallow, so no one else comes here. Only me."

"Why are there no crops planted?" He let go one hand and scooped a handful of earth. Rich loam trickled between his fingers. "It seems fertile."

"It's been fallow for several years, and hadn't recovered." The smell of wet earth cleared Gisela's mind, as though a flood passed through carrying all cares away. She'd face her fears tomorrow. For now, the sight of the flowering field filled her with gladness. Here, at least, she'd made a difference. "But now, maybe it has. It will."

At which point she noticed where they sat, at the end of the field. Movement caught her eye and she jerked to study the trail leading toward the village.

Nothing there but the wind blowing through flourishing trees and bushes. All the same, it brought back memories of her first dance in the field and how that had ended. How ironic.

Her shoulders shook with reluctant laughter. A few last drops of moisture glittered in the corners of her eyes, but declined to fall.

Stevan grabbed the hem of his mantle and dabbed at her face.

She pushed his hand away and cleared her eyes with the back of a hand. Although not so soft, skin on skin roused less soreness than the cloth.

"What did you find funny?" He tilted his head to one side. Voice light, and face bright, he invited her answer with a carefree air.

She could decline. Yet something about the set of his shoulders— and the intentness in his gaze—made her wonder how much he truly wanted to know.

He'd comforted her when she needed it. She could give him something back, small truths at the very least.

"Here is where I came to dance, and it's because of that I must go with you." She jerked her chin at the head of the trail. "That's where I saw her. The Terparchon. One time, early in the summer. She watched me dance, then ordered me to let her dig her fingers into my hands and feet. Didn't tell me anything, except that I was a dancer. And now I'm to be a princess? What do I know of that? Of anything, even the dances I'll have to perform? The spells . . ."

"I don't know what dances the princesses do in their chamber deep within the palace." Stevan frowned. A leaf, round and bright green, drifted down from overhead. He caught it before it could land on her head, and laid it on the ground. "I haven't even been there. But the dances at court balls are not so very different from those at the festival the other night."

"The princesses dance at festivals?" Gisela hadn't much considered what her life might include other than exercises and magic. And power wielded against the land as well as for.

"Yes. Often."

"Have you seen them do magic dances?"

"No. They don't do their magic in public although there are tales that once upon a time they'd go out and Dance anywhere, from a riverside to the top of a mountain. There are special chambers and buildings in every palace." He shook his head and picked up a stick to draw in the dirt. Line by line, he sketched an immense array of buildings and rooms that surely encompassed as much land as the village. Perhaps twice or three times as much.

Separate from all the other buildings, and yet encompassed by them if Gisela read his drawing aright, he outlined a square.

"The rest of us keep out." He tossed the stick to the side and tapped the square.

Only then did Gisela realize his other hand was still entwined with hers. She pulled her hand to her lap and his followed, not letting go. A harder tug and he likely would have, but she didn't test the theory.

"You've never pried?"

"No." He laughed, shoulders shaking.

"You weren't curious?"

"It wasn't my business. Not until very recently." Stevan squeezed her fingers, then let go. "I am not so different from you. Until this past moon, I was a scribe. A clerk to one of the royal ministers. Sub-ministers."

She reached for his hands and took them in hers. Turning them over, revealed the remnants of ink stains. Shivers of excitement trickled up her arms at the feel of the rough calluses from holding pen or stylus too long.

His fingers quivered within her grasp. His breathing shallowed, then emerged in a sigh.

But he'd stopped his story, right at the point where he'd caught her interest.

"What happened?" She looked up at him, hands still cupping his.

"The Terparchon danced with me at a ball—I blame my brother for that—and decided I was what Amara calls a compeer. Someone born to partner princesses." His hands turned within her grasp. Pushing backwards, he laid her hands in her lap and withdrew. Wrapped his arms across his chest. "That's why they sent me here. As bait, for you."

"Bait?" The word made no sense.

"A lure. Attraction. Amara claimed any princess would be drawn to dance with me. Not least one unaware of her power and standing."

Gisela sat right next to Stevan, practically in his lap. Nevertheless, without moving he withdrew from her. The air between them became a vast gap.

"And that is why I declined to lie with you that night."

"I don't understand."

"What were you offering, when you asked?" He stroked her cheek with a finger, leaving a burning warmth behind.

"The pleasures of the body." She cupped her head, covering the spot he'd touched. Her other hand flattened against the ground. The steady beat of the earth beneath helped her keep from reeling. As well she was seated still, for she did not know how many more unexpected shocks and realizations she could face.

"For one night. You did not think I would stay or you leave with me." He shook his head. "But I knew otherwise. That we would be bound in the same direction for much longer than you guessed. It wouldn't have been fair of me. It would have been taking advantage of your lack of knowledge."

"Kind of you." Though for a moment she wished he hadn't resisted.

That she'd had a night of celebration before facing the loss of her world.

"Because I want more." He caressed her other cheek, though his own ruddy cheeks flushed redder. "As I told you that night, ask me again at the next full moon and you'll get a different answer."

At which he turned shy, and ducked his head. Pulled away and rose to his feet where he towered over her.

She sat unmoving, turning his words over and over in her head. A new life away from the village, filled with unknowns. The power in her dance and the potential for its misuse. Someone who wanted to live and love with her, in this new life. It was all too much.

"If you're not ready at the next full moon, then the full moon after or any moon after." He smiled down at her, though his hands shook as he helped her to her feet. "If you ever decide you are willing to risk a life with me, all you need do is ask."

He escorted her back to the village, bowing over her hand as he left her at the door to her chamber and walked off.

Only after she'd downed a pitcher of watered wine and laid on her bed to rest did she allow herself to ponder any of the changes and realizations of the day.

Of which his offer was the sweetest.

A compeer. She'd never heard the word, yet the syllables held a sense of rightness and balance.

Someone to turn to and share with as they both entered the magic of the dance.

She dreamed of the dance that night. Of matching with him in twisting limbs as the beat of the earth pumped in their blood.

Then roused in the darkness to sit bolt upright and clutch the covers. She might not know much of the rulers and their attendants, but some things were no secrets. That the members mated in twos and the occasional three.

That rather than holding all children in common, bloodlines mattered.

If he wanted children, she could not bear them.

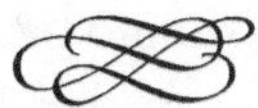

CHAPTER 13

Mud covered Gisela's foot. Thick and gooey, it clung to her skin. Resisted her attempts to yank her leg free. She stood at an angle, left foot dirty but resting on comparatively firm ground and the right stuck. Her hands held the skirts of her tunic and mantle to the knee, giving a clear view of the slick, yellow guck adhering to her skin. Adjusting her girdle, she twisted the cloths so the leather strap kept her skirts high. She wiped sweat from her forehead with the back of one hand. Damp hair clung to her scalp and neck.

Rain no longer cascaded from the clouds. Only stray drops pelted from the tree branches arching over the trail. The sky remained overcast and the air humid but otherwise pleasant. Certainly filled with the fragrance of grasses, grains, and flowers all growing in abundance. A glance in any direction would reveal a dozen or more shades of flourishing greens—a glance anywhere save directly down.

Gisela had spent many a day in the council chamber listening to traders complain about the condition of the tracks in the district without paying much heed. The trails near Foleilion might grow slick with mud or ice on occasion, but remained passable. How much worse could the path to the main trade road be?

If only she had advocated for improvements. Too late now.

Two days into the trip destroyed any interest in travel. Never having drifted farther than the other Escalli villages, she'd spent much thought on what she left behind and the trials she might face when she reached the palace—and almost none on getting there.

Stevan and Amara and the company had made their way to the village well enough; how hard could it be to walk the reverse? With all her dancing in the field, Gisela should be well suited to the trek.

Alas, walking along an uneven track for hours on end proved different enough from dancing that, although her body was accustomed to regular movement, she ached. Her step started out sprightly before settling into a slog. By the end of the first day, she lifted her feet only as far off the ground as necessary to shuffle along. A brief stint jouncing along on the back of the cart convinced her walking was preferable.

At least she no longer wore the dreaded sandals. She'd doffed them shortly after the cart stuck in the first large mud puddle. Heavy rain overnight left the bare ground wet and mucky. Here and there, the gray sky reflected in pools of water that had yet to seep into the earth. No matter how much mud clung to Gisela's feet, stepping in the pools rinsed her skin.

The narrow track passed along a dip between a field and forest. On either side, uneven banks sloped up. Patches of grass and large boulders covered both sides, as did thick roots from the tall trees. The result channeled rain into the ground along the track rather than letting it seep into the field or run off.

Whoever had thought this a good place to pass?

Curses and grunts rang out from behind as Stevan and half of the guards lent their strength to get the cart through the muck. The donkeys brayed and struggled as they forged on. The humans pushed. Most had streaks up legs, along arms, and across faces and chests. One of the guards had a solid smear of mud along the top of his head, having run a mucky hand through. All had rucked up their tunics above their knees, showing shapely legs now amply striped in thick wet earth.

Quite a sight to see, even dirtied as they were. If Gisela's gaze lingered longest on Stevan, she doubted any took the time to notice.

Gisela's offer to assist had been gently declined.

Amara had not offered. Wrapped in two layers of mantles to keep off the damp, she passed along the edge of the muddy ruts and escaped with only a thin layer of mud coating her feet.

If only luck had favored Gisela as well.

The muscles in her back and thighs protested as she bent over and wrapped her hands around her ankle.

Yanked once. Twice. On the third, her foot came free with a vengeance. Clods of earth splashed all around. The force of the release nearly toppled Gisela, except Stevan's solid body braced her. His muddy hands fastened on her upper arms and her torso pressed back against his.

They held onto each other as they hobbled to the side of the track and dropped onto the narrow verge. Covered by a mix of grass clumps and gnarled tree roots, it offered little in the way of comfort but was preferable to treading further off the track into the field stretching to one side or the forest to the other.

The ground welcomed Gisela with a soft thrum. The resonance eased the ache in her legs, but only for a moment. Running her hands along her legs, she massaged her sore muscles. Found a knot in her right calf and pressed hard. Drew in a deep breath, held, and then let it out slowly. The muscle twanged as tension released. Although improved, a residual ache remained.

Farther down, the others had freed the donkeys from the mud puddle although not the cart. The wheels remained nearly a third covered with muck as most of the dirty company likewise settled onto the verge to rest.

Emmi and Rik lifted skins of wine from the cart and poured generous mouthfuls for all who wanted. Other servants tended the animals. Gisela drank the wine gladly, swishing some of the tart liquid around her mouth to clear the taste of mud.

"How long did it take you to travel here?" Gisela looked back where the track curved in the distance, around a high hill.

"A matter of days." Stevan picked up a stray pebble and tossed it into the puddle. It sank with a gulp. "The way was not this bad. The summer storms hadn't started. We're fortunate not to be walking in pouring rain, though this is hardly any better.

"The summer storms?"

"Beginning around midsummer, great storms roll in from the ocean and drench the land, at best. The winds have been known to whip houses from their foundations. They grow worse, then weaken as summer turns to fall. The court remains at the summer palace in Yaras to face the storms, as the princesses ease their rage." Stevan frowned, brows wrinkling. "Haven't you endured them in Foleilion?"

"Our summer storms are mostly the same as you saw while you were there. Nearly every afternoon, a squall will pass through and drop rain before moving on. They rarely last long." She rubbed her soles against her legs, sending clumps of flaking earth to roll down the slope. "And though they leave us with mud, I don't recall ever seeing quite so much of it."

"I can see the road in the distance. In good weather, we'd cross the distance in half an hour or less." Amara remained standing, perched high on a thick root that raised her nearly a length above the muck. She shook her head, mouth turning up to one side, as she gazed down at Gisela, Stevan, and the rest. "It'll take longer today."

Gisela's arm muscles trembled as she rubbed her calves and ankles. Little though she'd liked the previous day's travel, she'd found passing over dry earth more preferable.

"Must we continue on in this?" The notion of a long slog through more mud sent a shiver up Gisela's spine. "Is there nothing that would dry the earth, just a little?"

"Only a Dance, though even a lesser one could. There's a Dance for almost everything."

Amara pronounced dance the same way everyone did. Yet somehow the way she said it roused a resonance in Gisela, a warmth as though she'd stepped from shadows into a pool of sunlight. Soon, she'd learn what Amara meant, what kind of Dance was more than the measures and movements enjoyed at festivals and casual gatherings.

But not, evidently for healing conditions such as hers. A flash of disappointment flooded through her, even though she'd not imagined the possibility until it was withheld.

"Dance." Gisela tried to replicate the emphasis, but failed.

Stevan glanced back and forth between them, brows narrowing in a frown. Perhaps he hadn't heard the difference.

"There's no way to describe it that does it justice." Amara closed her eyes and tilted her head back. "When done right it is a melding. Bringing disparate forces into harmony. Achieving balance. Once you've Danced on purpose, not by accident, you can never mistake it for anything else. Balls and hops at taverns are mere exercise in comparison."

The older dam pressed clenched fists against her chest, arms tight at her sides. Her torso expanded and contracted with deep, shuddering breaths. Air hissed through her lips as she exhaled.

"You miss it." Stevan rose. Though standing on earth, not the root, he was tall enough to lay a comforting hand on Amara's shoulder.

"Always." A shiver racked her, then the tension drained from her body. She opened her eyes and ducked her head. "But I am no longer able to Dance as I did before."

"Why not? You're in better shape than Gisela or I. Surely—"

"It's not just a matter of body but mind and spirit." She jerked away from his hand.

Stevan retreated, shoulders turning inward.

Without thought, Gisela rose and stood next to him. She nudged him, tucking her hand in his. He grabbed tight.

Amara noted the movement and gave them a tight smile. "My apologies. But I know myself not fit. I leave things unbalanced, so it is better if I content myself with teaching others."

"But you're not content." Gisela waved at the mud. "Couldn't you do a little one here, on the track?

"I must be content. It is required of me." The other dam shrugged. "Didn't you hear me say I am unbalanced?"

"Well, so am I." Gisela reflexively touched her temple, where the purple streak had yet to fade.

"It's not quite the same." Amara shook her head.

Gisela slumped. Stevan laid warm hands on her shoulders, fingers digging deep to the point Gisela moaned in relief as tension dispersed. She leaned back into him as he spoke over her head.

"Could you teach Gisela?"

Amara paused, then leapt down onto the trail. The mud squelched, sinking her down far enough that her toes vanished from sight.

"I'll show you something that might work, but you must be the one to Dance and dry the road." The elder offered Gisela a hand. "I'll only participate as much as needed to ensure the cart wheels are not trapped. And you"—she jerked her chin at Stevan—"can keep time and watch that Gisela does not use too much power."

Gisela clasped her hands together to keep from twitching. What had she wrought? A simple hope to ease their travels had ensnared her. She'd thought Amara might dry the ground—not her.

Thick damp earth oozed under Gisela as she left the verge to stand in the middle of the track. Feet together. Arms loose at her side. Back straight. Head raised.

Slow pulses moved through the goop surrounding Gisela's feet. She tapped her thigh to catch the beat.

Then startled when Amara rapped her nose.

"Not yet."

"Don't we Dance to the earth's beat?" Gisela let her hand hang loose. The thick smell of warm, wet earth filled her and made it hard to focus.

"Not if we want to change matters in a way the earth has no interest in." Amara circled Gisela, feet sliding through the mud. "Now first, you must set limits. Think only of this stretch of track, not the field or forest. From here to where it joins the stone road."

A glance in the direction Amara pointed showed nothing but a mucky track, with trees and crops to either side. Yet the words stone and road formed a picture in Gisela's mind: of the track, except lined in stones to make for an easier passage.

"Just the track."

"Good." Amara crossed her arms and tilted her head. "Now, if we're drying the track, where does the water in the mud go?"

"Wherever it would?" Gisela shrugged.

"So you wish to speed the process up? Or bring sun to bake it or a wind to absorb it and wick it away?"

"I don't know." Gisela took a deep breath and resisted the urge to stamp her foot. "Isn't that what I'm supposed to be learning?"

"Dances change the world, however small. It is important to consider as many of the consequences as you can in advance. This is true even when the earth asks you to Dance something for it. The best Dances are those that balance the needs and interests of all parties, and . . ." Amara leaned in, so her face lay only a breath away from Gisela's. "Do you understand me even a little?"

"We can't just change one thing, because everything is connected." Gisela stared back, refusing to back down.

"That's a start." Amara squelched back to the edge of the track, heaving a sigh. "Now, what's the earth's beat?"

Finding it again took little effort. Gisela clapped her hands. The slow, lazy beat sapped energy from her body. Standing straight became work, as her torso wanted to sway.

"Enough."

Gisela squeezed her eyes shut and shook her head, trying to banish the somnolence creeping over her.

Amara had Stevan start a fast, sprightly beat. Much perkier. Even from a length away, the crisp clapping brushed some of the cobwebby feel from Gisela's mind.

"Find the rhythm between the earth's beat and Stevan's." Amara shifted so she stood halfway between Gisela and the cart. "Think about what you want to have happen, the track drying. Dance until that's all you hear—until that's what you're Dancing to. Then stop— and be sure to end with your body touching Stevan in some way."

Two beats, and she had to find a third between them. With no further help from Amara, some teacher she was. Gisela shifted—or tried to. Mud clung to her feet, sucking at her and resisting efforts to pull away. Her legs settled into a slow back-and-forth movement without actually lifting toes or heels. An itch crept across her shoulders. She rolled them, fast and then faster.

How long it took she never knew. Only that her legs followed the earth's beat and her arms Stevan's. Her poor torso suffered. Muscles in her abdomen of which she'd been unaware began to ache.

A third beat began to pulse in her hips. She made small circles, then larger as the thrum expanded from her mid-section to reverberate in her legs and arms.

The earth firmed beneath her feet, growing warm and lifting her. Letting go of her soles. She twirled around, her skin rippling with energy as the air heated and wicked moisture from the earth. Light filled her eyes, turning the world into a haze in the distance.

Life and joy and happiness thrummed from the tips of her hair into the deepest recesses of her body. All sorrows faded, drained. Her whole being became light, mere thistle-down floating on the breeze. Her hair dried and stood out from her head.

Gisela barely remembered Amara's last instruction. Some instinct had her twirl over to Stevan before a wind could blow her away.

His arms wrapped around her, and the energy sank through him back into the earth. She slumped against him, body still aquiver. Skin exquisitely sensitive to the press of him against her. The taste of his sweat on her lips as she tucked her head against his chest.

Only then did she dare open her eyes, in time to watch a glowing Amara give a leap—and the wagon likewise lift before settling onto dry ground.

CHAPTER 14

orget weariness or inexplicably stained clothing or the general lack of decent bathing facilities, Stevan considered the lack of privacy the primary problem with travel. Every time he turned around, someone watched or brushed by, or hummed.

He slogged on along the road, gritting his teeth so as not to say anything too rude or unforgivable. It was his own fault he walked close to the hummer. Rik led the donkey cart and, unfortunately, had no musicality whatsoever. They wandered from tune to tune without warning, all the while never managing to be in key.

Stevan's own choice placed him right in front of the cart, in the middle of the procession.

Yet at the same time, it was the best option. The most courteous. He'd ceded the places closer to the front to Amara and Gisela. They had only two guards preceding them, leaving them with clearer air while he had to follow behind, breathing in the dust kicked up by additional pairs of feet. Stevan brushed at his clothing but never managed to get them quite clean. His throat remained dry, and no matter how often he resorted to well-watered wine he couldn't be rid of the taste of dust.

Stones lined the road, worn almost even by the repeated passage of wagons and carts and feet over the decades since they were first laid. The dust came from between the stones, and from the dry earth to either side.

They hadn't seen a drop of rain since the day Gisela dried the track.

Hot, dry, dusty weather might make any man ill-tempered. Increase a tendency to stomp. Grit teeth. Tap fingers restlessly against his thighs.

Stevan blamed the lack of privacy instead.

Gisela walked in front with an easy stride, hips rolling from side to side. The straight lines of shoulders and back remained steady in contrast.

Remaining behind deprived him of the proximity needed to talk to her. Save that the things he wished most to discuss warranted distance. Not between them, but between them and everyone else. The very thing he'd not managed to arrange at any point. Only times for more general discussions about the weather, scenery, and court.

All because they were traveling in company.

If only they were at the palace. Immense and rambling and a font of nooks and crannies. It held hordes of people, as every generation added on to the rambling assortment of buildings. Some part was always under construction, and another falling apart. Between them and the extensive gardens, an inventive explorer could always find some measure of privacy.

But they hadn't arrived yet, and before they did, Stevan wanted time with Gisela. Alone, or at least where they might speak without being overheard. A chance to ensure she was prepared for the organized chaos of the court. To discuss her Dance, and how she'd clung to him afterward. Her arms had wrapped around him, head pressed against his chest, and bolts of energy passed from her body through his and into the ground.

She laughed at something Amara said. A light, clear tone that rang out over Rik's humming and the constant plodding footsteps of humans and donkeys.

The sound lifted his spirits, no matter he had no idea what she'd found amusing. A small chuckle escaped him at that realization.

And she heard him. For a moment, her head turned just far enough to glance back.

For eyes to meet.

He smiled.

So did she, before turning away. Facing front. Setting her shoulders.

Though her hips kept swaying, circling.

Somehow he'd find a way.

Less than an hour later, they topped a rise and began to descend towards a village halfway down. The lake spread out before them, wide enough the far side was no more than a sandy blur against the horizon. Likewise, the palace appeared in the distance as only a smudge along the lake shore.

They wouldn't make it there tonight.

The village, on the other hand, lay well within reach. It had a lovely, multi-floored inn with a garden at the top.

No sooner did Stevan see it, than he began to plot ways to draw Gisela with him up to the garden.

Alone.

He waited through the bustle of their arrival. The reservation of a suite of chambers. The disbursement of their belongings to those rooms, so that all in the party could—in strict order of rank—take advantage of the inn's bath house and plunge pool.

Hair damp and newly trimmed, and the stubble cleared from his face, he donned fresh loincloth and tunic, and the cleanest of his mantles now sponged free of dirt. The barber had rubbed his head with a cloth bearing a light, musky perfume, of fir trees and high places.

Thus refreshed, he tracked Gisela down to the common room. Similarly cleansed and perfumed, she leaned against a wide window and watched the hustle and bustle in the inn-yard below. She too wore fresh attire, a light purple mantle that complemented her coloring. Declining to don another pair of sandals anytime soon, her bare toes dug into the soft, flat rush rug covering the stone floor. Thick walls, also of stone, kept the rooms to a tolerable temperature despite the heavy sunlight.

Already her skin started to glisten with moisture. He was sweating. A breeze blew by, but not enough to offer true ease.

"There's a garden above us." He stood at the opposite side of the window, giving her space. "With refreshing breezes, and a lovely view. Would you care to see?"

She didn't respond immediately. Her head remained tilted downward, face toward the courtyard. One of her hands slipped up and under the damp hair trailing down her neck. Lifting the thick locks, she angled her shoulders to catch the breeze. With a sigh, she let her hair fall and turned to face him.

"More breezes?"

"I promise." He held out a hand.

After a moment's consideration, she laid hers atop his. His fingers curved instantly about her fingers, skin soft and warm and redolent with a perfume that made his nose itch. He kept his grasp loose and easy as he led the way to the stairs, and up and out onto the rooftop.

The sun had begun to descend, and shadows lengthen. These allied with the breezes to ease some of the day's heat.

Wide-lipped basins and vases, and long rectangular stone fixtures, boasted a dazzling array of plants. Tall ferns with delicate leaves. Short trees only a few hands taller than he with thick canopies that offered pools of shade. An abundance of flowers in all shades of purple, pink, and red. Without the breezes, cooler here so high above ground, the floral scents might be oppressive. Instead, it made for a heady mixture: lush and damp from earlier rain or watering.

Gisela oohed and aahed over the plants, asking a myriad of questions. He pled ignorance too many times.

"The palace gardeners will know, I am sure. This is lovely, but less than one thirteenth what you will find in the gardens when we arrive tomorrow."

"Tomorrow." She ran her fingers along the fronds of a fern. "So soon."

"All travels must end some day." A breeze lifted scents of bread and meat cooking, making his stomach rumble. He drew in a deep breath. "Are you looking forward to joining the court? Nervous? I am."

"You?" She turned on her toes, bracing one hand against a tree trunk. "But you're—"

"Newly raised to a compeer and with little notion what is expected of me." He shrugged. "As I told you once before, we have much in common."

"And many differences. You have some knowledge of life at court."

"Some, yes. But you'll catch up. We're nearly there, after all." He led her to the waist-high balustrade surrounding the garden. Pointed down the hill at the palace splayed out along the lake shore. The gilded roofs of the main buildings glittered in the burnished light. "We'll arrive before the midday meal."

"So close." Gisela drew back, brow furrowing. "Why did we not press on today?"

"Would you want to arrive tired and dusty from the road?"

A pause, then she shook her head. Began to smile, small though the movement was.

"As well, this small delay means we will arrive back thirteen days from when we left to find you. An auspicious number."

"Indeed, the best of them all save one and two." She turned back to lean against the balustrade, head turning this way and that. "Which is the palace?"

"Nearly all. It sprawls, and the town curves around it, from the river harbor to the lake shore in a great arc." He reached over her shoulder to point at the ships sailing to and from the docks out into the wide waters. The light, floral fragrance clinging to her skin made him a little dizzy, but he resisted the urge to stroke her hair. "The palace grounds are laid out in a solar pattern. The royal residence is the sun, that half-crescent shape by the shore."

"So large." Her shiver shifted her back to lean against him.

"It holds all manner of chambers and suites. I haven't gone in it often, got lost once. Or twice."

Mosaics covered the floors and walls. Tapestries hung in chambers, alongside wooden furniture with intricate carvings and glittering arrays of candlesticks, ewers, and items for which he had no words. Quite different from the plain, white-washed walls of the manor he'd grown up in. He'd learned to use the mosaics and furniture to decipher his way, as he couldn't merely memorize numbers of turns.

So many things to learn, but she didn't need to hear that now.

"The buildings running out from the center, like rays of the sun, hold ministries and barracks and servants' quarters. Between them are gardens and practice fields for the guards."

"Where do you live?" Gisela glanced back at him, with a small smile.

"I share a room on a top floor with another scribe, about there." Stevan tried to point, then gave up. It was too far distant. "I'll likely be moved, but no one's told me where."

"Or where I'll be put either, I suppose." Her sigh pressed her body more firmly against him.

"No, but this much I can tell you. You see that seven-sided building at the center, within the curve of the royal residence?" His cheek brushed hers.

"Yes?"

"That's the dancing pavilion. Where the princesses go every day to . . . do whatever it is they do."

"Right by the lake and that gray spot." Her hair brushed his neck as she shifted, then pointed at a pale-gray circle near the pavilion. But what is that squarish building on the far side?"

With the exception of the palace and pavilion, almost all the buildings were square. Stevan had to align himself with Gisela's arm to track down what she was pointing at, then nodded. The one spot he'd forgot to include.

"That's the children's palace."

"The what?" Her body stiffened, a sudden motion that made him step backward to give her room. Her arms pinned tight against her side and a muscle jumped along the side of her neck.

"Given the size of the court, and the number of servants and guards required to keep all safe and functional, there are many families with children." Stevan circled around to lean against the railing close but not right next to her. Where he could gesture at the scene below, but also watch her from the corner of his eyes. "Several generations ago, one of the Terparchon's ancestors decreed children should not be separated from their parents but allowed to travel with the court. She had small palaces built for her children and those of her attendants and servants. Tutors and nurses care for the young when their parents cannot. Some of the wealthier families do not let their children mingle with those in the children's palaces, but the Terparchon's children all played with others regardless of rank."

It should be good news, yet Gisela's torso remained stiff. Her shoulders hunched and head drooped.

"Don't the Escalli do likewise? Care for children gathered together?" Stevan had passed by the nursery often enough, and the cacophony of children's laughter, calls, and tears was unmistakable.

"Yes, but Escalli children don't belong to specific parents. It's known who sired and bore them, but they're kept as a shared treasure. I thought . . . I was taught that it was different for others. For the courtiers." Her voice dropped. "I didn't think they would have children there with them."

"Why not? Children belong with their parents, except when work doesn't allow for it. Most of my older siblings have marital contracts, and the few times I've gone home the place was overrun with their offspring." He'd shared a room with five of his nephews on the last visit.

She didn't respond. Her hands wrapped around the balustrade, knuckles white.

Stevan drew in a sharp breath, near choking on the thick scent of smoke wreathing up from the cook fires below.

Escalli held children in common.

"Did you leave children behind?"

"No." She blinked and touched the fading purple streak in her hair. "I am unable to bear children."

Back straight, she held onto the railing as though only it kept her standing.

"That's the first time I've said it aloud." A lurching laugh broke from her as she turned wide, bright eyes his way. "It's strange. I always assumed I would be able to. Never even considered not, though there are always some unable. Our children belong to us all, not merely those who sired or bore them, and yet . . . ever since I had to dye my hair purple instead of pink, I haven't been able to face the nursery and the nursery guardians."

He put a hand on one shoulder and squeezed to offer comfort. No words sprung to mind.

But words weren't necessary. She leaned into him, and again he held her close. He'd never given the matter of having children much thought. He had quite enough siblings and several times as many nieces and nephews. All the same, he understood at least some part of the pain she might feel—of not being able to do something, whether or not he wanted it.

So he folded an arm around her. Rocked her. Brushed kisses across her hair. Didn't say it would be all right somehow because it wouldn't and she'd know that better than him.

When her rigidness eased, she turned her face toward his. He patted away the dampness in her eyes. She straightened the set of his tunic and mantle along his shoulders.

The result was two pairs of lips in close proximity.

He stole a kiss. Soft, warm, gentle. Pulled back and waited for her response, her choice.

Tilting forward, she lifted her face to his for another kiss.

"Gisela? Are you—Oh!"

Having missed the signs of Amara's approach, they sprang apart and rocked against the balustrade with the force of their movement.

"I am so sorry, I'll just go back—"

"No need." Stevan licked his lips to savor the last sweet taste of Gisela. "I was just pointing out the palace. I'll go check on dinner."

"Stay." Amara patted his shoulder as she made an arc around him to the far side of Gisela. "I apologize for my interruption. I wanted only a brief word, in case there is not a chance to say this much tomorrow. But it applies to the both of you in different measure."

"Both of us?" Gisela shifted back against the railing, away from Amara and Stevan.

"Do not let the other princesses make you feel less than what you are, Gisela, which is a princess and their equal. Even as you, Stevan, are a match for any of the compeers. But if you ever do . . ." Amara stretched out a hand to touch the streak in Gisela's hair. The younger woman stood strong without flinching, although her hands tightened on the railing. "Go stand upon a Shadow of the Moon for a little while and you may realize how much power and life you still have in you."

"The Shadow of the Moon?" An odd note entered Gisela's voice. "There's one here?"

"Yes. They're uncanny things." Cold rippled up Stevan's spine in memory of the times he'd passed across one, at the summer or winter palace or up in the hills of his youth. He pointed to a small circular area set in a clearing surrounded by trees. A spot that seemed to absorb light and not give back, although it wasn't dark or shadowy gray in color but rather an unnatural grayish-green. "It's dead. There's no life there at all. Deader than dead."

Upon which he understood Amara's reasoning. In such a place, one could not help but feel the presence of one's own life in contrast.

"Then why build the palace so close?" Gisela stared at the spot. "I presume it was here first, or after?"

"The Shadow was here first." Amara stood next to Gisela, shoulder to shoulder. "Nearly every Terparchon has pursued the goal of building palaces next to all twelve of them someday, even though only eight lie within Codaros' boundaries."

"Twelve?" Gisela shuddered. "An unnatural number, too easily divided."

"I heard there were thirteen." Stevan tried to tote them up in his mind, since Amara continued to linger and Gisela had a distracted air.

"Twelve." Amara grunted. "People may claim there's a thirteenth Shadow, but that's not but a shadow of a shadow. Things grow there; only weeds, but they flourish. On the true Shadows nothing grows, they are so far out of balance. But I interrupted you." She stepped back, a smile on her face. "I will have dinner held for you."

Although she left, the mood had changed. Gisela held onto the railing, hands loose although her body vibrated with energy as though a lute string recently plucked.

Stevan remained at her side. A sliver of the moon rose above the lake—so faint it barely cast a reflection in the glittering waters. Time remained before the moon grew full. The interruption might have set matters back, but they'd made progress toward the next time it grew round.

He now knew one of her sorrows. The law of balance meant that, if he determined to continue a courtship, he would have to offer her a corresponding sorrow or weakness in turn.

Yet the way Amara had worded her advice concerned him. That he and Gisela were the equal of any other compeer and princess he accepted.

But was a compeer a match for a princess outside of Dancing? Compeers' names weren't commonly known the way princesses were. Stevan combed through his memories, but couldn't recall noticing any other than the royal offspring and one of the royal councilors. On the other hand, he'd heard many jokes about how fast the princesses burned through partners, even before being raised to that rank.

He desired Gisela, but not at the cost of being scorched.

CHAPTER 15

For a day Gisela dreaded, the morning dawned entirely too nice. A hot sun burned as usual overhead, but ample breezes blew in off the lake to cool the procession's descent. A lovely mix of puffy white and pale-gray clouds marked the otherwise bright blue sky, save for a faint hint of dark gray along the horizon. Thanks to a brief rain shower prior to dawn, feet, hooves, and wheels kicked up little dust from the road, yet faced only a few spots of mud all easily avoided.

The lightest and loveliest of Gisela's new tunics flowed about her. Embroidered flowers and stars enlivened the hems of the pale violet gauze. Today's mantle, of deeper violet, had originally concealed the embroidery, but Emmi managed to take it up.

"You shouldn't have. I could have sewn it myself."

Emmi had waved off Gisela's protests. "That's not your place anymore," the other dam insisted. "You Dance, I sew."

And clean and mend and so many other tasks, not least of which was lining Gisela's newest sandals with soft cloths. Thus the violet-dyed straps, which criss-crossed her feet at different angles than the previous day's footwear, didn't chafe her skin anew.

To think that Gisela, who'd once rarely worn anything on her feet, now had so many pairs of sandals. And clothes. And needed take little time in caring for them.

If this were a taste of the luxuries she'd find at court, she stood atop a slippery slope and might be all-too-easily corrupted.

Yet, Emmi had summed up what Gisela could do in recompense quite neatly.

She would Dance.

But what kind of Dances might she work? Drying the road was the merest trifle, no doubt. Easing storms and coaxing water in times of drought, those she would not mind at all assisting with. On the other hand, she now believed previous Dancing Princesses could have destroyed her Escalad, though she did not know whether they had.

What if she were asked to help mete out destruction to others?

Ilburna had made clear to Gisela her first duty was to the Escalli through service at court. Dancing in exchange for tax abatement. The use of her eyes and ears to feed news back, as she could.

When Gisela posed that same question to the older dam, after admitting the power of dancing, Ilburna had closed her eyes and sighed. She had no answer for Gisela then. The next morning, before Gisela left, she passed on only a few pieces of advice.

"Do as little harm to others as you can." Ilburna had cupped Gisela's head within her hands. Her fingers trembled, sending sympathetic resonance through Gisela's cheeks. "For all else, trust your own judgment. We trust in you."

Gisela would have to remain strong and resist temptation.

First she had to walk downhill.

This proved trickier than expected. Flat-topped stones lined the road but had settled at a slightly different angle, so that each step required adjusting her stance. After the first few hours, her ankles and legs ached far more than arms and shoulders.

She spoke less, focusing instead on keeping her breathing even and her eyes on the road.

Amara and Stevan kept pace. They gave occasional grunts suggesting they found the descent troublesome as well, but managed to speak off and on, pointing out this feature or that in the town and palace below.

When they reached flatter lands, the two fell into step behind her. The town walls began to loom in the distance. The gilded palace walls rose beyond.

The road down the hillside joined with others, with an increase in traffic. Carters and peddlers toted wares in donkey carts and tall backpacks. Traders led convoys with attendant guards to ensure the safety of their goods. The stony surface might be more even, but now Gisela had to keep aware to dodge spots marked with urine or feces the rain had not washed away.

Amara made changes to the order of their procession on the flats. Two guards led, as before.

Gisela followed, with Amara and Stevan behind her and two more guards. Then Rik and Emmi with the donkey cart, and the last guards at the end.

Even as Amara rearranged their order, she drew from the cart a thin circlet of silver twined with gold. Burnished to an impressive brightness, it drew all eyes. The maker had engraved a pattern of hands clasping hands around the edge. No one else might see, unless they came close.

But all saw the glittering brilliance gracing Gisela's head.

The metal itself didn't weigh much. It sat light across her brow and along the sides. Yet it grew warm, even hot, as she walked. Made her head sweat more than the rest of her.

The more so as it drew attention.

First from Stevan, who dropped his chin low and bowed, his light green mantle fluttering and the thick, gold embroidery at throat reflecting light back in dancing circles. When he raised his head, his eyes had a watery sheen. He took a step backward, dropping into formation behind her even though she'd nodded for him to join her if he would.

Respect—and rejection? His withdrawal to walk behind was only slightly eased by his evident admiration. Which did little good alone. Bitterness flooded her mouth.

The others' open approval gave a little balm. Amara, Rik, and Emmi all beamed at Gisela's new appearance. Although dressed well, in varying shades of blue and purple, their lightweight tunics and mantles were pale and subtle in color, allowing her darker shades to draw attention.

The guards marching before her stood straighter, shoulders high.

Before, their procession mingled with the others with little difference. With the addition of the circlet, all changed. Passers-by drew back and gave Gisela and the others more room. Carters and traders pulled to the side and bowed at the waist, shallow or deep, as they passed. Even rich traders bent their heads and offered signs of respect.

Moreover, they all watched her. So many eyes and unspoken thoughts. The air around seemed to thicken, making it harder to breathe. Not merely a trick of heat and humidity, but something more. As though the breezes lifted hopes and expectations from those watching and draped them upon Gisela.

The weight of unspoken expectancy grew heavier as they entered the city. The air grew hotter, thicker, as stone walls grew to either side. Gisela snapped her mouth shut more than once, on realizing she gaped at the massive buildings. Some had three, four, and more stories. Plants grew on balconies from some upper levels, dripping the occasional leaf or flower petal. Elsewhere, cords stretched across the street from building to building. Damp tunics and mantles hung to dry, occasionally falling upon those walking below.

Here and there lay open spaces, gardens and plazas filled with multi-colored blooms, fruit trees, and vegetables plants rising knee- and waist-high.

Sandals slapping against the stone-lined streets, the guards led a twisting way. Forward several paces, then turn and to the right. To the left. Then left again.

Gisela would never find her way out without assistance. There was no place to go but forward.

To the palace.

A lump formed in her belly. Despite hurried lessons on the road, she only half-remembered how to greet the Terparchon and Marchon. Or anyone at court, for that matter.

Walls of gray stone stretched out to either side. Flecks of gold and copper within the stones caught select rays of sunlight and magnified them. Soldiers stationed atop appeared as spots against the bright sky. After no more than a breath or two of looking at the wrong section, Gisela blinked several times and turned away. Spots continued to jiggle in her eyes as she focused on a different section of the wall—and the gate.

Gridded doors set into an arch in the wall lay open. The bars themselves were a dull gray, both up-and-down and side-to-side. Each place where they crossed bore an intricate cast animal or bird, from donkeys and oxen at the bottom to falcons and eagles in flight up high. All different, all with some touch of colored enamel even if only on the eyes or as beads of blood on claws or talons.

Guards in boiled leather armor and red capes stood watch at the opening. The smells of sweat and leather hung so thick about them Gisela swallowed to dispel the taste. All but one carried spears and had long knives strapped to their waists. The exception, with a sword as well as knife and a copper circlet across his pasty, sweaty forehead, moved forward to block the way.

The guards marching ahead of Gisela swung to either side, leaving her exposed to move forward alone.

Her steps slowed, faltered.

The sword-bearer frowned and squinted at her.

"I don't know you. Who comes?"

Amara and Stevan caught up with Gisela, framing her.

"We bring the new princess." Amara waved a hand at him. "Let us pass."

The other continued to gaze at Gisela for several breaths. Then moved on to glance Amara's way, and gave a half-bow.

"You've been much looked for." Half-turning, they snapped their fingers and jerked their head.

A tan youngling made of all arms and long legs, dressed only in a red loincloth, leapt from the shadows beyond the gate and streaked off across the wide plaza. His sandaled feet slapped the stones, setting up a mute echo as he went.

"Has there been trouble?" Amara took Gisela's arm and urged her forward. "There seems to be no one about. Most unusual."

"The Marchon and Terparchon have each gone hunting, taking much of the court with them." One hand on sword hilt, the guard stood aside to let them through. "There's little enough business at this gate with them gone, though the south gate still sees much traffic."

Amara continued conversation with the guard for some time. Gisela heard both voices, but the words passed through her head with little understanding.

Mosaics covered the plaza floor and surrounding walls. Minute polished stones added up to immense creations. Giants in white, red, black, and brown gazed out from every wall. Some carried weapons and fought. Others played sports—throwing discs, running, leaping, and more.

Below her feet lay an ocean of blues and greens studded with purple, red, and golden fish of all sizes and shapes. The plaza stones absorbed sunlight and gave back some heat, warming her feet despite the protective layer of her sandals. The warm air carried a salty aroma that dispelled the sweat and leather of the gate.

Across the wide-open space lay the only building not decorated with mosaic figures. In sharp contrast, the walls were white-washed until they gleamed so bright as to draw the gaze despite the competition.

Anyone walking up or down stood out.

Emmi, Rik, and the other servants and guards slid off along the wall. Donkey hooves clopped against the stone pavement, with a lighter ring than out in the streets. Gisela turned to follow them, but Amara laid a hand on her arm. Pale lavender skin shone bright against Gisela's violet sleeve.

"We go in the front. Not the back or side. Chin up, my dear." White teeth flashed as she smiled. "Remember, we need you here as much or more than your people do."

"So you say." Gisela allowed Amara to lead her across the ocean mosaic to the stairs. Stevan followed behind, his mere presence reassuring even though he said nothing. A warmth and protection at her back.

At the top of the stairs, doors parted.

To Gisela's intense relief, only three people exited and descended the stairs.

Princesses all, for each wore a circlet matching hers.

First a dam reminiscent of Amara in form and ease of movement, albeit little else. Bright red hair sprang from the new arrival's head, scarcely tamed into a long braid down her back. A dull silver-colored mantle barely stood out against a dark gray tunic. The colors combined to leach color save undertones of green from the dam's skin and give her an appearance of ill-health.

"Jola." Amara whispered in Gisela's ear. "Born and raised near the winter palace. She's been a princess for a decade. These past years she's partnered with the Terparchon and Marchon's elder daughter."

Next to Jola strolled a tall, lanky figure. Long limbs connected to a short torso, but they nevertheless moved with liquid grace. Shoulder-length locks of dark brown wreathed a face only a few shades paler. Their face was smooth-shaven, save for a few hints of stubble along the pointed chin. Their light orange tunic bore bright gold embroidery at neck and ankle. An artist had dyed the mantle draped around them, for it featured swirls of three different shades of orange against a red background.

"Heron." Amara again provided the name. "An eleee from across the northern river. A princess these past five years. They came to it late, although some of the other princesses started much older than either of you. I think you will find much in common with them."

The third princess started down last, but ended first. Short and delicate, but with ample curves at breast and hip, she bounced with every step. Her circlet threatened to slide off her wealth of tight, night-black curls falling to her collarbone. She too wore a silver mantle, but over a deep blue tunic that brought out sapphire undertones in her sepia-colored skin. Her hands and arms rose and fell with each bounding step, graceful as wings on a bird in flight. Seven gold bangles around her right wrist and three silver on her left chimed with the movements.

Her momentum had her tripping off the stairs and nearly barreling into Gisela before she came to a sharp stop. She grabbed Gisela's hands and pressed them in warm fingers.

"Oh, I am glad to meet you. Now I'm not the youngest anymore."

"This is Danissa, born and raised at court, who's only been a princess for a year." Amara wrapped her arms around the shorter dam's shoulders and squeezed.

"I'm the youngest princess by years and time dancing. But no more! You'll be the last of us until the next changeover." Danissa wiggled out of Amara's grasp, still holding tight to Gisela. "Though I'm sure I'll learn a lot from you all the same. Everyone teaches me all the time. Even Ylena, who always had her nose so high in the air she hardly noticed the rest of us. But my father said he'd not seen anything so moving as your dancing in a long time, not since Amara still Danced, so maybe we can practice together and some of it will rub off on me?"

Gisela blinked "Your father's seen me dance?"

"He was with the Terparchon when she found you. Idan? Her first counselor?" Danissa let go and took a step back. She folded her arms over her chest and tilted her head.

The pose called forth vague memories of an elder with Danissa's skin and build but long white hair wrapped around his head, and a deep, resonant voice naming Foleilion.

"He's also the longest serving of the compeers. There are some who say the Terparchon only took me on as a princess because of him." The other princess heaved a sigh as she abandoned the serious pose. "But they've only ever seen me at court balls—not Dancing."

"I'm sure you are a fine dancer." Gisela smiled.

"You need do nothing to encourage her confidence." Heron's voice was low and musical, with faint lilt that made their pronunciation closer to Gisela's people, though not the same. "But praise is always welcome."

"Oh my, yes. Do not look to the Terparchon for praise for she rarely grants it. We are never quite good enough for her liking, no matter how well we accomplish her desires." Danissa bounced on her toes. "But come. Let us show you around, all that you will need to know before the rest return."

"The rest?" Gisela glanced around the open area. Few others stood upon the stones—but above, faces shone at nearly every window.

"The other princesses." Jola gestured at the city beyond the gates, her wrists fluid and graceful and eye-catching. "Some are in town. Others on a hunt with the Terparchon and Marchon. The three of us were chosen, or volunteered"—a smile at Danissa there—"to remain behind. We did not want to overwhelm you with the need to meet, and remember, all of us at once."

"Very politic choices." Amara nodded at each in turn.

The note in her voice sent a chill along Gisela's spine. "Oh?"

A second turn around showed even more faces at the various windows, all looking down at her. She stiffened, keeping her lips closed in a smile so no one might hear her teeth chatter. Twined her hands around soft folds of her mantle to hide how her fingers twitched. The sun seemed to shine even brighter overhead, light reflecting from every side until the world was awash and colors faded in her sight.

"Jola and Heron usually Dance with the Terparchon's daughters as their compeers." Amara waved a hand at the youngest. "And everyone likes Danissa."

"Not everyone." A shadow passed across the young dam's face.

"Nearly everyone likes Danissa. So to have these three to welcome you is a statement of support."

"We're prepared to like you." Danissa quivered, each and every curl seeming to jiggle independently. Her circlet shifted, but never fell from her brow. "Even Ylena might, so long as you don't choose Todor as your partner for the Dance."

The new names went in one of Gisela's ears and out the other. They meant nothing more than syllables, save for the three princesses before her.

"I thank you for the courtesy. I'm prepared to like you as well."

Gisela managed to smile at Jola and Heron, then wider at Danissa as the younger grabbed her hand and squeezed it.

"Come, there's so much to show you and so little time!"

Danissa would have swept Gisela up the stairs and away without ado, but Gisela paused to glance back. To seek support or encouragement from Stevan and Amara—and in hopes one or both might accompany them.

Amara only smiled and nodded, gesturing for Gisela to accompany the others.

Stevan smiled as well, but a shadow crept over his face and a hesitancy hung about him Gisela didn't understand.

Danissa escorted Gisela up the stairs. Jola and Heron fell in only a few steps behind. Drawing a deep breath, Gisela mounted step after step, rising as high as any building in Foleilion. Dizziness gripped her, slowing her feet as she refused to sway or fall.

Or to glance back again and see Stevan watching her but doing nothing more.

Danissa drew Gisela into a large room, bigger and more elaborate than any she'd ever seen, but called it only an antechamber to the reception hall.

Gisela forged ahead on her own, aware she must form connections and alliances with others if she was to serve her people . . . and if she wanted to survive.

But her back grew cold. How quick she'd learned to rely on Stevan's presence so close by to shield her.

CHAPTER 16

*S*tevan paused at the fourth landing. Planting his sandaled feet firm on the smooth, gray stones, he leaned back against the interior wall. Only small puffs of air moved, no breeze or even whisper of a caress despite the long, thin window looking out over the city. He raised a hand to his throat. His mantle had ridden up during his climb; the band of green and gold embroidery rolled over twice to form a heavy ridge. Wrapping his fingers in the fabric, he yanked hard. The cloth unfurled and settled lower on his chest.

He breathed easier, though the gray stones blurred together and so discouraged him from proceeding onward.

For days, he'd lain on the earth, at Amara's bidding, and absorbed subtle details of the world around. Unbidden and unwanted, that same awareness unfurled to reveal how high he'd risen and the full extent of the layers of stone-on-stone that were all that prevented him from crashing down.

He'd climbed these stairs—and others as similar as to make little difference—hundreds, thousands of times, in his years. Never once had he refused a climb or experienced fear of heights.

Yet a fervent disinclination to rise any further weighted his feet and pulsed in his head. He had to force himself to leave the wall, to climb the last array of steps to top floor. It stretched out a fair length, far enough the window at the distant end was little more than a rectangle of light.

Alternating squares of light and shadow lined one side of the corridor. Each of the half-dozen wide windows had a pair of stout, thick shutters that could be adjusted to let light or air in, or shut completely when one of the many storms blew across the lake. This late in the afternoon, they were a mix, some open and others partly shut.

Across from them sat a thick wall punctuated with regular doors. These had louvered panels at top and bottom, to increase air circulation. Most were open at the top, letting sweet scents swirl up from the gardens far below.

His footfalls echoed. No voices, except in the distance. A halting snore from behind one door and whistle at another. Most of the clerks and scribes who shared these rooms were off at their labors.

He no longer had a key to the chamber he'd once shared with others.

Why return?

Habit, most likely. At least once or three times a day, he'd walked this way. Not long, but enough days and nights he knew the route with ease. As soon as Amara left him, after nearly dragging him from Gisela's side—and an accounting before one of the Terparchon's aides —he'd retreated having forgotten he no longer belonged.

Stevan trudged down the floor to stand before the door to his old room. Shared, then, with three others, none of whom he'd known well. Something he'd regretted when he first came to court, but found more palatable since. The few times he'd interacted with them between elevation to a compeer and leaving to find Gisela, they'd fawned on him. Not because they understood his new station—for that matter, neither did he—but desiring some part of the increased status and access to power that would come his way.

Their motives were natural. He'd have done the same if one of them were elevated, albeit likely with more reticence. Perhaps he would continue some of the acquaintance. What harm in reminding himself of who he was before?

A scribe who enjoyed dancing.

Versus a compeer.

A lost compeer, at that, with no knowledge of what place to go to lay his head. Or find his belongings. Someone had moved them, but forgotten to tell him.

Still more aware of the building's height than ever before, he descended with care. Kept one hand brushing against the wall, in case his feet slipped. The haze that clouded his vision eased the lower he went—the closer to solid ground.

When he finally set foot off the last step, a thump and thrum against the soles of his feet gave him a start. He nearly lost balance, but slid against the wall and steadied himself. Then bent and patted the earth.

"I'm glad to be down, as well." With no one in sight, he dared ask, "I don't suppose you know where I'm to go?"

No answer. Not a surprise.

He could traipse through the palace complex until he found someone in the know. Amara, no doubt, or one of the Terparchon's aides. All of whom had assumed he knew already, or were testing him, or keeping him in his place by making him ask.

Rather than do anything so active, he retreated into the shadows of the nearby gardens. The walls around had a small alcove with enough space for one person—or two if they were small or narrow hipped— to sit and take a rest. He settled down onto the stone seat, still warm from the sun or from whomever had last sat there, and leaned back against the likewise sun-heated wall.

This was one of the gardens that mingled beauty and practicality. A mix of flowers, fruits, and vegetables. Stake fences lined a nearby portion, supporting beans and peas. Cucumbers and squash. Redberries. Other plots held carrots and turnips, leafy greens, fennel, garlic, and more.

Whichever gardeners tended these plants had come and gone.

They left behind the smell of moist, freshly turned earth. A faint moisture hung in the air, as roots and leaves greedily sucked in water.

Only a few people remained, all in simple knee-length tunics slung over one shoulder rather than both. Half in sandals, the rest bare of feet. Bustling here and there, as they filled baskets with those vegetables needed for dinner.

It smelled familiar, homey. As a child, he'd often taken refuge in the kitchens from those in his family who considered him unwanted or too much under foot. The head cook hadn't paid him much attention, except when he brought a passel of fish. But two of the under cooks had welcomed an extra set of hands to chop or stir.

One of the cooks called to another in a voice similar to Amara's.

She'd certainly had words with him recently.

If not for her, he would have followed Gisela and the other princesses into the main royal residence. Might know now where she roomed, and how she fared.

But Amara had kept him at her side instead, her fingers wrapped tight around his arm when he went to follow.

"Let Gisela find her place as a princess on her own, and you yours as a compeer, before you make any long plans."

Her words still burned in his head.

They held truth. Neither he nor Gisela knew what awaited them. They needed to learn who to trust, to listen to, and of whom to be wary.

Yet Amara had been a courtier for a very long time, since she once was a princess. She'd no doubt forgotten how lonely it could feel to be new and uncertain—one small person within the great machine that was the court. If she ever knew to begin with.

His first, tentative days at court remained fresh in his memory.

Confusion. Trouble finding his way around, remembering names, or distinguishing between people he'd just met. Awkwardness as he tried to recall manners he'd thought ingrained when he met rulers and those they entrusted with great power.

Surely Gisela would appreciate not being left alone to find her way. The other princesses might help or hinder, for all that three had come to welcome her.

Alas, too late now to go back and be her guard and helper. He'd let Amara hold him back. The result? He didn't know where anything was save himself, and he sat where he no longer belonged.

Lacking enough energy to move and tackle the task of finding his new place.

Or, to start with a smaller goal, finding his possessions.

"Here he is." Rik's voice preceded their arrival by no more than a breath.

The stomp of Brenn's boots on the hard-baked ground nearly drowned out the softer slap of as Rik's sandals as Stevan's brother strode hard on the eleee's heels.

"I heard you were back." Brenn strode over and shook his head. He wore a red mantle thrown over one shoulder, the tunic underneath a strong pink, rather than his usual uniform.

Stevan found small satisfaction in the casual attire, indicating that Brenn had chosen to search for him on his own time.

"Of all the parts of the palace open to you, this is where you end up?"

"Don't you ever miss the kitchens, back home?" Stevan leaned back and lifted his chin.

"No. The food's better here, and no one throws rotting vegetables at me." Brenn shuddered from head to toe, an exaggeration.

Albeit not by much. Their siblings had enjoyed a number of food fights, if only when their father and stepmother were away. When the elders were present, decorum ruled the day as much as children were capable of it. No smushing mushy lettuce heads against the wall. Instead, an offender might be summoned to one or the other parent's chambers for chastisement. Smacks on the behind or stripes with a length of wood.

"I preferred getting hit with vegetables," he said.

"That's because you were small and good at ducking." Brenn scowled, eyebrows drawing together into a single line. Then he gave a smaller, more genuine shudder and held out a hand. "You got the worst of it, but you're out and away and will never go back. You'll dance with princesses any day now."

"Already danced with one, though she didn't know she was a princess then." Stevan smiled. No matter what he faced when he joined the compeers to partner the princesses, he had that success to fall back upon. Slapping his hand atop Brenn's, he let his brother pull him to his feet.

"Did you, eh? Fast worker." Brenn patted Stevan's back, a warm thump very similar to the earth's. "Let's go take a sit over a skin of wine and you can tell me all about it."

"Sounds good." Stevan ran a hand through his hair, combing the thick strands. "Though I've no notion where I'm to sleep now."

"Your quarters are in the princesses' wing, on the first floor. A very nice arrangement, too, a corner room with windows on two sides the better to catch the breezes off the lake." Rik clicked their tongue as they took in the state of Stevan's hems and the set of his mantle. "Your belongings and the remainder of your new wardrobe await you."

"Who moved my things?" Stevan had known someone else would have had to do it, but that was different than bracing himself to find out what might have been thrown away as of no value.

"I saw them transported myself." Brenn brushed his hands together. "They're all there, some left for you to unpack and choose where to dispose." He turned to Rik. "I'll take Stevan there. Perhaps you can scare up some wine?"

"Some food might not go amiss, either." Rik nodded. "If you're willing to allow me to draw on your stipend, I can arrange everything."

Stevan waited for Brenn's agreement, but instead find his brother regarding him with impatience.

"Well?" Brenn jerked his head at Stevan.

"*My* stipend?"

"From the court, fitting for your new position." Rik's voice dropped, although the cooks were far enough away they wouldn't hear, and he said a number that made Stevan's head reel.

He bobbed agreement, still stunned.

"Excellent. The food and drink will be ready directly." Rik sauntered off.

Brenn watched them, then shook his head with wry grimace. "That's a second piece of luck for you, or a third or fourth at the rate you're going, getting on Rik's good side. They counsel the Terparchon and Marchon when they want, but prefer working for compeers as a daily matter. Something about similar roles and greater understandings."

Something in Brenn's words almost struck a chord, but Stevan's stomach growled and he lost hold of his thoughts. He followed his brother, still in something of a daze.

Within minutes, they walked through the garden entrance to a large, white-washed building close to the lake. Several buildings had better sites—the Terparchon and Marchon's quarters, the princesses' dancing pavilion, the grandest of the audience chambers. Nevertheless, this constituted a part of the royal dwelling. He now had two chambers for himself, plus a semi-private water closet allotted to him and his closest neighbor versus communal sanitary facilities at one end of a long corridor.

The smaller chamber held shelves bearing Stevan's new wardrobe, boxes containing his old wardrobe and belongings, and a bed. A thin blanket of blue-and-white striped linen covered the mattress and two lumpy pillows. A sweet lavender perfume emanated from the shelves, proof someone had taken time to layer protection against insects. It had a wide window, shutters thrown back to show the view of the gardens and the far edge of the Shadow of the Moon beyond.

A matching window in the larger chamber—big enough to host five or seven comfortably—had the shutters closed, but adjusted to let air through while minimizing the glare off the lake. He peeked through, blinking hard twice and pinching himself at the choice lake view.

The angles of doors and placement of the windows combined to ensure a light breeze circulated, drying the last of Stevan's sweat from his skin. Not one but two reclining sofas stretched out in an L-shape. Light cloths covered them, matching the blanket. On the only wall unbroken by door or window hung a tapestry—a mass of blues and greens and purples portraying a sea chock-full of fish with a single figure on the shore casting a fishing line in.

"Your choice?" Stevan nodded at it as his legs folded beneath him. He dropped into the nearer sofa.

"A gift, to celebrate your new station." Brenn settled himself with more ease onto the other sofa. "You can replace it with that old painting of home, if you want. I thought I'd give you something new to go with the older. Keep what you will, though if I were you I'd be rid of most of your old clothes now you're wearing the Marchon's hand-me-downs."

Rik had been and gone, for the table between the sofas bore a tray with bottles of wine and water, goblets, and a platter of vegetable rolls wrapped in vine leaves. The infused oils used in the rolls set Stevan salivating. He maintained sufficient control to offer his brother, as guest, first choice of food and drink.

"You start in." Brenn waved at the rolls. "I'll pour."

Stevan wrapped his fingers around the first taut roll and took a bite. Onion, garlic, and a sharp redberry tang hit his mouth. He shook his head at the burst of flavor, then settled in to the mix of leftover vegetable ends and the chewy leaf rolled around the whole. One alone served to settle his stomach and banish the last vestiges of dizziness.

Brenn made a hmphing sound, and filled the goblets partway with red wine in unequal allotments. He added more water to balance them out. Stirred the results with a glass rod, then pushed the pinker one in Stevan's direction.

Stevan sent him a tight glare—his older brother took liberties—but allowed it this once. Even with his belly filling with food, a lighter hand with wine made sense. Despite the watering, the wine held a tang that soothed his throat.

"So, you brought the new princess back. Well done." Brenn lifted his goblet in a toast, then knocked back half in one long draught. "The Terparchon will be pleased, and just as well. She's been up at least once most nights pacing the rooftops and staring out over the lake at any word of dark clouds—praying, so I've heard, that the next great storm doesn't manifest until the princesses are at full strength."

The mere mention prompted Stevan to glance over at the window. The angle of the shutters allowed a glimpse of the sky. Peaceful enough, save for wisps of white clouds. As he turned back to his meal, he caught Brenn also checking the sky, and shared a grin of relief. Then indulged in a second roll.

"Word's out the princess's well-grown and pretty, but fairly unassuming." Brenn swirled wine in his goblet before taking another sip. "She'd best show some spine. Whether she likes playing for power or not, she's in the middle of it now. Taking Ylena's place? With Jola and Heron welcoming her into the lot? Dancing with Todor?"

Stevan stiffened, tension creeping into his back and shoulders. He laid the roll aside, half-eaten.

"Who says she'll be dancing with Todor?"

A pang struck him at the idea of her Dancing with anyone else. After their impromptu Dance on the road, he anticipated with great pleasure in doing so again. As for dances at court balls, those everyone mixed and mingled. Gisela could, and would, dance with whomever she pleased.

Amara hadn't addressed with whom Gisela would Dance as a princess. Stevan's stomach clenched, the food he'd consumed turning heavy in his belly. He'd made the error of presuming he might get to partner Gisela. In truth, he had no knowledge of how princesses and compeers were partnered.

The princesses would need one less compeer if they accepted Stevan as one—but in that case, were one to be let go, it would not be Todor. He had experience. Peerless connections. Even the potential to someday become Marchon, should he beat out both sisters, and raise his chosen princess to be Terparchon.

What could Stevan offer to balance that?

"Well, now, that's a twist I hadn't expected." Brenn leaned back and tilted his head to one side. "How serious is it?"

Stevan's tongue deserted him. He ducked his head and shrugged.

"That serious." Brenn put his wine aside and reached over to clasp forearms with Stevan. Skin to skin, he gripped tight. "Best of fortune to you. May you be both worthy and rewarded."

Before Stevan found words to reply, or managed to subdue the flush of blood to his cheeks, a hard knock broke their rapport.

Leaving Brenn to finish his wine, Stevan rose and opened the door, then stiffened yet again.

No less a personage than Nefeli stood there—the oldest of the Terparchon's children, Todor's elder sister, and partner to Princess Jola. Solidly built and a hand shorter than Stevan, she wore shades of yellow and orange this day. These combined with her gold-tone skin to give her the appearance of a statue, save for the array of short black ringlets curling out from her head.

"May I enter?"

A polite enquiry, since both knew he couldn't deny her without good cause.

"Of course." He stepped back and bowed. Glanced around the room and didn't see a third goblet, but he'd only had one sip from his. Surely he could clean it well enough. "May I offer you some wine?"

She declined with a smile as she entered. Her lightweight slippers shuffled against the stone floor making hardly any sound, yet heavy enough to raise reverberations from his heels to his teeth.

"Captain." She nodded at Brenn, acknowledging and dismissing him in a single word.

Brenn bowed and shot a speaking glance at Stevan as he departed.

He left the door open, but Nefeli shut it. The latch caught with a snick.

"We will want no other ears to hear." She settled onto the sofa where Brenn had reclined.

Stevan eased back on the other. The fabric was warm beneath him. A bitter tang bloomed in his mouth, and he risked a quick sip of wine to banish it. Kept the goblet cupped in his hands, the better to remain still.

"How may I be of service?"

"No, it is I who come to help you." She wove her fingers together and gave a half-laugh. "Of the compeers who partner the princesses in the Dances, there are four born to the task, five now with you. The rest have learned to mimic what we do, but their capabilities are limited."

"'We?'" He set the goblet aside and bolted to sit straight up. "You are a born compeer?"

She nodded.

A million fragmented questions filled his mind. So many he couldn't form a single coherent response for several beats. At length, he gave up. She hadn't moved, just sat waiting for him. "There is so much I don't understand. Amara didn't really explain much," he said.

She'd trained Stevan, true, but he'd watched Amara working with Gisela. The older woman hadn't showed him anything she didn't also share with the princess.

"I've developed a greater awareness of the world around me thanks to Amara"—Stevan shrugged—"but most else she shared with me thus far boils down to stretches and exercises to fit me as a partner."

"Amara was a princess, and they do not appreciate all that we do." Nefeli's eyes flashed and her mouth tightened. Setting her hands on her knees, she leaned forward. "My mother does not, and never will. She identified you as a compeer, but did she offer you any training?"

"No. Though I was sent away almost immediately to bring back Gisela." The excuse slipped out. But it was the truth, as well as a polite way to ensure he didn't accuse the Terparchon of neglect to her own daughter.

"She would not have thought of it either." Nefeli flicked her fingers in the air. "Dances have been shown to be particularly successful when more princesses are paired with true compeers, rather than those who only mimic. Nevertheless, my mother considers what we do a matter of instinct. We are believed to be able to be in the right spot to brace and support our princesses because we become so subsumed by the Dance as to be part of it."

"But that is not the case?" Shards of memory flashed through him: watching Gisela dance in the field as she lost her way, providing the beat and then bracing and supporting her as she dried the track. Both times he'd been aware of her and her actions in ways new and strange —and acted only on instinct.

"Not for me. Not yet. Only the eldest of us, who knows the most and has Danced near as much than the rest of us put together."

He nodded, watching her with narrowed eyes. She'd come to give him information, certainly, but only that? Why not hope, even reach, for more?

"If by this you offer me training, with you or another, I accept."

"We who are compeers by birth meet regularly to practice, apart from the princesses, and to talk. You are most welcome to join us." She extended her hand. Her grasp was firm and decisive as they shook. "And the night after any Dance, we always gather to discuss how things went from our perspectives and consider ways we might do better."

A rill of excitement sent his heart pounding, even as giddy waves of relief rolled through him. He hadn't realized how much he'd dreaded and feared having to fight for a place and hold it against all comers. Yet her welcome struck him as genuine, and warmer than he'd hoped for.

Which made him bold enough to share a remaining fear.

"Will there be any resentment against me for displacing one of the other compeers?"

"Hmm." She tilted her head back then shook it. "I think not. There are never enough of us. One of those who mimics will have to step back."

He nodded, teeth clenched in his jaws. One of his worst fears made real: to have to battle for a place. She might blithely say one would step back, but who? Not her, and surely not her brother, even though Todor would be the most natural in that the princess he paired was unable to dance.

No, Stevan would likely face many dancers who, though they were not natural compeers had years of experience and did not wish to give their up places.

Unable to keep all his tension within, he blew out his cheeks in a sigh that made her laugh.

"Do not fear to share your mind with me or the other true compeers. We do not lead and we rarely shine, yet an active compeer can help shape any Dance and bring better, stronger, greater results. I consider us of equal import to princesses in making a Dance succeed." Nefeli's smile turned bitter. "But even if you do make that difference, do not expect my mother to ever recognize it. She takes the part of the thirteenth princess. Yet even when my father joins as her partner, she still Dances alone."

The Terparchon had found him, yet by Nefeli's warning would never truly value him. Regrettable, but not concerning. Rather, the new fear that filled him after Nefeli left was how Gisela might view him once she was brought fully into the ranks of the princesses. Would she consider him a match and equal, or no more than a step on the way to greater partners than he?

isela woke well-rested and sprawled across a thick mattress with her torso deeper than her limbs. A tricky position, for every move made her sink further. The soft linens made things worse. They shifted beneath her, soft and slippery to the touch. She had to grab hold of a hank to pull herself upright.

All was strange, herself included. Yesterday's tour of much of the palace complex had featured a visit to the private baths provided in the princesses' dancing pavilion. She'd been steamed, swabbed, oiled and massaged. In the process, the attendants eased most of the signs and soreness of travel, and more. Lifting her hands, she twisted them this way and that. Between the water, lotions, and oils, some of the ink stains had vanished from her hands.

So she lay, clean and naked, under a soft blanket that kept out the early morning chill, in bounteous bed hung with nets from the ceiling to keep out any insects that might flit through the wide, open windows facing the lake. The shutters were fastened to either side, leaving nothing to obscure the long view. Warm pink and orange light from the rising sun reflected off the lake, casting rippling patterns on the white-washed ceiling. Few shadows filled the room, save along the wooden floor and its many braided rugs. All was light and color from the pale peach walls, to the tapestries decking the walls with images of people dancing, to the shelves bearing more clothes than she could wear in a month.

Luxury.

And strangeness.

So few sounds. Only a few voices broke the silence, and those in the distance. Speaking, at that, rather than breaking the dawn with coos and shrieks of joy as lovers celebrated the start of another day of life. She hadn't noticed so much the night before as she wished, too busy drinking in all the new sights to remember any one in particular —but a few princesses entered chambers such as hers without company.

Did most people at court sleep alone as a matter of course?

Birds sang. Some of the light, lilting calls were familiar, but several strange, not least one composed of two long, low notes followed by a trill.

The breeze sifting in through the open windows brought the aromas of bread baking and meat cooking. Only enough to stir an appetite, suggesting the kitchens lay far distant from her rooms.

Gisela strove to rise, but every time she pushed up on one side she sank on another. Losing patience, she rolled over until she dropped out of the bed onto her side atop a thick rug of blues and pinks braided together. The impact knocked the breath from her lungs, and roused twinges of pain in her elbow and knee. These eased soon, although deeper soreness lingered in her legs.

Once up on her feet, she raised her arms high into the air on a long stretch. The bones along her spine and shoulders settled into place. Although still cool, the day promised to be warm with summer's full heat.

She pulled the top loincloth and breast band from those piled on a low shelf. Plain they might be, with no adornments or embroidery unlike some of the other pieces, but they were still of thinner, softer fabric than she'd worn until the fateful day her world changed.

She'd met the other princesses and been presented to the Terparchon, all giving her a warm welcome. Or, at least, showing pleasure that she'd brought their numbers back up.

Nevertheless, her stomach growled and rumbled—and the queasiness was not from hunger alone.

Feet planted on the rug, she went through the routine Amara had shown her. The sun sequence, then birds, and last plants growing from the earth.

After which she remained prone on the floor with her arms extended. Even with the rug cushioning, the surface was hard and unyielding beneath her. A far cry from the warmth and shelter the ground offered when she'd learned the sequences in her home and then along the road. The earth lay too far away.

Still the exercises soothed her spirit and her belly. It no longer rumbled with anything but an edge of hunger.

The Terparchon had summoned Gisela; she had not come by choice or desire. If she were sent from court, she might regret, but she had a home to return to. Foleilion and her people would take her back, whenever the need came. With disappointment, no doubt, if she did not manage to last long—but they would welcome her all the same.

She drew in a deep breath until her chest rose high.

Then leapt to her feet at an unexpected knock on the door. Bare moments later, metal scraped against metal. The latch lifted and the door opened to reveal Emmi on the other side. She carried a covered platter in one hand, the other wrapped around the door handle.

"Oh, you're up already, are you?" The older dam slipped through the narrow opening and let the door close behind her. Her light blue mantle was tied at one shoulder, leaving her paler tunic visible at the other. Savory aromas of cinnamon and berries rose from the dish in her hand. "I thought to leave your breakfast for you, to start your first day. Mind, you may not have such service all days—much depends upon the kitchens and the moods of the cooks. Yet there's such a lovely set of fruit rolls today, I could not but bring you a few."

"I hadn't . . ." At home, Gisela would have slipped over to the kitchens to get her breakfast. "I didn't realize anyone would bring me food, or I'd have left the door unlatched. I would have sworn I'd locked it." Gisela glanced at the door and shook her head, only realizing a beat too late she'd spoken all her thoughts.

"It matters not whether you locked it or not, I have the other key." Emmi set the round dish on a small table by the window. Lifting one hand, she wiggled her fingers. "I am one of those who serve the princesses. I will tidy and clean your rooms most mornings, and see to your clothes and laundry."

"I see."

This meant Emmi would provide even more assistance and service than while on the road.

"Does everyone at court have servants to clean and launder for them?" Caring for fine fabrics and vibrant colors would require more skill at washing than Gisela had learnt.

"Most do who can afford it. For the princesses, it is one of the comforts given back in return for their service. Do your part in easing the storm we're bound to have in the next day or two,"—Emmi nodded her head at the sky and the deep pinks fading from the eastern horizon—"and we'll be in balance."

"You never wished to dance yourself?" Gisela lifted the cover and inhaled the warm scents of fresh baked sweet rolls.

"Not I, though there are others with such dreams." The other clicked her tongue.

Gisela picked a slice of pastry thick with cinnamon spots and ruddy berries, and paused food partway to her mouth.

Emmi turned away, to flip through the tunics and mantles piled on the shelves, but Gisela had caught a glimpse of her face. Of blankness, and caution.

Rethinking her words, she bit her lip before biting into the sweet.

Better to listen much and think before she spoke, as she learned the ways of the court.

Emmi laid out suggested attire for Gisela to don. A light pink tunic and a darker mantle nearly as deep and ruddy as the dawn sky plus sandals decorated with matching ribbons—and a cord of braided gold and silver silk to bind around her forehead and keep her hair back.

And ensure no one mistook her rank.

Danissa's arrival in similar attire, albeit greens rather than pinks and three green-enameled bracelets on each wrist and ankle, did not fully resign Gisela to the cord of rank. All the same, Gisela kept her mouth shut. No sense in antagonizing anyone soon after her arrival, as she had yet to learn what was acceptable to ask or not.

The more so as she appreciated the younger dam's consideration in stopping by to escort Gisela to the dancing pavilion for morning practice.

"Because we didn't want to presume you'd remember after all we showed you yesterday. Not that the way is so very difficult to find, but timeliness always matters to the Terparchon as she has so many calls upon her time." Danissa led Gisela along the hall and around a corner to an interior staircase. "Jola and Heron went ahead, but we're not late. I'm always careful about that since I made the most awful blunder my first week as a princess. Inexcusable, really, since I knew better having grown up here, but the Terparchon was kind enough to forgive me. I've not tried her a second time, not yet."

Danissa's light, cheery voice echoed in the stairwell along with the clatter of their sandals against the smooth wood.

"Thank you for your kindness in keeping me from making such an error."

"No thanks needed. It's a pleasure to finally not be the youngest and least. You might think that the other princesses would give me credit for not being a know-nothing when the Terparchon finally allowed me into their ranks but no." Danissa waved her hands in the air as she bounded down the stairs. "The older, longer-serving princesses always tell the younger what to do, even when the younger know it better than they. It's a tradition."

"Indeed." Gisela laughed. "I shall be sure to allow you to tell me what to do when needed."

"I appreciate that." The other princess ducked her head and gave a rueful chuckle. "Though I fear all the others shall continue instructing me alongside you regardless. There will need be many more changeovers before I rank among the seniors, and changeovers are never easy. There are always adjustments and shifts, and princesses and compeers dancing with different people after than before because they suddenly match better."

"And how is it that you know so much to begin with?" Gisela winced as they left the stairwell and turned through an archway out of the building. Her sandals fit and no longer chafed, but she missed the feel of the earth beneath her soles.

Rectangular stones formed a pathway through a vibrant garden to the nearby pavilion. Bright flowers in verdant yellows, reds, and oranges bloomed to either side; low to the ground close by the path and rising waist-high further away. Floral scents mixed and mingled with the ever-present moistness of the breezes crossing the lake. A gull squawked overhead as it flew toward the water. Bees buzzed in the distance, and yellow-black butterflies massed over the orange flowers in joyous array.

A spate of flutters similar to butterfly wings pattered in Gisela's belly.

In the near distance, the pavilion itself loomed high. Shorter than the other buildings in the complex at a mere two stories, it nevertheless drew attention. For one, it was heptagonal—a startling choice given that even those people most fixated on the powers of prime numbers, accepted and endorsed buildings featuring even numbers of sides. The gray stones alternately gleamed and presented a dull appearance in random array. The first floor had no windows, and doors on only three of the seven sides, but banks of windows along the second floor caught the light and refracted it. A peaked roof rose above, covered in gray slates that continued the semi-random mix of light and dark.

Danissa led Gisela along the path to the nearest entrance. She came to a sudden stop square in the center of the path and set her hands on either hip. The arched doorway loomed before them. The doors were made of intricately carved wood burnished to a lustrous red-brown. The carvings were inlaid with precious stones and metals, and pierced in several places to allow airflow.

Between them and the door stood a tall, broad sire with short dark hair bound back from his head by a length of copper rope. A soldier, perhaps, given the leather breastplate and arm and leg bands he wore over his knee-length tunic. His sandals bore small wings of copper and a long knife hung in a plain sheath from the belt wrapped around his waist three times. A strong odor of leather and sweat hung about him.

"Captain Brenn, whyever am I not surprised to see you lingering here?" Danissa shook her head at the sire.

He smiled down at the young princess, though his gaze flitted back and forth toward Gisela and lingered longer on her. "I have ample reason to visit and pay my respects, princess. Now more than ever." He bowed to Danissa, then to Gisela.

"Truly? I would have thought you to abandon us and spend more of your time lingering about the healer's wing these days." Danissa waved a hand, nearly dislodging the cords around her headband and setting her curls twirling. "All sorts of things might happen there, after all."

"I know where I'm not wanted, and can take no for an answer." Brenn shook his head, a muscle twitching in one cheek. "If you had thought further, you might have anticipated my presence here. After all, my youngest sibling is now a compeer and I come to wish him well on his first day dancing. Perhaps tease him, too."

"Of course, I had forgot. Gisela—" She turned and flashed a bright smile and white teeth. "This is Captain Brenn of the Palace Guard, brother to Stevan whom you know. Captain Brenn, the newest princess, Gisela."

Brenn bowed again to Gisela, smile genuine but eyes quick to take in every detail of her appearance and action.

Before either had a chance to speak more, hasty footsteps echoed from behind Gisela and Danissa.

Gisela turned to find Stevan clipping along the path at speed. He'd fastened his deep purple mantle over one shoulder with a brass pin this day. The folds of materials, and the lighter-weight tunic of pale gray below, billowed behind him. Twined cords of gold and copper at his brow glinted in the sunlight.

"Good morn, Gisela. Danissa. A lovely day for dancing, is it not?" Stevan's face stretched wide with a broad smile as he caught sight of Gisela, sending a rill of warmth through her. Then he glanced beyond her, and his lips twisted to one side. "Brenn, what a surprise to see you here."

"I couldn't let you dance without wishing you well."

"Couldn't you?" Stevan grimaced, then managed a nod. "Just see that you don't interfere."

"It's not my place to interfere, or approve or disapprove. You're an adult, fit to make your own choices. I only wanted a glance, to start." Brenn clapped his hands together. "Moreover, I had other reasons for coming here this morning. A summons, for one."

With exquisite timing, the doors opened. Although they had to be heavy, they moved silently without so much as a creak of a hinge. A solid dam about Gisela's height stood on the other side, dressed in much the same fashion as Stevan—gray tunic and purple mantle fastened over one shoulder—except three entwined cords bound back her hair instead of two: gold, gold, and copper. Although she did not particularly resemble the Terparchon, she had something of the ruler's manner; Danissa whispered in Gisela's ear that this was the Terparchon's eldest, Nefeli, a compeer.

Nefeli did not seem to notice Danissa, Gisela, and Stevan. Instead, she fixed immediately upon Brenn.

"Oh, good, you're here."

"Your messenger was . . . persuasive." Brenn bowed, then stood square before her. "How may I be of service?"

"If Ylena will not go of her own will—" Nefeli's gaze drifted, then bounced about between Danissa and Stevan before fixing on Gisela. "Princess Gisela?" She bent her waist in Gisela's direction.

"Yes." Before Gisela could say more, Danissa leapt into the breach.

"Compeer Nefeli, this is indeed the newest princess, Gisela."

"You are very welcome, and I look forward to dancing with you at some time. Perhaps now, however, Danissa might show you the beauties of the garden for a brief while?" Nefeli shifted in place and blocked the doorway. "I fear there are yet some preparations to be made to the pavilion."

Something in Nefeli's delivery, or the way her eyes lingered on each, gave Danissa a warning. She jumped in place and gave Gisela an utterly fake smile.

"Of course. You simply must see the Shadow of the Moon before the dance. Morning is the best time of all. I was just thinking this would be the perfect time."

A small shiver rippled through Gisela. Stevan laid a hand against her back, although his face showed puzzlement. The warmth and pressure eased her nerves.

Danissa grabbed Gisela's hand, but before she could pull her away, a sire appeared behind Nefeli. A little younger and with a slight resemblance to her, but a greater one to the Terparchon of Gisela's memory, in coloring, but most especially in his long face with deep eyes and thick brows. He, too, wore a purple mantle over a pale tunic and a cord of gold, gold, and copper around his head. His lips were drawn tight, and embarrassment flashed across his face.

"It's going to happen sooner or later. If it takes place here, we can at least keep it dagger short."

"That's right. Let her in. Let her see me and know her time is limited." A high voice, shrill with an edge of pain, carried over uneven thumps behind him.

"I am sorry this must mar your first day." The Terparchon's son winced and stepped aside, nodding to Gisela.

"You couldn't stop her?" Danissa hissed at him, slipping between them. "The healers shouldn't have let her out. Surely they wouldn't have if not given an order."

He shook his head, eyes half-closed. Nefeli, too, seemed abashed as she stood off to the other side.

Behind Gisela, Stevan drew in a sharp breath. His hand closed over her shoulder, squeezing. She stood stiff as a board waiting for whatever it was that the Terparchon's heirs were allowing to happen.

Only Brenn appeared unmoved. Feet spread wide, he crossed his arms over his chest and waited. On second glance, the tic had returned to his cheek.

Gisela faced the door as the thumps grew closer.

"Well?" A lovely dam in nothing more than a gray tunic stumped into view. Fair hair streamed down her back. Her light skin revealed every line of shapely muscles pulled taut. Brown eyes glared out of a face limned with pain and determination. She wavered as she stood on one foot, crutches propped under either arm. Bandages and lengths of wood kept her left leg straight, but she did not let the toes touch the ground.

After one quick glance around, she focused on Gisela. Anger and hurt vibrated from her so forcibly that they practically manifested as waves in the air, pushing everyone else back and away. Stevan drew a sharp breath and stepped back, his hand slipping from Gisela's shoulder and leaving a chill spot behind.

"So, you're the new princess. Come to claim my place, my partner, my glory. Go ahead. They're yours." The other dam gritted her teeth, swaying. Her hands wrapped tighter around the crutches, knuckles nearly white. "But don't expect to keep them for long. I'll have them back. Soon as I heal, I'll take all back."

Gisela blinked, unable to move amidst the palpable anger and pain. No one else moved either, or spoke.

"You'll have to walk first." Brenn broke the silence. "You can't even stand on your own feet."

"How do you think I got here?" The injured dam flashed her teeth at Brenn.

"Sheer stubbornness, but that won't get you back. You're already about to fall." He waved a hand at her crutches. "You gave Gisela an ultimatum, so here's one for you: you can stay here and drop, and watch Gisela dance off with your place and partner, or I can carry you back to the healers, and put you that much further on the way to retrieving everything you say you most desire."

"Don't dare touch me." Her anger lashed out again.

Gisela raised her arms in front of her face, a moment before an invisible force struck her. Pinpoints of pain blossomed, manifesting as dozens of small red welts appearing along her forearms.

"That kind of trick may work on princesses and compeers, but not on me. I have no magic." Brenn stepped forward, making his body a shield between the dam in the doorway and the others. "Your choice, princess."

Ylena swayed, crutches creaking beneath her. Beads of sweat rolled down her face, and the tendons in her neck stood out.

Sympathy bloomed in Gisela. Of course the injured princess welcomed the change as little as she. Was equally if not more scared about what would become of her.

"Let him take you back." Gisela moved to Ylena's side in time to brace her as one of the crutches started to slip. "If I'm to win anything from you, I want you well for the winning."

Ylena stared at Gisela for a long moment. Her eyes fluttered closed and a shudder rippled through her, then she slumped against Gisela and nodded. "Very well."

Brenn gently elbowed Gisela out of the way and swooped Ylena up. He threw her over his shoulder. Her body jerked, air rushing out of her lungs. The crutches fell against the stone floor with a clatter. Gisela picked them up.

"Lean them against the wall outside the door." He jerked his head at the archway. "I'll collect them later. I hope you stay." He gave her a broad smile. "You'll be a breath of fresh air in the court."

Then off he strode, with Ylena grumbling that he'd hefted her over his shoulder rather than carrying her in his arms. His voice carried as well as hers as he went, telling her the position was better for her leg because he could make sure it didn't get banged that way.

"You handled that very well." Nefeli nodded at Gisela, a degree of respect in her voice. She elbowed her brother. He stared after the departing pair, but started and nodded agreement before both withdrew inside.

"Did that truly have to happen?" Stevan returned to stand at Gisela's side, arm to arm and shoulder to shoulder.

"Knowing Ylena, it would have sooner or later." Danissa sighed. "It should have been later, if the healers had managed to keep her in bed longer. But it is not surprising she managed to drag herself here. She's one of the most powerful princesses seen in a long time. A fact she knows well, as do the rest of us. We still wonder who tripped her."

"Is it verified?" Stevan asked. "It was only rumor when I left to get Gisela."

"Not proven, but no other princess doubts it." Danissa stared at her hands, voice lowering. "To give Ylena her due, she was also not only powerful but graceful. Any dancer can fall, but in such a way?"

Gisela had not understood the reference to tripping at first. Compassion flowed in her. No doubt the injury being an act of malice stung enough to make the whole situation worse.

"Is Gisela in danger?" Stevan put Gisela's fears into words.

"Not now, not yet, I think." Danissa grabbed Gisela's hand and squeezed. "Ylena flew high. Powerful, ambitious—and not caring who knew it. She wooed Todor as her compeer, knowing that would give her a chance to be named the next Terparchon. If you seek power, then you'll court danger, but if you are content to be merely one of the princesses, as I, you should be safe enough."

Stevan stiffened next to Gisela, setting up a small breeze along that side of her body.

"I have no desire to rule." She shook her head.

He sighed, tension slipping from his body. Opened his mouth to speak, but Danissa got there first.

"And on that note, we are due to dance." The other princess wrapped an arm around Gisela's shoulders as she and Stevan escorted Gisela into the dancing pavilion.

A hall wide enough for three to walk abreast led past the princesses' private bathing rooms and chambers for massage and contemplation. The hall also featured a fountain along one of the walls. A seascape carved in bas relief from light-gray stone with purple-blue streaks included fishes leaping from the waves to spout water that fell into a long, low tray below.

Then into the central arena. Here all was light and space. Although the circular chamber had no windows on the lower level, windows wrapped around the upper level along with a walkway so that the Terparchon or whomever she chose so to favor might watch from above. At the apex of the ceiling seven smooth glass panels allowed midday light to stream down and illuminate the vibrant floor.

Layers of paint on smooth wood created an awe-inspiring vista. Unlike the mosaics covering other palace floors and walls, this did not portray legends from the past or moments of spectacle in the land's history. Instead it featured a seemingly random assortment of stars and shells, flowers and leaves, flames and waves, and a myriad of other images all mashed together. Yet the very way in which they were combined resulted in a sense of movement, as though they shifted place when glimpsed out of the corner of one's eye.

The one in the second dancing chamber immediately below, where none but princesses and compeers ever went, and where they worked their magic, on the other hand . . . But Danissa, Jola, and Heron had to a one shivered when they mentioned that room the day before, and Gisela had not asked further questions at the time.

Even with the injured princess's accusation, Gisela had found in herself only sympathy when outside. Once within the pavilion walls, and in particular within the large chamber where the other princesses and their partners were stretching and preparing for the day's practice, all changed.

Nothing about this resembled where and how she'd learned to dance as a child, or an adult.

Gisela didn't belong. It did not matter how kind and gracious the others might be as they trickled over in ones, twos, and threes to exchange polite greetings.

"Are you all right?" Stevan whispered in her ear, after Danissa went off to greet an older sire whom she much resembled. "If I had known Princess Ylena might—"

"It's not that, not her. I don't belong here. I'm nothing like any of the others."

He took time to consider her words. His mouth opened and shut, and he glanced around. Then his lips quirked to the side in a half smile.

"Nor are any of them alike to each other. Look again. You belong at least as much as I do."

Since he'd done her the courtesy of pondering her words, she returned the favor. Studied the princesses—denoted by the gold and silver cords about their brows—and compeers—marked by gold and copper.

Although they all seemed more at ease than her, in their fine clothes and sandals and jewels, there was truth in his words. All differed from each other. Body types from thin and gangly to lushly curved. Heights ranged from short to tall, ages from Danissa's likely late teens to her father who had at least four more decades, and appearances likewise with every color she'd ever seen of hair, skin, and eyes represented.

"Give yourself time." Stevan's hands braced her shoulders before he stepped back and began to stretch himself.

Across the floor, Danissa waved and gestured for Gisela to join her.

Before Gisela moved, Amara arrived. She stood out from all the others, not only for her unusual lavender skin but as the only one not wearing cords of rank across her forehead. Nevertheless, no sooner had she clapped her hands than all rendered her full attention.

"The Terparchon will not be present until later in the morning, if then." Amara strode to the center of the floor, standing atop the seven-point star fixed there in shades of gold, silver, and copper. "She's asked that I to see to the morning practices, as we need to be ready for the storm season. There's warning one may be forming over the lake even now. Therefore, take your pairs."

The order made no sense to Gisela, until she noted princesses matching up with compeers.

But the numbers weren't even. The room held one more compeer than princess.

All the others quickly formed twos: Jola with Nefeli; Heron with a younger dam who had been introduced as Nefeli's younger sister but whose name Gisela didn't remember; Danissa with her father Idan, who seemed spry but tired. They spread themselves out around the circle, leaving one twelfth of the space for Gisela.

Two compeers remained: the Terparchon's son and Stevan.

Both stepped forward and bowed, waiting for her choice.

The one courtly and wary; the other reticent and resigned.

Far more comfortable with Stevan, Gisela stretched out her hand in his direction—but Amara stepped between them.

"It is best not to have the new princess and new compeer together, when both have much to learn." Amara shook her head, with an apologetic look in either direction. "I will take Stevan as my partner for the exercises. Gisela, dance with Todor."

Gisela didn't desire power, or to dance with the sire who'd partnered Ylena, but she no longer had a choice about the latter.

How much choice she would she have about anything?

CHAPTER 18

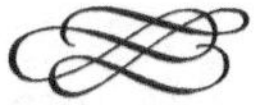

*D*espite the heat of summer, a cool draft wafted up through minute cracks in the floorboards. Enough to set up a chill through Stevan's body, especially where lines of sweat dried. His loincloth, tunic, and mantle could not keep away the cold seeping upward. Even the shoulder where he'd tied his mantle, tucking it under the arm, grew goosebumps along his skin despite the layers of cloth in the knot. The brass buckle keeping the knot tied absorbed the cold and radiated it back.

Occasionally a breeze brought in a gust of steam from the nearby bathing rooms, but not enough to counter the dank stench of iron welling upward. The piece of warm bread spread with yogurt and honey that he'd consumed for breakfast turned to lumps of heavy snow or even ice within his belly.

In that moment, he desired most of all to turn his head and learn if others likewise suffered.

He set his teeth and fixed his gaze on the ceiling high overhead. The wooden beams holding panes of glass aloft at the center gleamed with warmth and light. Yet the cold slipped into his head to change the view. Golden lengths of wood turned gray to reveal bars of iron within. Glass grew cloudy and turned to a fog so thick a person walking through would not see so much as their own nose.

A few blinks and the illusion dispelled.

Stevan remained chilled. His muscles and joints tightened. Faint aches seeded his legs, arms, and back. They grew vines, snaking through his body.

Who could dance this way? He should be up and stretching, growing warmer and looser.

As opposed to slowly turning into an icicle in the middle of summer.

In the distance, a single pair of sandals clicked as Amara circled the floor. All dancers save she lay on their backs slowly chilling. Or so he presumed, having not heard any of them rise.

No, not merely presumed.

Knew.

For though he did not move and had yet to dance in the chamber in any way whatsoever, something in him tracked the location of every other person. Ever since the first day he joined a throng dancing for joy, he'd experienced heightened consciousness of those around him. As a gift it wasn't worth much. Kept him from painful clashes with others on dance floors. Mostly. He'd still tripped his share of times over the years.

All the same, here in the stillness and cold, he registered more than so many people being present around him. He knew who lay where, and how fast their hearts beat.

Along this section of the chamber were arrayed the compeers. Amara had made introductions so fast that half their names escaped him. She skipped mentioning which compeers came by it naturally versus which mimicked. Nefeli had yet to let him know, but while lying on cold wood Stevan came to his own conclusions. Nefeli, of course, and Idan whom Stevan had recognized from long service at the Terparchon's elbow, and a few others.

Likewise, a picture formed in his head of the room indicating where each of the princesses lay. His mind skipped over the others— those he recognized, those he had yet to meet, and those who confused him—in favor of Gisela. She was as cold as he by the hitch in her breath.

His awareness seemed to spin, turning a spiral and with each revolution deepening his understanding of his surroundings—first and foremost the people.

Then Amara clapped her hands and all his extra consciousness burst as sudden as a bubble boiling up from water.

Rising from the floor in a single, smooth motion, he moved into the first of the stretches Amara had shown him during the trip to find Gisela. He managed to match her and the others in a regular progression from movement to movement.

First his head, arms, and upper body reached, stretched, retracted, and repeated. Then on down through the torso, legs, and feet.

All solo, each working at their own pace although no one that he saw or sensed was far off from the others.

Why the fuss about who partnered whom if they danced alone?

Until they didn't.

From exercises done in place, they took hands and skipped in a wide circle. Pair followed pair.

Although dry and smooth, Amara's fingers slipped through his hand time and again. Maintaining hold required constant adjustment through the various circles. Skipping, leaping, twirling.

How he held his body mattered, as did finding the proper angle to complement his partner. A buzz of power zipped along his skin. When he aligned his movements to those of Amara's, it crackled along his skin and gave him more energy so that the exercises invigorated rather than tired him. In contrast, when he fell out of alignment, the buzz nipped and stung. A few welts on his hands and thighs, and he took increasing care to match Amara.

All the same, he kept an eye on Gisela. She smiled as she traced circles on the floor, graceful and lithe. Yet certainty welled within him that she was not completely comfortable with Todor's hands on her. A hesitancy marked her movements as she shifted from leaping to twirling, which required two hands joined. Moreover, an element of her discomfort seeped up into him from the floorboards.

When he turned away from her, his ability to track the dancers expanded. Perhaps due to the circular nature of the floor. Or the awareness that had blossomed since the interrupted dance with the Terparchon, after which she proclaimed him a compeer. Or Gisela's dance in the field.

It was not Gisela alone he followed, will-he nil-he, but everyone. A relief, on the one hand, because it made her one of many rather than a sole focus. But a mixed blessing, because the more he breathed, the more information and unasked-for knowledge flooded through him. It was as though he'd connected to the dancing floor to experience the weight and pressure of every foot that stepped on it, no matter how firm or tentative.

The knowledge didn't come whole-cloth but in pieces that he had to choose whether to track and put together or not.

He knew too much and too little. Which details mattered? He might pay attention to the way Idan favored his right side in twirling and occasionally winced when he came down heavily on one foot or another. Should he care that Nefeli and Jola matched each other best of all the dancers, nearly breathing in the same measure?

That for all his calm appearance, Todor was tentative and performed the steps only a little better than Stevan? An oddity that troubled Stevan, for Todor's younger sister Zora was far more assertive. Indeed, she danced more like a princess than a compeer, despite partnering Princess Heron, except for an oddly heavy step on the floor.

How did Stevan even know? Why was he sure that he could be blindfolded and yet walk among the dancers' still bodies and know who was who, and which princesses?

Too many questions without answers.

At least he had managed to adjust to Amara's slipperiness. The occasional odd step when her whole body jerked and turned limp as though hung from strings. The way she regularly leaned to the outside and had to be gently coaxed back in.

Amara certainly hadn't lied about her imbalance.

He needed to talk more with Nefeli and the other compeers, at the first opportunity.

But more urgent was the desire to speak with Gisela. Amara had separated them because they were both new, but that was also a reason to bring them together. To let them learn in company rather than isolated and all too aware of their lacks, the more so as they'd already danced together often enough to have developed an ease approaching that between others who had partnered each other much longer.

Then Amara set them a new set of exercises. This involved practicing specific movements mimicking storm winds, rain, and flood.

"The better to give the Terparchon possibilities in easing storm-falls." The elder turned in a circle, taking care to meet every dancer's eyes. She demonstrated these, slow and sure.

Stevan struggled to follow. Pretending to be the wind proved the easiest but most tiring. It involved extensive twirling, leaps, and hand movements. Always moving, always changing, never remaining in one place for longer than a breath.

The turn to rain let him catch his breath, and spend more time in one place or at least moving slower. Stretch, yes, reaching high and then hand movements tumbling down. Much hand and arm action while torso and body drifted this way and that, often driven by those dancers imitating winds.

Last but far from least, the flood steps brought him low. Crawling on hands and knees or even lying flat and undulating against the hard floor. Never rising very high. Always swaying and seeking the path of least resistance.

These became more involved than the earlier exercises, the more so as Amara broke them into three groups. Each worked their way through the movements in rotation. Wind dancers, rain dancers, and flood dancers all had to interact with each other. Weave around the floor in intricate patterns.

Now experience mattered. Amara and Todor's familiarity with the movements let them guide Stevan and Gisela, and reduced clashes and crashes. Amara had everything down cold despite her balance issues.

The same did not hold true of Todor, who never aligned his body quite right to Gisela no matter how he tried.

By the end, sweat covered Stevan's body. Even with the windows open at the upper level, the smell of warm bodies in motion filled the air. His muscles ached, but he'd aligned himself enough with Amara to end with more energy than he'd started.

Seeking out the fountain near the entrance, he dashed lukewarm drops against his face. Cupped his hands under one of the spouting fishes and drank deep. Other dancers formed lines at the remaining spouts or sought out the other fountains.

Then Amara summoned them back for one last exercise.

This time she ordered them to line up along the walls.

Stevan took a place near the fountain, the distant trickle of the water a pleasant underscore to the soft shuffle of sandals on wood as Amara rearranged them to place all the compeers on one side and princesses on the other.

And gave to each a length of cloth. A blindfold. Stevan ran the soft, dark fabric through his fingers.

"I will assign you each a role." She turned a slow circle, once she had them all where she wanted them. "Wind, rain, or flood. You are to dance in your role through the room until you find a partner with the same role. Princesses find compeers, compeers princesses. Once you've found a matching partner, pair up without ever touching each other."

Whispers and glances circled the room. Stevan joined in the second, but not the first. From the astonishment, and resistance, on various faces, this represented a variation from usual practices.

He stroked the fabric a second time, holding it up to the ceiling. The fine weave allowed little light to pass through. They'd all be dancing without sight. Although hardly an activity he'd have sought out, he did not fear it. If anything, nervous energy made his whole body vibrate. He ached to discover how much he truly did sense without seeing.

"A warning," Amara pitched her voice to be heard over the whispers. "You may not touch anyone during the course of this dance. If you do—and I will know—you must remove your blindfold and withdraw to the edge of the room."

"Why?" Zora stepped away from the wall, body stiff and chin high. "What purpose could this possibly serve? If we do this, surely next you will stuff our ears as well, that we cannot hear each other."

"I shall keep the suggestion about stuffing your ears under advisement. It's not a bad idea. But not for today. Blindfolding you will be enough." Amara drew back, away from Zora, but her voice rose in power and impact. Every syllable resounded throughout the chamber. "Remember, o child of radiance, how dark it can be down in the Dancing chamber. Even with lanterns at every corner. A true Dancing Princess is able to Dance and work magic whether or not they can see. Or hear. Move or breathe."

The air in the room grew taut for a moment, then Zora jerked her head in acknowledgment and retreated to the wall.

Across the chamber, Gisela fumbled with the task of tying her blindfold. One foot tapped restlessly against the floor.

Lifting the cloth in his hands, Stevan laid it over his eyes. The sudden cessation of light made him shiver. The fabric seemed cool, even cold, against his skin. Bowing his head, he tied it tight at the back.

His breaths sounded louder in his hears, but otherwise his senses didn't change. He still tracked Amara's passage around the room by the press of her sandals against the floorboards. Couldn't hear what she said in anyone's ears, no matter how hard he tried. Even when she reached the compeer nearest him.

Then she rose up high enough to cup her hands around his ears and whisper.

"Flood."

He quenched his instinctive urge to sink down and begin the movements. Waited until she'd finished the circle and picked up a drum.

"Here is your beat." Three slow even taps, three fast, then back.

Stevan delayed leaving the wall for three full rounds of the beat, letting it sink into his bones and the flow of blood in his veins.

Becoming a flood, he dropped low. Crouched and slunk along the floor. Sometimes moving fast, other times slow. Stretching upward slightly, as though swelling with added waters and swallowing a beast, hillock or house, then falling low again.

His calves and back ached, but also sizzled with the energy of the dance.

His other senses compensated for lack of sight. The movement of air around his body shifted to alert him when someone approached. So too did the different scents of peoples' soaps or perfumes mixing with their bodily odors. Those dancing the part of winds breathed fast and frequently. Rain dancers changed their breathing patterns often as they moved from heavy falls of water to soft and then back, but otherwise remained steady. Flood dancers such as he drew long, deep breaths as they flowed about the room.

As before, he registered when anyone stepped upon the floor. Without vision, he couldn't put names and faces to a good half of the other dancers. But he tracked where Gisela moved. By her long, low, slow steps, she too danced as a flood. The whole of the room separated them, but he headed that way, determined to dance the flood with her even if they couldn't touch.

Todor danced as rain—and so could not partner with Gisela this time.

A third of the way across the floor, a twirling wind nearly took Stevan out. They both dodged at the last minute, Stevan with a sharp almost whistle.

Occasional curses as others bumped into each other—or brushed by and had to be ordered out by Amara—distracted him as well.

Yet not enough. He met up with Gisela two-thirds of the way across the chamber. Had she headed toward him consciously or not? No matter. As two flood dancers they faced off, slipped to one side then another.

Then danced together.

In joy—and agony, for they couldn't touch.

Heat and power zinged between them, easing his aches and helping him dance longer. Savor his triumph. Exult in the pleasure of dancing, success, and how well they paired. Above and beyond, a new wave of confidence flooded through him in time with his movement. The Terparchon and Amara were right: he was a born compeer, with something of value to offer.

When the drumming stopped, he stood up and removed his blindfold. Without thought, he mirrored Gisela as they removed the fabric from their eyes and stared at each other in perfect harmony.

Several voices interrupted. Nefeli and Idan approached, the latter's steps heavier than before, both calling Stevan's name. He glanced their way, and when he turned back Gisela had vanished from the room. As had Danissa . . . and Todor.

CHAPTER 19

Gisela leaned back against warm wood planks. Neither smooth nor rough, the slightest shift in either direction resulted in a most wondrous rubbing of her bare skin. She wore nothing, the better to enjoy the steam bath. Thick air heavy with moisture and heat drained tension from her body. Even the heated floor beneath her feet eased overstressed muscles and helped erase sore spots. The scent of sweet pine tinged with flowers she couldn't identify further relaxed her.

Her hand fell to her side and wrapped around a handleless clay mug. Decorated in a simple blue and red pattern, it was warm but not hot to the touch. Lifting it, she drank deep. As with the clay, the water remained notably cooler than the air. A faint aftertaste of mint lingered on her lips as she set the mug back down.

She let out a soft sigh, echoed by others in the room. Some sat, as Gisela, and others lay flat. Whenever the air began to dry, someone would rise just enough to lift a full dipper from the pail of water and pour it over the hot stones in the center of the room. With a hiss, clouds of steam gusted up to fill the room again.

Since leaving the dance floor, Gisela had rested in the steam room apart from plunging into the cold-water baths in between luxuriating in the warm humidity. She knew better than to stay too long. Foleilion had its own bathhouse, small despite serving all of the villagers. The only way to luxuriate there was to bathe very late at night. She'd never enjoyed so much room and time before. Yet the dancing pavilion included not one but two bathing complexes, for the princesses and the compeers, should they choose to remain separate. Such luxury.

So easy to keep putting off rising to leave.

Other parts of her new life she might resent, or enjoy with a tinge of guilt. Given how the dancing exercises had wrung Gisela of energy, she refused to allow any shadow to her taking pleasure in the baths.

Here she might rest. Upright or upon her back, either way her sore muscles found ease. Aches dulled. Pain slipped away. Even the tender spots in her feet faded.

Though she indulged in bodily relaxation, her mind was elsewhere. Still in the dancing chamber so nearby. Whenever she closed her eyes, the last dance returned to fill her with energy and peace. In darkness, she'd exulted in being a flood sweeping away all before her —while avoiding other dancers. Other princesses. She'd existed in her own space, tracing and retracing steps and ignoring others save when she needed to shift to keep from brushing them.

Until Stevan found her. No matter that she hadn't seen his face until they removed their blindfolds, she'd recognized him. Noted the ease with which he aligned his body to hers. The spark of energy between their skin as they all but touched.

His solidity. Although his movements matched hers, portraying a flood, he'd seemed to her instead to resemble an immense rock so firm in its foundations that the mightiest flood could not shove it so much as a hair. No, nor even make it sway.

Todor'd given her no such assurance, verbal or physical. Based on appearance, Todor and Stevan were of an age or nearly, and both likely a few years her junior. Yet the royal scion struck her as the younger and less reliable. Gisela had no quarrel with his partnering her in the exercises. He'd braced her competently, ensuring she didn't fall and righting her the few times she started to slip.

But that was all. When it came to Dances that invoked power, she'd rather ally with the tree than the sapling. The more so as Stevan attracted her body, mind, and movement.

Even though all they'd truly done, apart from the last dance, was exercises. Most frustrating, too, for the movements were so limited. Why those particular sets of actions for winds, rains and floods? So separate and restricted. The floods to stay low—could they not flow high? The winds to be always moving, but surely they might circle in one place or vary more. The rains so . . . simple.

"Why?" Gisela had asked Amara after, while they both sat in the steam bath.

The older woman had only shrugged a shoulder and given a half smile. "These are the movements the Terparchon considers most useful in easing lake storms. Enjoy the rest of the day."

Upon which she wrapped a towel around her torso and left the chamber.

Almost all of the princesses departed before Gisela. One by one they slipped away. Some paused to exchange pleasantries, including Jola and Heron, and others merely smiled. Until only two remained.

Gisela lingered in the baths partly because she had not yet determined what she was supposed—or allowed—to do next.

Next to her sat Danissa, bent over and bracing her elbows on her knees with her head in her hands.

The air began to dry, and grow less comfortable.

"One more bout of steam?" Gisela leaned forward to wrap her fingers around the blue-and-white ceramic ladle. Only one more for her, and then she'd leave to plunge in the pool and . . . whatever she might discover lay next.

Danissa waved a hand but said nothing, returning it to brace against her knee and thrusting her fingers into her curls.

Gisela lifted the ladle, then let it tilt so half the water ran back into the pail. The remaining drops she drizzled over the hot coals. Gouts of pale-gray steam billowed up. The air grew moist again, her skin slickened, and she sighed.

But not so hard or loud that she missed the sniff from the other princess. Danissa's shoulders had yet to ease in the heat. She kept them hunched up by her ears.

"Did you strain yourself in anyway? Or drain yourself?" Gisela echoed queries she'd heard other princesses exchange earlier, while stripping to enter the baths.

"No." Danissa straightened and tossed her head, then slumped back against the wall. "Not me."

The odd note in the other princess's voice puzzled Gisela. Even more troubling, Danissa had said so little and lacked her usual vivacity. Gisela shifted on the plank bench, just enough to be able to glance over without being obvious, or straining her neck.

She waited as drops of condensation or perspiration rolled down both bodies and the steam began to ease again.

"It's my father. He wasn't on the floor at the end of the storm exercise. Brushed another compeer, the merest touch but Amara noticed." Danissa waved a clawed hand through the last wreath of steam. "Though even if she had not, he would have removed himself. Too honest to remain."

"That's not common?" A shiver ran down Gisela's spine. She'd participated in dances where the numbers of participants dwindled as people made mistakes and left. Sometimes such a dance would be called at an impromptu occasion, but not often. Usually when a passing caravan of traders offered to teach villagers the latest dances.

Yet at the depth of winter, the full moon celebrations always end with such a dance. The more people who fell away having made mistakes, the worse the coming year was thought to be.

Was it the same here?

"Most unusual. Others get knocked out when we do competitive exercises, even when not blindfolded which is more often the case, but never him. I haven't seen it, not since I became a princess." She turned an agonized expression toward Gisela, eyes big and damp. "I asked him how he was doing, what was wrong, but he said nothing and sent me away."

"Perhaps he was embarrassed?"

"Or ill, and does not want me to know." Danissa's hands curled into fists.

"You might ask him another day, when the memory is not so fresh for him."

"Oh I will. He's always told me I can tell him anything. He gets me to do so even when I promise myself I'll keep secrets from him. Never big secrets, only little things. Yet he keeps things from me, and that's not right. He should share. I will make him share." Some of Danissa's energy returned. She sat taller, straighter, and her words tumbled over each other again. "Somehow."

"I believe you." Gisela frowned at the coals. Better not to risk another pour, but to go back out . . . and do what? Setting feet firm on the warm floor, she rose and stretched. Arms high overhead, then curving outward to fall back by her sides. "If I may, where are we supposed to go next? Back to the chamber to learn more dances?"

"Did no one tell you? However not? It was posted along the eastward door, though you wouldn't know to look on your own." Danissa rose as well, doing a few toe-touches and rolling her shoulders. "Ylena's unexpected visitation quite drove that from my mind, but I would have thought Amara or Jola or Heron might have mentioned. The more so in the event you do not know how to read. You do, don't you?"

"No, no one told me to look, and yes I know how to read. The common alphabet." Gisela sighed, blinking her eyes against sudden memory of holding the council scrolls for the last time before passing them on to her former apprentice.

"That is all most use here, save those from the northern mountains." Danissa yanked the door open.

Cool air rushed in, raising goose bumps all along Gisela's skin. She wrapped her arms around her chest and huddled, anxious not to lose the warmth and flexibility.

Outside lay a rectangular hallway bare except for a line of shelving along the far wall. Two piles of cloth lay folded atop the shelves, both thin and small from the distance. The ripple of water flowing resounded from the right where the baths lay. To the left sat a wooden wall with a closed door that led back toward the dancing chamber.

Danissa rose on tiptoes across the stone floor to the shelves. Gisela mimicked her, finding the stones warmer than expected albeit still chilly compared to the steam room.

The shelf proved to bear small wooden plaques along its length. Each displayed the name of a princess, letters first carved then painted in bright gold and silver. Already someone had added Gisela's name, and above it sat one of the two piles of clothes.

Likely Emmi had placed them there, or someone who'd taken a degree of care, for they were placed in exactly the right order for donning. Clean underthings atop a pristine tunic in pale yellow gauze. Then a slightly heavier weight mantle in gold with pale yellow suns and flowers embroidered along one side. The folds of the mantle held a broach of entwined gold and silver to fasten the mantle at one shoulder and let the decorated side flow free. Instead of a circlet, a simple thong of gold-tinged leather to pull her hair back and off her neck.

Of course, beneath all else, another pair of sandals.

"Scholars, too, read other alphabets. The palace libraries are quite choice, most particularly at the winter palace. But the one here has ample holdings, if you have any interest." Danissa pulled a rich pink tunic over her head.

"Yes, but first I need to know where I am supposed to be next." Gisela grimaced but donned the sandals before tunic or mantle, so her feet might adapt to the constraints as she dressed.

"Oh, the time is ours do as we will. Afternoons, at least. Mornings we have practice always, save the occasional off day. From noon to evening meal is ours to choose." Danissa paused long enough to tick off the times on her fingers. "Sometimes our presence is requested as attendants for court occasions or hunts. To judge competitions. Evenings, likewise, are usually free save that some of us must attend any court function, and if there is a dance we all do."

"Then I might do anything for the rest of the day?" Gisela paused, tunic bunched about her waist. The idea of *not* having her day set for her, at least for the first weeks or months, hadn't occurred.

"Unless you have been asked for specifically, yes." Danissa gave a sharp nod as she threaded the ends of her purple mantle through a broach that matched Gisela's. "Mind, you shouldn't stray from the palace without escorts—or without permission because we might be called for a Dance at any time and so the Terparchon or Amara needs to know where we are, to track us down if necessary. Otherwise our time is our own. Most princesses have one hobby or another; things they enjoy doing besides dancing. Jola teaches dancing, she's organized schools in half the cities in the country. Heron weaves and embroiders and makes the most beautiful scarves and tapestries."

"And you?" Gisela eyed the other dam, unable to guess where her interests might lie.

"I dabble. I've let each of the other princesses show me what they enjoy. I can recommend that as a way to get to know them. Some of them do go on and on, but I've learnt things I never expected." Leaned in close, Danissa dropped her voice even though they were alone in the room. "Ylena, of all people, introduced me to the libraries. She will read anything she can get her hands on, no matter how boring. I would never have thought. Though there are some very interesting texts there, and good-looking librarians as well!"

Gisela thought better of Ylena based on the news. If only the other hadn't been the princess whose injury opened the door for Gisela's forced recruitment.

"What do you enjoy?" Danissa knelt down to fasten her sandals, glancing up between grunts and yanks on the straps.

Gisela's mind went blank. She laughed, wincing at the bitter tone audible even to her. "When I was home, in Foleilion, my joy and pleasure was slipping off to dance in a fallow field. Yet dance has now become my new livelihood, so perhaps my old position—being a scribe—shall become my new hobby."

Danissa rose to face Gisela, face tilted up but head leaning to one side. She pursed her lips, then gave a wry smile. "If you are a scribe, you may like the library here. Shall I take you there?"

"Why not?" It might at least smell of home, for surely there would be ample ink and parchment.

They left the pavilion and walked straight into the heat of full summer. Bright light shone down, nearly blinding in its strength. Though the indoors had not seemed cool to Gisela while she was there, leaving showed how much heat the thick walls kept out. Gisela blinked rapidly against the brightness as sweat dewed her body. Her whole self seemed an uprooted plant blowing this way and that on the wind.

"Let's take the long way through the gardens." Danissa jerked her head to the side, though Gisela had to squint to see the motion. "It's shadier there."

"Shade would be good." Gisela followed in Danissa's footsteps.

They turned to the side onto a path made of flat, oval stones in varied grays. The steps wound between banks of flowering plants and trees. Masses of blues and purples bloomed against leaves in varied forms and shades of green. From long, narrow, and palest green to broad and deep. Thick tree trunks stood tall, all well-grown and mature with ample foliage arching overhead. Rays of light passed through, but much of the path lay in shadow.

Shade alone eased the heat beating down. The trees bore the brunt instead. Walking within the shady confines, Gisela paused now and then to hear breezes rustling through the leaves, and feel their caress wick the remaining drops of sweat from her brow.

"An excellent choice." Gisela lifted her face to the wealth of branches and leaves overhead. "I could remain here all day."

"No, we should have gone the other way, through the other gardens." Danissa stopped and stood stock still, body stiff and tense. "I come this way so rarely I forgot this is why."

Gisela glanced over Danissa's shoulder, but nothing explained the other princess's regret. They'd reached a clearing of some sort, wide and circular and nearly as large as the dancing pavilion. One line of oval, gray stones led straight ahead on the other side of Danissa, but stones also lay embedded in the ground to either side, tracing wide arcs around the perimeter of the open area.

A dazzle of butterflies in golds, blues, and reds darted around the edge of the opening, doing their own dance above the blue-green sun mosses that covered the earth with their velvety growths.

"It's lovely. Those mosses must be a delight to dance on." Gisela slipped around Danissa to kneel and stroke a hand over silky leaves. "Do we ever meet here instead of the pavilion?"

"Do not wish that." Danissa shook her head, shifting her weight from foot to foot as though stepping on hot coals. "The moss is wonderful to dance upon, yes, but as for the rest. The center . . ."

"What's wrong?" Gisela rose and stopped. There lay a perfectly round section of earth clear of all mosses and greenery. White and chalky, it had ridges and dips that resembled the moon when full.

"That's one of the Shadows of the Moon."

"I thought you wanted to show it to me. That's what you said this morning." Gisela didn't turn away from the pale spot nearly glowing against the moss.

"Then I wanted more to help you avoid meeting Ylena. It was the first thing that came to mind. The worst thing so often is. But you've seen it, now, so you know and can describe it if you are ever asked. Sometimes ambassadors and visitors from other lands ask about these, and it can be quite tiresome to answer when one doesn't know. So you do now, and we may go on to the library. It's just around the edge and a few paths further."

"I'd like a closer look. You can stay behind, if you'd rather. Or I'll meet you at whichever point leads on to the library." Gisela took a step forward, then glanced back at Danissa.

"I will escort you." The younger remained in place, stiff and straight. She set her teeth in a fixed grin, eyes wide and round.

"Truly, it's not necessary. We can meet elsewhere. Over there perhaps?" Gisela pointed one-quarter around the clearing, where a path led off back into the trees.

"No. It's better not to be alone here. But"—Danissa's tone shrank to a soft whisper—"if you don't mind being quick about it?"

An urge washed over Gisela, to forget the matter and go off with Danissa as she so clearly wanted. She resisted. This was the type of site the old Terparchon supposedly desired to the extent she destroyed Escalad and drove the Escalli into their new home far away. Gisela might never see that other site, but she could at least view this and maybe gain insight into what the dead ruler had valued so highly.

She led the way along a path of well-trodden stones to the center.

The round of chalky earth was big enough for three or five people to lie down and curl within. The color seemed off, lacking the silveriness of moonlight and instead holding the tinge of aged bone. Then the relative cool of the clearing bore in upon her. The sun shone overhead, surely as bright as before, but lessened. The Shadow drew it in, swallowed it whole.

No breeze blew through the clearing, but Gisela's skin remained dry and warm rather than hot. The still air held a taint that hit the back of her throat as though she'd swallowed a mouthful of soured milk.

Gisela remained several feet back from the shadow itself. Not close enough to touch. The ground of the Shadow appeared hard and sharp. Unweathered by the elements. Except . . . around the edge, bits flaked off. Or was the Shadow growing and absorbing the earth around it?

The trees' ample foliage ended with the edge of the clearing. None of the trunks had limbs growing out over the mosses, toward the Shadow of the Moon; nor signs such limbs had been removed. The closest trees seemed almost to be leaning back and away.

A faint ringing began at the back of Gisela's ears. Distant, as though someone far away had struck a gong. Or screamed. She shook her head, but the impression remained. It made her dizzy. She blinked and rubbed her ears with fingers growing chilly against heated cheeks.

A sense of wrongness flooded through her. The Shadow reminded her of the fallow field, only worse. Withering. Dying. Dead. Despair formed a lump within her. Her arms grew heavy and legs wobbled. Hard to pull away. The chalky earth called to her. She almost stepped forward, except memory of the fallow field also brought to mind the last time she'd danced there. Bidding it farewell. Stevan balancing her and cradling her as she wept.

Behind her, Danissa shifted from one foot to another. Her mantle rustled, disturbing the silence, and the ringing faded away.

Gisela turned in a circle, fixing on Danissa. The other had her arms crossed and shoulders hunched. Desperate to go, but unwilling to abandon Gisela. Shaking her head a second time, Gisela nodded at the closest path leading away.

"Shall we go?"

"You do not wish to see any more?"

"Not today." Gisela turned her hands out to either side. "I thank you for coming with me. I regret I didn't listen and stay away." Only a half truth, for Gisela would have wanted to come close some time. Still might, but not alone. Danissa was right about that.

"The old Terparchon—not the current one, her mother—she used to host picnics and court dances here and on the other Shadows of the Moon." Danissa started along the path away, glancing back every few steps as though to be sure Gisela was following—or perhaps that nothing else trailed along farther behind. "She died when I was young, but I remember having to go along with my father and hating it."

"The Terparchon treasures it?" Gisela glanced back herself, and saw only empty air. Not even butterflies or insects seemed to dare the area close to the Shadow.

"All the Terparchons have, or so my father says. The empire possesses eight now, but that's not a good number. Sooner than later they'll want to get them all. The old Terparchon never let anyone else walk on the Shadow of the Moon, but she would dance on it with glee." Danissa sighed, relief clear in every inch of her body, as they reached the more natural shade of the canopy of trees. Stopping for a moment, she shuddered and gave Gisela a rueful glance. "The old Terparchon—she's not much missed. The current Terparchon has her oddities, and you have to get to know them, but she's much nicer to dance for. Even my father will admit it if you get him drunk enough."

Gisela made no protest when Danissa set a quick pace on to the library.

A chill remained, no matter how far they went from the shadow. Its very unnaturalness lurked in the back of her head. So horrid. Worse than the fallow field. Gisela pulled her mantle closer around her shoulders and tucked folds around her arms. All the same, she didn't warm even when they left the woods and gardens to walk bright, hot paths between buildings.

No matter how fast she moved, or how hot the sun, she stayed chilled to the bone until they reached the arched entrance to a tall building of silvery stones—and met Stevan hurrying along toward them.

CHAPTER 20

*S*tevan's unexpected promotion brought many benefits, some he'd admit publicly and the remainder never. Of those he would claim, new clothes ranked high. Shallow of him, perhaps, but practical as well.

The summer heat no longer bothered him so much as he wove his way from one side of the palace to the other. Tunic and mantle, both in shades of green-blue, flowed around his arms and legs but wicked away moisture. His sandals lacked patches to the underside.

And all were clean without his having lifted a finger. The second clean outfit in one day, the clothes he'd worn dancing having been whisked away for laundering.

If he strode along a little faster, bounced a little higher with each step, it was from the sheer pleasure of being able to cross an open-air courtyard from side to side without hugging the shadows in a vain attempt to avoid overheating.

Gray stone buildings rose high to either side. Matching stones paved courtyards, save where raised beds nourished trees and flowers, or fountains rose to toss drops of water high. These were rougher stones than elsewhere, the buildings newer and paths less trodden and so not yet worn smooth.

Fewer mosaics adorned the walls—room left for rising generations to leave their mark. The most decorative parts were often the floors and paths. The stones beneath his feet were myriad small ones set in the earth to form patterns. One courtyard boasted stones adding up to a starry sky. Another was decorated with waves teeming with fish.

They made walking much more interesting, even if one did have to step carefully to avoid stray stones lying slightly higher. The stones channeled whatever waters fell from the sky. Though dry now, under the hot sun overhead, bits of moss already grew here and there waiting for the next deluge.

He'd walked these ways many times before, back when he sharing rooms on a high, hot floor. Unlike other, grander, parts of the palace, he knew what lay within these walls. Which ministries filled this building. Whose overworked clerks labored on the other side.

Now he'd didn't belong—he passed through.

But his new coworkers had welcomed him. At least Nefeli and Idan and the other born compeers. For well over an hour they'd all sat together in the shade outside the dancing pavilion, exchanging stories and hints and tips.

Giving him advice, but in a kindly fashion that did not demand he immediately act on any of it. Just as well, with so many offerings from the best ways to lift and support princesses to many of their individual quirks and preferences. Better to listen and let the suggestions sink in. Whatever made sense would float to the top, and those he'd seek to make second nature.

He licked his lips, clearing away the last lingering drops of the yogurt-smeared flatbread he'd grabbed for a snack when he passed the kitchens.

Tonight, the court would feast to celebrate Gisela's arrival . . . and the looming departure of some ambassador or another . . . and at least three or four other purposes as well. The Marchon and Terparchon had perfected the art of honoring as many people at the same time all the while convincing most of them that they were the primary reason for the celebrations.

Gisela would likely not be taken in.

The heat of noon-day sun sent most people inside thick walls that held the night's chill, or in the shade somewhere. Even when on the track between Foleilion and the court, he and Gisela and Amara stopped for lunch and naps.

Stevan didn't mind being sent off on an errand this day, not in light clothes. Not when he returned some service to those who helped him.

Particularly when it meshed with his own inclinations and interests.

Despite the heat, some others were out walking between the buildings: the secretary to minister of defense, clerks who toiled for the treasurer. Stevan nodded and occasionally exchanged pleasantries. He avoided longer conversations and project a friendly air to show he hadn't grown too big for his sandals since his sudden elevation, but also appear a man with a mission of some urgency. Someone who knew where he was bound.

Which he didn't, at least . . . not exactly.

He knew not when or where, but whom he was headed toward.

Quite an odd feeling to be tracking a person rather than heading to a place. Energy raced through his skin, keeping him on edge. His skin heated the longer he walked, making him all the more glad to wear cool clothes.

The uneasiness in his bones made no sense. Tracking should seem a natural extension of his ability to know where Gisela was at her village, or where people were on the dance floor.

But this wasn't the dance floor, and he didn't seek Gisela . . . or, not only Gisela.

Idan and Nefeli had explained it, but making sense of it all required time.

His powers extended beyond the dance. Or should. The more he used them off the dance floor, the more natural he'd find them on.

Apparently a natural compeer could, if they put their mind to it and practiced, track at least one and as many as several people across varyingly vast distances by feeling their steps on earth and stone. Or a compeer might cast a wider net upon a smaller field, and learn something of everyone who walked there. Or various combinations between.

Stevan tracked Danissa on purpose, to deliver a message. He'd find Gisela near Danissa. They followed such a similar trail that surely walked together. They headed toward one of the newer, squarish buildings that sat near the guard barracks. As Stevan drew closer, he became aware of Brenn not too far away, pacing around a large square.

That was only one part of being a good compeer: cultivating awareness of his environs and the people surrounding him.

Much as he wanted to see Gisela again—indeed he'd jumped at the errand as an excuse to head her way—the other parts of being a compeer, such as drawing and channeling power or grounding it when a princess overextended, intrigued him more.

Tracking people, knowing where they were, made his skin itch. Phantom noises plagued him—the whistle of a whip or switch about to strike. When he whirled around, he faced only empty air.

Still, Idan had asked him to find Danissa and see if she would attend on her father. To explain his decision to withdraw from being an active compeer to advising only. This guaranteed Stevan a place in the next Dance; albeit partnering Danissa, should she agree, rather than Gisela.

How could he say no? Particularly when Idan framed it as an opportunity to test and stretch Stevan's tracking ability.

Even if it meant hurrying ever faster, no matter that it made him sweat more. Struggling to draw in deep breaths as he tried to outrun the inexplicable sounds chasing him. Desperate to reach Danissa and deliver his message before whatever invisible force caught him.

He spotted Danissa and Gisela together on the stoop of the library. The tall building with its high, arched windows rose up behind them. Against that, they appeared smaller and drawn in upon themselves. A light sheen of sweat made their respective skins glow, but rather than seeming overheated both shivered. Their mantles and tunics clung close to their skin.

Gisela smiled at his approach, but Danissa managed only a flicker of movement along her mouth.

He yanked open the door to the entry hall and encouraged them to enter. This was but an anteroom to the library itself, though large enough to encompass many people. Empty at the moment.

The air was cooler than outside, albeit not by much, and tinged with a dusty tang. Baskets hung on the largely unadorned walls. Each held a wealth of luminescent mosses that offered the only light. Faintly green, the moss light complemented no complexion but held less risk of fire.

At the center of the wall to the right sat a fountain in the shape of an immense pink spiral shell. Water trickled from the tip down the sides before falling into the basin. Beneath hung a dozen or more mugs from hooks set into the stone. The last wall featured immense double doors to the library itself, both pierced by a series of grates that allowed the librarians to look out. The wall to the left held three small alcoves, each with a bench and a degree of privacy.

Sandals clacked against the tiled floor, with its subtle pattern of browns, greens, and golds meant to represent layers of books. Every footstep raised an echo, as did the princesses' shivery breaths. Stevan ushered them into the center alcove. Retrieving two of the mugs, he filled them with water and left them to drink. For himself, he stuck his cupped hands into the cool fall and drank straight from the source.

One of the librarians opened a door a hand's breadth, just far enough to stick out a pale face topped with a mass of tousled brown hair. An instant later, a tall, thin body draped in a double layer of green tunics slipped out. Slippered feet made a soft shushing noise. The librarian patted hair down, giving Stevan a courteous nod.

"How may I be of service? Do you wish to consult the library?" Wide brown eyes glanced at the women in the alcove, gaze lingering on the broaches that proclaimed their rank.

"Perhaps, but not quite yet. If we might have a little time?" Stevan nodded back.

"Of course." With a last look at the princesses, the librarian retreated and let the door click shut behind him.

"Gisela wanted to see the library." Danissa set her mug on the floor and stood up, dusting her tunic and mantle although both appeared spotless to Stevan.

"And so she shall, if she wishes. But drink well, first." He refilled Gisela's mug; Danissa shook her head when he offered to do the same for hers. "No liquids are allowed farther than this room."

"I didn't know you were headed here." Danissa glanced between Stevan and Gisela, eyebrows arching. "Or perhaps you hoped to meet us?"

"I did, yes, but for reasons other than what you may suspect." Stevan didn't meet Danissa's eyes. "It's you I was asked to find."

Both stiffened and looked straight at him for a long moment. Gisela shifted to glancing between him and Danissa, concern clear on her face. Danissa merely seemed surprised.

"Your father would like to speak with you. He's in his rooms." Stevan tilted his head in the general direction.

"Is he well?" Danissa held very still.

Stevan drew and expelled a deep breath, turning his hands out in unspoken commentary. "He says he is."

"He would." Danissa turned to Gisela, then Stevan, then back and forth until she finally settled on giving Stevan a glare before facing Gisela. "If you don't mind, might I leave you in Stevan's hands?"

Scarcely waiting for Gisela's assent, Danissa stalked through the antechamber. Her footsteps quickened with every step, sandals slapping against the tiles by the time she was out the door.

Gisela watched her leave.

Stevan watched them both.

"He seemed tired this morning." Gisela pursed her lips. "I only met him once before, but he reminded me of many of the elders on the council—determined to go on and do what they consider their duty no matter what anyone else said."

"An apt description as far as I can see, though I know him only a little better." Stevan shrugged.

"I didn't know I was headed here until a little while ago. Danissa and I told no one." Gisela set her half-full mug on the floor and twined her fingers together, a puzzled expression on her face. "How did you know to find us here?"

"There's more to being a compeer than dancing." Stevan stood still, feet firmly planted on the tiled floor. Nevertheless, movement thrummed in his heels: an echo of Danissa's steps headed across the palace complex at a rapid rate. A faint whistling sound from behind made him jerk and whirl about, but no one was there.

"Such as what?" Gisela rose, tunic and mantle hems fluttering around her ankles. The fabric no longer clung quite so close to her figure as before, to Stevan's regret. She peered around him, brow further furrowing. "Were you looking for someone?"

"No, I heard . . ." The whistle echoed in his head, more distant but still audible. Again he turned around to find no source.

"Be at ease." Gisela gave him a gentle shove, enough to send him reeling into the alcove.

He dropped onto the bench and scooted back into the corner where stone surrounded him on two sides. Nothing and no one could sneak up behind him here. Filling her mug, she brought it to him and pressed it into his hands.

"Your turn to drink deep, and tell me what is wrong."

He obeyed only so far as to take a long swallow. Enough to wet his throat, but no more. All the same, his voice was rough and words scraped his mouth when he spoke.

"I can follow people. Find them, by tracking where they step on the ground. That's not . . ." He grimaced. "I'm not sure how to describe it. A knowing or . . ."

"Such as when you found me dancing at the fallow field?" Gisela settled onto the bench next to him, radiating warmth and comfort.

"No, that was as much because I watched you leave the village and followed you." He met her eyes. "This is more. At practice, I knew where everyone was on the floor. When I found you while blindfolded, it wasn't by chance."

"Hmm." She didn't look away. "It must be so distracting, particularly here where there are so many people. How do you manage?"

"I only track those I'm most interested in. It used to be my family, but then—" He stopped, his own words repeating in his head.

He tracked his family? Why had he said that and not merely that he tracked Brenn? Drawing in a quick breath, the air whistled through his mouth. All at once, voices overlaid each other in his ears. His father's, stepmother's, other siblings.

"Where is she? I know you know. You'll tell me if you know what's good for you."

"I warned you, boy, keep your mouth shut on things that aren't any of your business."

"Tattle-tale, you better not spill my secrets or you'll get it this time."

Voice after voice demanding to know where someone was: he, she, she, he, they. Then the same voices yelling at him for having told on them. Always angry at other people—and at him.

The crack of a whip.

Swish of a switch.

Smack of a hand slapping his face.

Lashes landing on his back. He hunched. Pulled his arms in against his chest. Ducked his head. Pain bloomed from neck to buttocks. He ground his teeth, rocking.

Soft arms wrapped around him. A welcome voice crooned in his ears. "Shh. Easy now. You're safe here. Nothing's going to harm you. You're safe."

He let his head fall onto her shoulder as shuddering breaths racked his body. But the pain and voices of the past eased their hold, while leaving unwelcome knowledge behind.

"I could do this all along. Ever since I was a child, except . . . I forgot. I didn't want to remember."

"You've been a compeer that long?" Gisela stroked his hair. He shifted to cuddle closer to her, and she didn't pull away.

"Perhaps. I guess. But no one recognized it, especially me. At first, when I popped out word of where this person or that was, usually one of my siblings who'd run off to avoid punishment, no one believed me." Stevan drew back, though he wrapped his hands around one of hers to keep the contact as long as he could.

"If I hadn't seen evidence, I might have trouble believing you." She twined her fingers with his, squeezing. "You don't need to tell me, but I admit to being curious. Why did you forget?"

A lump grew in his throat, sourness filling his mouth. Swallowing hard, he continued. "When people did believe, things got worse. My father and stepmother were a bad match. My father wanted money and a mother for his children. My stepmother wanted higher rank. Neither got as much as they expected, so they sought consolation elsewhere."

Her eyes flickered at that.

"You do know that most people in Codaros form marital alliances in twos and occasionally threes? And restrict their, ah, sexual activity to within marriage rather than . . ." He halted, rather than try to describe what little he knew of her people.

"Rather than lying with whomever takes their fancy?" She huffed. "I daresay I know more of your ways than you of mine. In point-of-fact, many Escalli pair off or form triads after they've done their procreative duties, although as many do not."

"Fair spoken." Stevan's cheeks grew warm. "I wish more of my family were that. Both my parents constantly asked me where the other was. Scolded me, slapped my head, when I tried to keep from speaking. Then turned around and railed when I let slip where they were to the other. Sometimes my back still aches in remembrance."

"They hit you!" Gisela sat stock straight, body stiff and face radiating indignation. "They're no parents, no carers, if they did. Hurting you for their own deeds."

"Are children not punished among the Escalli?" An incredulous chuckle escaped him.

"Punished yes, but by being denied treats or made to do chores they detest. A guardian who is discovered hitting a child is removed and put to other tasks. At best." She stroked his cheek, her skin warm and soft to the touch. Eyes damp. "Children should be cherished. I'm sorry you weren't. And honored you confided in me."

The caring in her eyes loosened something within him. Bending forward, he set his head against her chest again and wept.

CHAPTER 21

*B*ooks, scrolls, and papers everywhere Gisela turned. The contents of Foleilion's small cache multiplied by thirteen or thirteen squared or more—so many the air tasted of ink and parchment.

Turning around and around, sandals scuffing against the wooden floor planks, and tunic and mantle swaying about her legs, she drank in the marvel that was the summer palace library.

Sturdy wooden shelves towered above her by at least a head. The highest held rolled scrolls carefully wrapped in varicolored fabrics. Her fingers itched to untie the cords—gilded, silvered, or plain twine with the ends dipped in dye of one color another. To unfold the soft lengths of cloth and reveal the treasures beneath.

Or to pull off one of the immense ledgers laid sideways on lower shelves and open covers nearly as large as her torso to read the contents. Would she even be able to move one on her own? Plenty of smaller books, most bound in bright colored boards, filled the middle shelves. Those more closely resembled the books she'd once cared for.

Then there were wooden boxes, gilded or plain, that held papers not yet copied into other volumes. If she dived into one, what might she find . . .

Caution held her back. So new to court and court life she might as well be a green bud barely poking its head above earth, patience was the better path. The safer. No sense doing anything rash until she knew whether the doing would endanger more than herself.

And her village's tax rolls.

Even though forbearance left a sour taste in her mouth. She'd waited years without complaint, trusting each cycle to show she'd finally conceived. What good was patience when it brought only unwelcome results?

One hand slipped out far enough to brush the binding of a burgundy book. Her fingers met lushly woven fabric, and a spark of energy shot up her arm.

She jerked back, grabbing her shoulder to keep from trying again.

Her hand landed, by chance or fortune, on the part of her mantle where Stevan had laid his head. The cloth was still damp from his tears. Some had even soaked through to the tunic below and not dried yet, leaving a cool patch.

This was all the more notable because the library was cool. Tall windows captured breezes and channeled them along the shelves. The underlying floor was unmatched stone, rough and unadorned with mosaics. The shelves sat on stones cut into triangular shapes, raised a finger's length or more above the floor. More triangular stones supported wooden floors and walkways around and between the shelves.

Wooden platforms around the edges of the large chamber held ample tables and benches set out for reading and copying. Clear, bright light from the sun through the windows and the ever-present baskets of mosses allowed scribes to view every detail of the works they studied.

The shelves holding the books and scrolls sat at the center of the room.

"This way, should a storm blow open the protective shutters, any damage from rain or wind might be limited to the tables and benches and not reach the treasured contents."

An elderly librarian, white-haired and face shrunken to a mass of light-brown wrinkles, bent to point out the high-water mark halfway up a supporting stone. His multi-layered tunics, in graduating shades from pale pink to deep rose, fell to his ankles. A thick leather belt wrapped three times around his waist, hanging low at the center loop, for several metal rings of keys depended from it. He'd covered his feet in strips of matching rose underneath the straps of his sandals, but was steady as he led the way around the chamber.

"The princesses have been kind to us." His voice quavered a little, and he nodded at Gisela's broach. "Even in the worst storms, they've shielded us from the heaviest downfalls and gales."

"I look forward to helping protect such an important place." So many folk had mentioned the summer blasts as evidence of the princesses' power and protection.

She smiled at the elder, but grew uncomfortable when he continued to stare at her. Rather than return gaze for gaze, she glanced away at the assortment of clerks seated at the tables. Most had two books or scrolls before them, one dense with text and the other blank save where the scribe laboriously copied in letters and forms. Pens scratched against paper. Pages rustled as they were turned. Occasionally a scribe drew in a deep breath after a turning.

Most also peeked her way now and then. She ignored them other than polite nods.

In a far corner sat Stevan, bent over a thick book as tall as his forearm. He'd stayed to escort her back after. Instead of following her and the librarian around the room, he'd asked for a book on trees of all things. Despite the distance between them, as he turned a page she caught a glimpse of a drawn tree that filled the paper from edge to edge.

He glanced up and grinned. Then turned back to his book.

Perhaps he'd noticed her stopping. Or whatever power let him track her footsteps shared other things, too, such as that she'd looked at him.

No one had told her about the powers of compeers, other than that they supported princesses and made their Dancing easier.

Then again, neither had anyone particularly instructed her in the powers of princesses either. Amara had shown her various exercises and steps, all of which raised some measure of power. This morning's practice had expanded her knowledge. Yet still so much remained a mystery.

One fragment of Amara's instruction stuck with her, nagged at her in stray moments.

Princesses raised power and directed it.

"But what matters most is what's in your heart." Amara had patted her own chest. "And how you express it in Dance."

Hence the practice of being rain and wind and flood.

Swallowing the burst of irritation burning the back of her throat, Gisela drew deep breaths. Each one bore the aromas of parchment and ink, of leather and preserved cloth. The special threads that stitched pages together within bindings. All familiar, albeit she was accustomed to a lesser degree, and that familiarity eased the tightness in her shoulders.

She had time. Her pledge to her village bound her here for years. What matter if she didn't find any answers on arrival?

Save Ilburna might not have so long to wait.

The village elder had mentioned fellow Escalli placed at court, one in the winter palace library and another somewhere. Gisela glanced over at the scribes and librarians rustling through the building. None gave her any sign of recognition or spoke with the brisk accents she already missed.

Jerking her head, she turned her attention back to the elderly librarian showing her around. He'd moved from the matter of water to discussing the treasures held here.

"We have at best a third as many volumes and rolls as the winter palace." The old sire shook his head and clicked his tongue. "But more with every passing year. You see we have the room." He gestured at half-filled shelves.

Some had as little as one volume laid flat upon them. Others contained one, two, or three covered boxes of wood specially treated to preserve the contents. The planks shifted not at all beneath Gisela as she slipped partway down the aisle. The librarian followed. Loosening some of the keys chained to his belt, he opened a selection of the boxes for her to peer into.

Most of the pages were thin and flimsy, or had the appearance of over-used parchment that had had writing scraped off so often they were nearly useless. Yet all had some words or numbers on them, mostly in the kind of cramped hand Gisela used for notes back in the days she'd documented the elders' meetings.

"Are these notes of value?" The lesser light between shelves combined with the narrow, scratched letters to make reading difficult.

"We will see." The librarian threw his hands out. "They came with the court this spring, and will go back in the fall. Clerks and aides sometimes come to consult them, or even remove them."

"How old are they?" She shifted further down, trying to read the lines on a particularly yellowed scrap of parchment.

"Most are recent. A season? A year? But some boxes go back and forth every year. That one there," he caressed the box lid, "has notes dating from the Terparchon's mother and grandfather's days."

Gisela's fingers twitched at the urge to page through them. Study. Search for more information about the loss of the Escalli homeland. She didn't fully understand the urgency welling within her. A distant voice in her mind insisted she already gave Ilburna the answer that yes, the old Terparchon could have and probably did drive them from their homeland.

But she lacked surety or proof.

Then again what good would proof do? Except give a little ease or direction to the deep burning anger that welled within her at how little territory the Escalli now occupied, and how little control they had over their lives and livelihoods.

And how little *she* had. Easier to be angry with the old Terparchon, whether or not she was truly guilty, than face the lingering resentment for her situation. For how fate blew her about, taking with one hand and giving with the other but not in equal measure.

And Gisela went along. Let herself be blown this way and that. Ordered here, sent there, commanded to dance.

Perhaps that's partly why she increasingly wanted to know the truth. Ilburna was right that knowledge was likely all they'd ever have, as it wouldn't change their situation. But Gisela found hope in the possibility that the old Terparchon was to blame for Gisela's people's misfortune. That would give Gisela someone, no matter how dead, to be angry with. To curse and lash out at, when she couldn't do anything to other forces.

Though it would require doing something other than going along.

Pulling away from the box, she let the lid fall.

Steeled herself to continue on the tour when what she wanted more was to sit down with the box's contents.

Turning, she discovered the librarian frowning at view through the window at the far end of the shelves. A small mass of dark clouds loomed in the distance over the water. Closer, the sky took on a greasy, yellow cast. Winds whirled over the lake, but all breezes had vanished. The air lay still and calm. Drier, and easier to breathe.

"That'll be a storm, no doubt." The librarian gave her an abstracted smile, eyes distant and calculating. "I regret that I must end the tour now, but do return another time. We are always happy to share our treasures. Now I must see about preserving them."

He clapped a friendly hand on her shoulder.

And somehow, within a matter of minutes, she and Stevan and most of the other scribes had vacated the building, only those employed by the library remaining behind. The scribes scattered off in a dozen directions, several muttering about supper.

Gisela remained, shocked by the speed with which she'd been shunted out of the library. The old sire had every excuse, if he believed a storm coming, but had he also noticed her interest in the old papers?

Distant clattering marked the shutters being closed over the windows, three at a time.

Quiet though the air lay, a current ran through it setting every hair on Gisela's body on end.

"The sky does have a storm-cast to it. We may be called to Dance before long." Stevan scanned the horizon, pointing out where the clouds merged and multiplied. "Maybe tonight, maybe morning."

"Do we Dance at night?" Gisela had never seen such a strange twilight.

"I don't know much more than you, but I've heard the bell that calls princesses, and compeers to Dance ring out at all hours. Even though it never called me before. You cannot miss it. Only infants can sleep through it. It always woke me out of sleep no matter how deep."

Both fell silent, waiting on it to ring. Bangs and clatters sounded from every part of the complex. Window after window turned dark as shutters closed. Only a few lanterns, and fountains here and there overgrown with the luminescent mosses, offered warm light to counter the greasy, yellow sky.

Except at the horizon, where thin silver beams fought to break through the clouds. The crescent moon hung above the lake before the storm swallowed it.

"Not long, now, until the moon grows full again." Stevan's voice grew distant and abstracted, though his eyes fell warm on Gisela when she glanced his way.

He said nothing more, but his silence spoke volumes. A flicker of power electrified the air between them. An illusion grew, from the power he'd begun to embrace—and the way he stood gazing down at her. Twilight turned to midnight. Their clothes shifted into thin tunics clinging to their skin after long hours of dancing. His refusal to lie with her rang again in her ears, along with his other words. His promise.

She now realized he desired a *yes* to last for days and months and years, not just a night.

If she decided to make the offer. Which she hadn't . . . yet.

A blink dispelled the illusion, returning her to the summer palace on the eve of a storm.

A tender, wry smile shone on Stevan's face.

"If you're not ready to make an offer at this full moon, hold off until the next one moon after. Or the one after that," he said, quiet but sure. "I'll wait until you know what you do or don't want from me."

"Why?"

"I have always loved to dance, but never did so with anyone who fit me as well as you." He took her hand, pressing it between his. In the growing quiet, their pulses beat in harmony. "No matter which of us leads, I can match you in the dance. And, I believe, in life as well."

They stared into each other's eyes. Longing rose in her, to dance with him in every way—but that very longing brought fear. The last thing she desired anywhere near so much had turned to dust and left only bitterness behind.

She looked away first. "I can't."

His hands remained warm around hers for a long moment, fingers squeezing in encouragement before he let go.

His promise to wait lingered in her ears, on her mind, for hours after.

CHAPTER 22

$\mathcal{A}$ week later, a deep bell tolled out, stroke after stroke to the count of thirteen. A long pause, then another set. The low notes resonated in every bone in Gisela's body, from skull to toes. Her teeth chattered.

The bell woke her from a deep sleep. Sleep of the innocent, even, for she'd lain down on her bed convinced the storm would not be too bad. Most of the court had dismissed the evening's greasy yellow sky as another minor gale pretending to be more than it would prove. Thrice this had happened so far—but this was a true storm. Heavy wind gusts battered the shutters and walls.

She pulled a thin undyed tunic over her undergarments, binding her waist with a matching cord. Thin sandals covered her soles, held on by mismatched, loosely woven orange and blue ribbons wrapped around her ankles. Strands of hair clung to her forehead, the rest she left uncombed and bound at her nape with yet another length of mismatched ribbon.

Sweat covered Gisela's body, most particularly her hands. She ran into Danissa in the nearly pitch-dark hall.

"This way!" The other princess shouted as she grabbed Gisela and led the way, but Gisela kept losing hold of her hand.

With every step came the howling of the winds and the tolling of the bell. It rang thirteen strokes at a time—thirteen thirteens in all. By the end, all princesses and compeers should be gathered.

Impossible to miss.

Gisela missed a step and crashed into Danissa's back at the edge of the stairwell. Reeling back, she grabbed hold of the frame. Bit her tongue as her slippery fingers grabbed the wooden doorway then nearly lost purchase. Dug her fingernails in to halt, whirling around.

"Follow me down." Danissa yelled over the howling winds. A dark, shadowy outline against more darkness, she passed through the doorway.

Gisela drew in a deep breath, swallowing the last of the blood from her lip. Right hand resting lightly against the stone wall, she followed. A little light trickled into the stairwell through gaps in the shutter-covered windows. Better than the windowless hall, but not by much.

Sliding one foot ahead then the other, she made her way to the stairs. Grabbed the railing and clung as she descended sideways, the better to keep hold and not fall. She slipped once, heel catching the edge of the stair rather than clearing it and moving cleanly down to the next. The tight grip on the bannister let her get her feet back under her.

Once on solid land, Danissa led the way through the door to dash across the courtyard to the dancing pavilion. An easy passage in daylight, for Gisela had made it often enough to find some familiarity in the dashes right, then left. Random wind gusts howled in her ears and nearly knocked her off her feet.

Only a few raindrops mixed with the winds, but those smashed against Gisela's arms and face as though bits of frozen ice. The wind and rain chilled her body, but not by much. Summer's warmth still held against the storm chill.

They made it safe.

Danissa stopped immediately inside the door to shake her head. A few semi-frozen raindrops loosed hold of her curls and splattered the walls.

Gisela darted around, and headed toward the great room where they always exercised. During those failed storms, a few princesses and compeers had practiced steps to ease winds and rains.

"No, this way." A form stood next to a door Gisela had not yet seen open. Flickering light from a lantern held in Rik's hand illuminated their face. "You're nearly the last. Go on down."

Gisela lingered, then followed again in Danissa's wake as the other princess moved around and passed through.

Another set of stairs faced them, wide enough for two to walk abreast. Stones lined either side, with a thin wood railing fixed on the right. No windows to offer even fragments of light, but Amara held a lantern high at the bottom. Between her and Rik, the stairway resolved into sharply delineated steps and overlapping shadows.

Turning sideways, Gisela wrapped her hands tight around the railing and descended again.

The door at the base opened into a room the equal of the dancing chamber above in size.

Here, however, all was gray and shadowy. Alcoves around the outskirts contained soft couches and stores of sweet-smelling breads. Three small fountains affixed to the walls—in the shapes of stars, fishes, and trees—provided a constant trickle of water. The soft tinkling sounds reached her ears easily; the layers of stone kept away the howl of the winds above.

A clean-smelling breeze bearing a hint of storm-scented moisture tugged at Gisela's tunic and then moved on. The air was fresh and easy to breathe, with no taint of sweat or staleness.

The floor captured and held the bulk of Gisela's attention. Unlike the smooth surface above, this was a mosaic formed of thousands of small tiles. All well set into the stone floor, but so unnecessary for they gleamed a uniform dull silver gray. Surely plain stone would have sufficed, or a good coat of whitewash mixed with ashes. She stepped onto the surface and off, grimacing. It wasn't slippery at all, but she'd felt the difference between the tiles.

For the first time she truly was grateful for the sandals protecting her feet, even as Amara had predicted all those days ago. A shiver rippled through Gisela, apprehension or a touch of chill in the air despite the princesses and compeers stretching and yawning.

A warm form approached from behind, stopping next to her at the very edge of the mosaic. Stevan's presence relaxed her, although anticipation and dread continued to reverberate in her body.

"You were right about the bell. I couldn't miss it."

"Nor I." Stevan touched her arm with his as they stood side by side. "Are you ready to Dance?"

"Are you?" She turned her head to look up at him; as she did, he wore a thin gray tunic and a layer of sweat. "This is your first time as well, is it not?"

"It's what we were made for." His hand brushed her.

She slipped her fingers into his, lacing them together.

"You speak truth."

Both whirled, without losing hold of each other, to find Amara standing behind them. Farther away, Rik held the door for Jola and Nefeli.

"We were made to Dance, to mediate between the forces of nature and the needs of humanity." Amara reached up and brushed a finger across each of their brows, Gisela then Stevan. "But be at ease, for this will not be a swift matter. The Terparchon will require only so many of you as necessary on the floor at any given time, to keep pace with the storm. At a guess, we shall be here through the remainder of the night and all of the day."

"Stay here?" Gisela turned, instinctively seeking the door. Now closed, only a faint glowing line betrayed where it lay. Stevan's grasp on her tightened, but his fingers shook as well as hers.

They were captives, no matter that they'd come willingly.

"Only until the Dance ends. All needs will be supplied. We have food and water"—Amara waved one hand at the fountains and the alcove containing sweet breads beyond—"and places to rest and do whatever is necessary." Another hand wave at the cushioned couches in the other alcoves, and a privy tucked off of one. "And I and other former princesses and compeers will tend to your needs."

A sharp clapping punctuated Amara's pronouncement.

From an alcove on the far side of the room marched the Terparchon. Unlike the other times Gisela had seen her, she was plainly dressed. Nothing differentiated her from the others, princesses and compeers alike. Only the small remainder who would not Dance—Amara, Rik, Idan, and a few others—wore anything other than a gray tunic and sandals with mismatched ribbons.

"The storm comes. Let us begin with two princesses each for wind and rain." Spine straight and head held high, the ruler turned in a slow circle. She summoned each princess and their attendant compeer with a crook of her finger.

Jola, Danissa, and two other princesses stepped forward. With a last squeeze of Gisela's hand, Stevan left her to join Danissa. He and the other compeers each placed themselves directly behind their princess.

A third of the way around the chamber, Rik placed a cushioned, backless bench just big enough for one person at the very edge of the mosaic. A dam Gisela did not remember having met or seen before seated herself and pulled out a flute. She blew a few notes, then began a soft meandering melody. The music floated in the air with no echo.

As wind and rain, the princesses began to move. Their compeers matched them, swaying as rain or whirling as winds. No dancer quite the same, but all graceful and lovely to watch. The Terparchon remained at the center of the mosaic, body swaying and arms tracing curlicues in the air.

A sudden gust of true wind somehow slipped into the chamber, bringing a hint of dampness and the taste of raindrops. The air grew hazy around the dancers. Gisela blinked, but her vision remained fuzzy. Then cleared—except it was as though the view before her had doubled.

The Dance and dancers remained visible. Stevan hooked a hand under Danissa's knee and braced her torso as she rose on the other leg and stretched her arms out. He lifted her high and twirled them around. Nearby Jola and Nefeli linked arms, back-to-back, and swayed in opposition to each other.

Yet another sight overlaid them. A dark and heavy cloud hung in place of Jola and Nefeli's heads and torsos, and their bodies shared space with torrents of rain. Where Stevan and Danissa moved, there blew a swirling wind. When Danissa pulled her arms and legs in, and Stevan lowered her to the floor, the swirling wind uncoiled into five or seven wind gusts, all heading in different directions.

Below, the floor changed the most of all. A miniature illusion of the palace and city grew to cover nearly half of the gray tiles. The royal residence stood knee-high on Danissa as she tiptoed around it. A matching illusory lake filled the remainder of the circular mosaic. An ever-increasing wall of dark rain clouds marched in from the far side. But Jola, Nefeli, and the other princess and compeer dancing rain encouraged them to empty the bulk of their water upon the lake before they reached shore.

Only the Terparchon remained unaltered. The images of palace, city, and lake turned slowly around her. With a hand gesture here, a toe pointed there, she directed the dancers where she wanted them.

How long did Gisela stand watching them with an open mouth?

Not long enough to prepare her for the experience of swapping in as Jola and Nefeli cycled out.

Todor laid a warm hand on Gisela's back as he ushered her from the periphery into the mosaic. Energy crackled to life within every cell in her body, welling up from the earth beneath her feet. The smells of the room—bread, sweat—dissipated and instead she breathed air redolent with rain.

Startling, she arched away from him. Her right hand rose high, and the clouds shifted. A portion burst. A brief torrent fell upon the lake shore close by the palace. Todor lifted his arm to match the angle of hers. He had not Stevan's ease at matching her. All the same, his gentle insistence forced her to curve her arm down, around, and back to her side. The torrent shifted, easing away from the royal residence to pound upon small buildings on the other side of the palace walls.

As she danced, she seemed to break into three parts rather than two as before.

Her body conducted the work. Arching, bending, weaving about the floor. Embodying and directing rain to fall here, not there.

Most of her mind watched not the scene in the dance chamber under the earth but from above as though she were one with the storm clouds. Amorphous and so laden with water that the winds could not move her fast.

Yet a small slice of her observed the action in the chamber. Watched the Terparchon direct her and the others upon the floor. Noted how the ruler made choices of where the winds spent the bulk of their energy, on land or over water, where the rains fell hardest and flood waters rose.

The time came for Gisela and Todor to spiral out and be relieved by other dancers. She spun over the edge of the mosaic, and then crashed to the floor. The crackling energy dissipated, leaving her limp and exhausted. Body drenched in sweat to the point her tunic and underthings clung to every muscle and sinew. Every muscle in her body ached, feet worst of all. Her stomach growled in hunger, mouth was parched, and she was in need of the privy.

Amara and Rik slipped gentle hands under her arms to lift her and carry her to a nearby bench. Rik left her and returned to help Todor to his feet. Amara remained beside Gisela. Ensured she had all she needed. Ample goblets of water from the fountains. A slice of bread sweetened with sugar and spices that drove all taste of sweat from her mouth. Access to the closest privy.

A cushioned couch to recline on afterward, so as to recoup her strength for her next turn at the dance. And basins of cool water sprinkled with healing herbs in which to ease her aching feet.

Gisela half-dozed, half-watched. The flutist no longer played, and instead the lyrical strains of the harp underscored the whirl of move-ment on the floor. The storm had shifted well over the coast, though much remained. The number of princesses and compeers dancing at the Terparchon's command had risen to seven.

Likewise, the ruler's control over the dancers increased. The hazy image of the city and palace grew in size, driving out most of the lake, until the tip of the highest building reached the Terparchon's waist rather than her knee. This allowed her to be more particular about where the heaviest rains fell, the strongest winds blew, and deepest flood waters gathered.

"Rest, my dear. You will be needed again, soon." Amara knelt next to Gisela, obscuring her view of the Terparchon and center of the dance.

By chance? No, given the glint of warning in the older dam's eyes.

"She chooses where the damage is worst." Gisela tilted her head to the side, watching waters seep into a single-level building at the edge of the mosaic.

"The Terparchon can't completely abate storm effects, so she must make choices." Amara's voice dropped to just above a whisper. "She has a care for which areas are best able to recover from flooding or wind damage, unlike . . . "

"The old Terparchon." Gisela finished the sentence, keeping her tone equally low.

"She protected what she valued first and foremost." Amara bent her head, coming so close her lips nearly brushed Gisela's ear. Her breath was warm, showing Gisela how much she'd cooled.

"And went after what she wanted?" No living beings showed in the illusory city. The flooded building might be a home, business, or something else.

Amara didn't answer. Drawing back, Gisela glanced at the floor. Princesses dancing winds leapt around, both lifted and lowered by the Terparchon's daughters, their compeers. Stevan and Danissa oozed along the floor in the distance as thick, turgid waters filled another building farther from Gisela.

Slow anger seeped into Gisela with every flood surge, each tree toppled by the wind. When she cycled back into the Dance, she fancied she heard the shrieks, moans, and groans of those suffering from the storm damage. People who might have been harmed by the storm by chance—but instead took harm due to the Terparchon's choice.

Her feet hurt more with every step she took, as she and the others Danced until they wore their shoes through. All at the command of the Terparchon.

Better than her mother she might be, but that only increased Gisela's fury at the old, dead Terparchon. The earthquakes that drove the Escalli from their homeland must have been the old Terparchon's doing. Surely one or two princesses alone could have eased the later quakes, if not the first.

The haze over the mosaic dissipated when the Dance ended. Another lingered in Gisela's eyes. She saw the other princesses and the compeers as though from a great distance. Stevan's concern registered, but only for a moment as he was swept away by fellow compeers as Gisela climbed the stairs in company and sought the bathing chamber with other princesses. She didn't argue, glad that he wound up in a different part of the baths.

She wanted him safe from the anger burning within her—or perhaps she feared he'd somehow drain it from her and put off the conflagration to some other day.

Time spent in the baths did nothing to ease her ire. Neither plunging in cold water nor sitting in the steam room. Her thoughts spiraled, always returning to the surety of the old Terparchon's guilt. Increasing belief, since she'd suspected as much ever since Ilburna raised the topic. Convinced herself, but let it slide and do nothing.

How many times would this cycle repeat? Or she bear with repetitions?

Saying little, she trailed the other princesses as they dressed. Some others silent as well, letting her quiet go unnoticed while a few chattered all the while.

Pulling on a clean tunic and mantle, both in shades of green, failed to change anything. Donning sandals deepened the rage building within. Her feet bore lines where the dancing sandals had worn through. The muscles ached, and covering her soles with stiff leather made it worse. Making her way through palace complex, too much of it covered with intricate mosaics that made for chary walking, had no appeal whatsoever. Given a choice, she'd go barefoot upon grass or soft earth, such as that in her former home, rather than wear sandals across stone.

But she was given no choice. No one else complained or appeared to mind.

The clop of leather against stone resounded in her ears as she followed other princesses out of the pavilion.

Everyone stopped at the first step for a long moment. Near the end of the line, Gisela understood only when it came her turn. The air was light and cool and wonderful to breathe after the closeness of the downstairs. The remaining clouds in the sky were fluffy and light against the blue, faintly tinged with pink as the sun headed toward the horizon.

Nevertheless, more than one princess yawned. Heron first, and three more in the moment after. Chatter about whether or not to head to bed and sleep for days, if possible, filled the air.

Gisela took one cautious step after another until she reached the edge of the oval mosaic filling most of the courtyard surface. It faced the pavilion, and only someone leaving would see the whole as no doubt meant to be viewed.

Yet she'd managed to miss it before. At least, she'd registered the mosaic's existence but as little more than figures and colors. A stylized scene of conquest, perhaps.

On closer inspection, the full expanse hit her. At the center of the mosaic stood an ancestress of the Terparchon. A previous Terparchon, by the dam's stance and coronet, and distant resemblance to her descendant. There was no Marchon in evidence, only her in front of a bevy of princesses. Twelve, of course, with compeers standing in a line behind.

In this rendering the princesses and compeers were reduced to little more than outlines. No personality or distinctiveness about any of them. Indeed, whoever had designed the mosaic made them exactly alike. Same height, same proportions, same clothing in three layers of blue tunics each, graduated from dark to light for the princesses and the reverse for the compeers. Their faces featureless.

Only the image of the Terparchon had a face.

A prisoner knelt before her. Or perhaps crouched. The individual's head bowed so low that they, too, were unidentifiable except for the lavender-colored tunics they wore. Rips and blood stains marred their clothes. They lifted hands stained with blood to the Terparchon, perhaps asking for mercy.

Storms filled the upper portions of the mosaic with dark clouds save at the center where they parted to let through rays of silvery light upon the Terparchon.

Below the prisoner, around the edge of the mosaic, appeared pictured perfect images of the moon. A dozen to match the princesses and compeers.

And the supposed number of the Shadows of the Moon.

Stooping to one knee, Gisela brushed a hand over one of the mosaic Shadows. The cold stone had a roughness to it despite years, decades, even centuries of feet passing over it. Surely it should have worn smooth, but instead it was nearly as unpleasant as the nearby Shadow of the Moon. A layer of dust adhered to her skin, thick and tacky as old mud.

The previous Terparchon had wanted to possess all of them. Why —had an ancestor held them and lost the territory? None of the tales of history told in Foleilion indicated Codaros had ever owned their lands before them. The Escalli had lived there until driven out.

By a Terparchon who wanted possession.

"Gisela!"

Startling, Gisela rose to find Danissa and Jola standing before her. Neither showed any awareness or concern that they stood over the tiled images of previous princesses.

From the note in Danissa's voice, she'd been calling for some time. Only the three of them remained in the yard. Other voices echoed in the distance, none close nor could Gisela see anyone around.

"My apologies, I was . . . distracted." Gisela rose, rubbing her hands together to remove the dust. She had to work hard to get it off, until it finally cracked and fell away in large flakes. "What is this of?"

"That's the Empire Builder, the Terparchon who first brought the princesses together to Dance and protect the land from storms and floods and invasion and other disasters. Most of the mosaics portray her." Jola gave a harsh laugh and kicked at a loose pebble, sending it skittering across the tiles. "Nefeli dislikes this one in particular. Says it gives her mother ideas when she looks too long at it, as it did her grandmother before. They both talked about matching her—going out and acquiring new territories."

"Her grandmother certainly did that." Gisela stepped back to view the whole. The tiles between the Terparchon, princesses, and compeers' feet and the Shadows of the Moon resolved into a miniature map. No doubt of Codaros as it had been, for it did not stretch all the way along the Omirisi River where the Escalli once lived.

"Oh yes. Many." Jola ticked names off on her fingers. "Midrilia, Fayorth, Rorenber."

"And Escalad," Gisela said.

"What?" Jola blinked, then her mouth froze in a wide O.

"Isn't that the river land the old Terparchon built a spring palace on?" Danissa broke in before Jola could react further.

"Because it had a Shadow of the Moon." Gisela flicked the last fleck of dust off her hand and tapped her foot on the air over the mosaic Shadows rather than let her sole fall onto the stone.

"How do you know this?" Jola half-turned away, but her eyes watched Gisela closely.

"My people lived there once, until we were driven off. By earthquakes. So many that stone would not stay upon stone." No sense in hiding the information. Everyone who'd come on the journey to bring Gisela back knew where she came from. "Nature in action, perhaps, or destruction by Dance."

"I would keep that to myself, if I were you." Danissa grabbed Gisela's arm, fingers digging in and eyes flashing warning. "The Terparchon is not her mother. She does not send out guards in the night to bring unwitting prisoners and hostages into her keeping. Nor cry treason on those who did nothing wrong save offer unwanted opinions. All the same, it is better not to speak against any of the family. I will not mention this." Her head twisted to fix her sights on Jola. "You too can keep quiet, can you not?"

"I will not volunteer," Jola said, words dripping one at a time from her mouth. She licked her lips. "But if Nefeli asks, neither will I lie."

"She won't. I grew up with her and she always was one for keeping matters calm and not letting winds blow out of proportion." Danissa turned back to Gisela and gave one last squeeze, then loosened her hold. Her fingers left dull red marks on Gisela's skin. "So you may have this moment, but you must keep silent."

"Understood. I'll keep quiet." Though Gisela would send word to Ilburna when she had a safe chance. Let the elder know her deepening surety. Anger at the need for quiet flamed in her blood and bone. "But I'll have a Dance of my own first."

Memories of dancing in the fallow field flashed through Gisela. How she'd danced out her grief and bitterness. It took many visits, many dances, but then she hadn't known at the time that she was a princess and could change the world with movement.

She needed something similar now: a way to release anger and resentment so that they would not poison her, or cause her mouth to slip and antagonize those who ruled the land and moved her about at their whim whether she willed it or no.

Danissa had said that the old Terparchon used to dance on the Shadow of the Moon.

Gisela stalked off to do the same.

Danissa and Jola followed in her wake, calling for her to stop and asking where she went, what she meant to do.

No matter what they said, whether in ignorance of where she headed or once they began to suspect, they could not stop her.

No one could.

Anger drove her away.

CHAPTER 23

*B*eauty and peace greeted Stevan as he left the dancing pavilion through a side door that gave out onto the wide patio where the Terparchon and Marchon sometimes held revels. Clouds lingered in the sky, but light, fluffy ones that formed streaks of pink and gold as the sun sank toward the horizon. A pleasant breeze off the lake tugged at the damp strands of hair lying plastered to his head and neck, and wicked away the last beads of sweats from his time in the baths.

He'd grabbed a clean, old white exercise tunic from a heap left for any to use, his dancing tunic most definitely in need of laundering. The hem hit him at mid-calf, shades of his old clothes before his promotion. A sign of how comfortable he'd already grown in his new position that his lower legs felt cool exposed to the sun and breeze.

His dancing sandals had worn through at the ball of the feet, so he'd left them behind in a pile with the others. None of the extra sets of sandals left for compeers to use quite fit him. He'd settled for a pair a little too big even taking into account that his feet remained slightly swollen from the dance. He'd tied the straps extra tight.

An urge to go barefoot made him pause and consider removing the sandals, but practicality won the day. The patio showed evidence of the storm's passage. Plenty of downed leaves, assorted branches, and other things kicked up from who-knew-where lay scattered across the mosaic, concealing the vast majority of the stones. At least one jagged length of painted wood lay athwart a pile of leaves. It had broken off a shutter high above that now flapped loosely against the side of the royal residence. Otherwise, he saw few signs of real damage to the buildings.

Body relaxed and muscles at ease after a warm steam bath, more energy flowed in his veins than he'd have expected. Almost too much, for one of the muscles linking knee and ankle had begun to twitch. He might not sleep for hours at this rate. Scanning the sky, he noted the moon rising in the east. Nearly full, but not yet. He'd never tracked the moon's phases with such care before, but it would not grow for his wanting.

Sometimes patience hurt. A low, dull ache deep in his chest. He'd seen Gisela in the baths, but she'd left without a word. Not alone any more than he, but with other princesses, none of whom lingered here. Much as he wanted to track her, ensure she was well, he resisted.

He'd promised to wait.

So wait he would, but at least in good company.

Though he'd turned around in search of the moon, both of his companions faced the lake. Nefeli stretched her arms high and arched her back toward the sun. Beside her, Idan planted his feet wide but otherwise kept a more compact stance as he drank in the sunlight.

"A lovely night." Idan's chest rose high and fell in a slow sigh. "It almost never fails that we leave Dancing down a storm to such a sight."

"I'd rather it without the Dance beforehand, or the need at least." Nefeli turned her head long enough to flash a grin.

"Quite right, but let an old man luxuriate in the simple pleasures." Idan didn't move, though the corner of his lips tilted in a half smile.

"Old man?" Nefeli laughed, deep and hearty. "You may be slowing down, but I'm not so sure you won't live to dance on my grave."

"I would never! Dancing upon a grave is not a thing to do, likely to wake the dead to dance, too." Idan turned around, twisted lips straightening into a full grin. "I would dance *next* to your grave, in honor of your life."

The extra energy in Stevan's leg shifted to his foot. His toes twitched against the soft, worn leather of the sandals. It distracted him to the point he didn't notice Nefeli moving and so jumped when she clapped a hand against his back.

"You did well tonight." She gave him the small bow of equals rather than royal to courtier. "I look forward to many more Dances with you."

"Thank you. I count myself a credit to my teachers, then?" He quirked an eyebrow at her, something easing in him at this open acknowledgment of his contribution.

"Only if you insist." She stretched her arms, mouth gaping wide in a yawn. "But I, at least, am for my bed. Time to rest and dream, and not to dance!"

Stevan and Idan bowed and watched her slip through the doors into the royal residence. Idan jerked his head toward the path leading to the princesses' and compeers' quarters. Stevan fell in step with him, their sandals clapping against the stones as they walked.

Other footsteps sounded in the distance, but none near. Otherwise the area lay quieter than Stevan had expected. Most folk seemed unwilling to trust the storm had ended, and he didn't blame them.

For all the lovely colors in the sky and absence of heavy clouds, there was an odd energy in the air. A frisson that kept him on edge, as though a bird sang just high enough to be out of the range of hearing.

"Danissa seemed well." Idan's voice held no hint of the oddness. He rubbed his fingers together as he walked, a soft rustling more felt than heard.

"Yes, it was a pleasure to dance with her." Though a simple truth, it needed more when speaking with her father. "She moves well. Memorized the steps quickly, and made sure I knew where she wanted me to help her."

He'd found following Danissa's lead very easy. She gave ample indication of when she wished to be lifted and ways he could support and magnify her movements as they'd danced through the different roles, rain, wind, and flood. Yet dancing with her lacked the extra . . . excitement? connection? He couldn't readily compare dancing with Danissa versus Gisela, save that he didn't lose himself as much with the Danissa and his energy levels remained fairly even, while every time he danced with Gisela he wound up with more energy. And everything, even colors, looked brighter.

"I know it wasn't what you wished, but give it time." Idan led the way into the building and up the stairs.

"I am." Stevan nodded.

The air grew close and warmer here. Drier as well, leaching moisture from Stevan's lips and making him think longingly of the pitcher of water that had stood in his rooms when he left. Even warm, it would be worth drinking.

"And thank you for indulging an old man who wishes to see after his daughter's wellbeing."

They reached the door to Stevan's chamber. The older man swung around, a glint in his eye. His chest rose and fell more than it should, and he leaned a hand against the wall as he dragged in air.

"Nefeli had it right; for an old man you may well out dance us all." Stevan had thought Idan withdrew from Dancing as an active compeer in no small part to give Stevan a chance. Perhaps the elder had done so for his own reasons as well.

"Maybe, but if so only because I have waited and watched my step." Idan nodded for Stevan to open the door, and followed him inside. Closed it behind with a soft click, then leaned back against it. "You be sure to do the same. There should be more of us, you know."

"More who?" Stevan glanced about the chamber, lit by a single lantern resting on the low table between couches. Two goblets and a new pitcher of water sat in a bowl next to the lantern, condensation dripping down the clay sides of the pitcher suggesting a servant, perhaps Rik, had recently replenished the room.

"Natural born compeers."

A chill ran down Stevan's spine. He pretended it away, and walked over to the table. Lifted one of the goblets and gestured at the older man, offering refreshment.

"I'll not stay long." Idan declined, face grave and voice lowering. "I wanted to offer a word of warning, which you are not to pass to Nefeli. She knows, even if she will not admit it. All is not well here and never has been. Most natural born compeers burn out or take enough injuries to stop dancing within the space of five years, where princesses last at least ten. I should not be the exception—all compeers should last as long as I and not be carried off injured or accused of . . . Keep your wits about you. Never lose yourself too much in a Dance."

He refused to say anymore. Escaped through the door and let it bang shut behind him.

Stevan leaped across the space and opened it to watch Idan totter down the hall and slip into his own chambers at the far end.

He closed his door with more care. Pushing aside the empty rumbling of his belly and dryness of his mouth, he crossed the room. Opened the shutters with care, letting loose a small spray of water and leaves trapped in the edges. Leaned against the sill.

Even more colors swirled across the sky than before. Pink, gold, purple, and deepest blue. Somewhere the moon rose, although he couldn't see that part of the horizon. Nearly full by now. uch a small span of time since he'd become a compeer, met Gisela, returned to the palace.

How fast things changed, and kept changing. He no longer wished to be back in his former place and quarters. These became home more quickly than expected. Yet every time he turned around, he was reminded of all the things he didn't know, big and small.

Easier to ponder those he did.

The home he'd left, that he could still return to if he didn't mind being one of a crowd.

The place and work he had for now, for however long it lasted— and the pleasure he took in the work, the more so on those occasions when he'd partnered Gisela.

The hopes he held that when the moon turned full, Gisela would turn to him and agree to explore where their dance might lead.

He had no excuse to seek out Gisela but wishes and dreams. Yet now he knew he could find her by her footsteps, an urge itched at him to check on her. Just a peek, that was all, to find where she was.

He resisted, helped by an unexpected knock at the door.

Kicking off his sandals and shoving them under a couch, Stevan walked over to the door. Brenn waited on the other side.

An air of weariness hung about Stevan's brother. Brenn's tunic and short mantle, white and red respectively, were clean and free of rips or tears but well worn. Hair freshly oiled and slick against his head showed scratches along the left side of his face. His arms likewise bore healing scratches and several bruises.

"Congratulations on your first Dance. Will you let me in? I've brought you dinner." Brenn managed a half smile, lips twisting wider on the right than the left. He lifted his hands. One held a jug of wine, the other a small basket from which the smell of savory pine nut rolls wafted.

Stevan's mouth watered. His stomach growled so loud it nearly roused an echo.

Brenn's smile grew wider for a moment, then he winced as the gesture strained the new scab forming along his cheek.

Within moments, they settled onto the couches and divided the food between them. The wine as well, although Stevan mixed his well with water given the emptiness of his stomach. After a close look at his brother, he did the same for Brenn.

The older man gave him a long glance in return, but didn't argue for more wine and less water.

Only when Stevan had demolished his rolls, save for a few crumbs, and watched his brother's body slowly relax against the soft cushions, did he speak.

"You heard the Dance went well. In the barracks? Or someplace else." Stevan nodded at the bruises.

"The Marchon ordered most of the guards out into the city to help batten down loose shutters and ensure those without adequate housing found shelter. It got a bit tricky at points. This," Brenn gestured at the left half of his body, "came courtesy of an encounter with a tree that decided to fall. I count myself fortunate I've only scrapes to count."

"I hadn't realized you were out." Stevan tilted his head back, running through the hours spent underground. Displeased to realize he hadn't thought to check on his brother during his breaks from Dancing. If he had, he would at least have known Brenn was in danger even if he couldn't have helped. Other, perhaps, than trying to reduce the wind or floods there.

"What did you say?" Brenn sat upright, couch creaking beneath the sudden shift in his weight.

"I don't . . ." Stevan's cheeks grew hot as he realized he'd spoken his thoughts.

"You check on me?"

"I can, though I didn't. I should have." Stevan ran a hand through his hair. "I might've been able to do something this past night—"

"That doesn't matter. I knew the types of work I'd be doing when I signed up." Brenn waved a hand and shook his head as though a wet dog. "You can track my footsteps from a distance again? You've remembered how?"

"You know?" Stevan swiveled around, mirroring Brenn's tense seat on the couch, feet against the cool floor.

"Of course. I was the first person you tracked, or at least the first time you did so in such a way that all the family knew." His brother smiled again, more with his eyes than lips. "You were only three, so perhaps you don't recall that, but . . . I was mad and ran off, as children do. I don't remember over what. A storm was coming in. Thunder and lightning, the home kind of storm, not those over the lake. Everyone was worried and gathered in the great hall after searching everywhere, or so they thought, when you piped up with where I was. Told everyone not to worry because I'd curled up in the back of the larder under an old, empty sack. The rest of us, all of us children, used to tell the story over and over, as a reminder it did no good to run away because you'd only track us down."

"I . . . . must've forgotten." Fragments of memory slipped through Stevan. The boom of thunder. Whispered voices. The image of a much younger and smaller Brenn blinking sleepily at family crowding around.

"You wanted to forget. We kept telling you to at least pretend you'd lost the knack over and over. At least, I did and most of our siblings." A low growl escaped Brenn, a rumble as much felt as heard. "After watching father and second mother near tear you to pieces tracking each other and tattling . . . It took a while, but you stopped tracking any of us by the time you were, oh, seven."

A sudden ache bloomed in Stevan's head. An echo of the pain and determination it had taken to suppress the ability, perhaps, for he remembered hurting. Spending the winter crawling off into any small nook or crevice to press his head against cool stones to ease the pain.

He bent over, pressing the heels of his hands against his temples.

"I'm sorry." The couch legs groaned as Brenn settled down next to Stevan. Warmth seeped from his long body, and he laid an arm across Stevan's back. "We were all bigger than you, and older. We should've protected you. We didn't. *I* didn't."

"Father in a rage would put anyone off," Stevan mumbled, eyes closed and pressing against his head harder to push back the ache.

"Or worse, both of them." Brenn gripped Stevan's shoulder. "But it's not right you took the brunt of their anger, when they weren't aiming at each other, when it wasn't your fault you could find them anywhere."

"You couldn't have done anything. You aren't that much older than me." Stevan shook, but Brenn held him. Braced him.

Stevan's gift flared, feeding an echo of Brenn's pain into him. Then spiraled out further, inexorably seeking Gisela.

Found her.

The ache in his head doubled. Tripled. He forced it back. He felt her yearning for help.

Shrieking for him.

CHAPTER 24

Gisela stormed through the wooded garden, down the path toward the Shadow of the Moon. Her tunic and mantle swished around her calves. With every breath, cool air invigorated her lungs. Blood pounded in her veins. Step after step kept her muscles loose despite residual aches. Anger overwhelmed all else.

The sun shifted inexorably down to the horizon. The sky above flamed with all manner of shades from light pink to deepest red and purple. After one glance upward, she averted her gaze. Deliberately, rather than get caught in the beauty and lose her momentum.

Breezes whispered in the trees, almost as though spectral voices called to her alternately encouraging or warning. She ignored them even as she refused to acknowledge the patter of feet behind her. Danissa and Jola both sought to keep pace, but never quite caught up.

Gisela stopped for a moment at the edge of the open space around the Shadow. Shook her head at Danissa and Jola's protests and pleas for her to come back and rest and think about what she was doing.

Instead, she removed her sandals. Left them behind and stepped onto the grass.

Oh, the pleasure of walking on lush greenery with bare feet! She swayed, eyelids flickering.

In that moment might have allowed herself to be dissuaded from her purpose . . .

Except the Shadow of the Moon reflected the ruddiness of the sunset overhead. The stones gained a bloody cast, appearing as a raw wound in the midst of green beauty as though the Shadow lived and mocked her, revealing how it would look drenched in the blood of those who fell victim to previous Terparchon's lust for land and possessions.

The change of color increased Gisela's rage and determination to dance her own triumph upon it. She waved a hand to cut off the other princesses as they nattered at her.

"Enough. I am doing this. Go away or stand witness, but be silent!"

Gisela strode forward over the soft lawn, gaining strength and purpose as she drew closer. Soft shuffling sounds indicated the others followed.

Again, too slow to catch or stop her. Danissa's hand grazed Gisela's arm once, but Gisela yanked free with only faint scratch marks on her skin. Jola grabbed for Gisela's shoulders, but stumbled. As though the earth rippled beneath her feet. Whether to aid Gisela or not she couldn't tell.

Too late to wonder, as she reached the edge of the Shadow.

The bloody cast faded, leaving the circle glowing with silver light. The moon rose, barely visible between the branches, but there—nearly full—and the Shadow mimicked its light.

Nearly full. She hesitated a moment, seeking the faint glimmer of true moonlight through the trees. Memory flowed, of dancing under the last full moon. Beloved strains of music guiding revelers through familiar sequences of dances. Seeing Stevan for the first time. Meeting eyes. Taking hands. All the unspoken promises they'd made with their bodies in the dance, promises not yet made whole and complete.

But soon.

She couldn't take up the offer Stevan had made with the burden of rage and bitterness still upon her. This small circle of land had done nothing in-and-of-itself to offend her, yet it represented the forces that had inflicted pain and suffering upon herself and her people.

The previous Terparchon and her lust for land.

The current ruler who'd summoned Gisela with little care for her wellbeing, and couched it so that she couldn't refuse.

Even the whims of fate that arranged Gisela's body so that she couldn't conceive and contribute to the continuation of her people.

All of them out of Gisela's reach.

But not this symbol of them—this perfect circle of infertile land amidst a clearing overflowing with lush growth.

Drawing in a deep breath, she set aside her rage to begin the Dance properly.

She'd learned much about dancing since being plucked from her village. New stretches. Ways of moving that allow her to channel natural forces. How to use a compeer's strength and solidity as base and refuge when dancing magic.

All that slipped away. She fell back on the earliest lessons from the village elder. To begin as she meant to go on.

So she started in the exact way she'd used every time she visited the fallow field.

Remaining outside the circle, she tapped a foot against the earth to announce her presence and interest in dancing.

The earth responded sluggishly. As though torn as to whether or not to dance with her. Her toes received a mild pressure while her heel, farther away from the Shadow albeit not by much, experienced a more enthusiastic acknowledgment.

Kneeling, she laid a hand next to her foot. Asked the earth to choose the measure.

"What are you doing?" Jola's voice, echoed by Danissa a beat after.

She waved for them to quieten.

Again, the earth returned a double response. A faint baaa-baaa-baaa against her fingertips, near the Shadow. At the heel of her hand a quick pitter-patter. Together, it seemed as though the earth gave her the thrum of two hearts that did not quite beat as one. She touched her other hand to her throat. Her pulse fluttered back and forth between the two uncomfortably close beats.

The syncopation, and speed, spoke to her. Roused the rage she'd tamped down.

Standing, she stretched out her arms.

Lifted her right foot.

Then leapt and stretched her legs to travel as far across the circle as she could.

Landing hurt. The chalky earth was barren not only of any growth but any response. It gave her back nothing, not even the sluggish beat. Only resistance. Uncomfortable prickliness. Sullen warmth.

She'd lost the beats the earth provided, but had her own heartbeat. She Danced to that. Stomped and leapt. Growled and hunched her shoulders. Threw her arms and head back to scream defiance at the sky.

Her anger raised a response below. The Shadow began to glow red again, this time with accompanying heat and the occasional burst of steam.

Speeding up didn't help. The very air grew so warm it hurt to breathe. Dust filtered up from surface below. No, not just dust . . .

What had Danissa said before? That the old Terparchon used to dance here, in glee and triumph?

Or perhaps she'd done more. She'd been a Dancing Princess in her day, and knew Dance magic.

The old Terparchon had poisoned the ground.

Gisela danced on land inimical to life. With every step the unnatural earth took energy, power, will from her without giving anything back. Bits of poison floated in the air around her. The very air tasted bitter, of bile and ash.

Resisting, Gisela slowed her movements. Imagining her heartbeat when calm, comforted, contented. Ceased to pour power into the hostile ground and instead invested it in keeping herself alive.

Danissa and Jola stood beyond the edge of the Shadow, horror on their faces. Their hands raised and pressed against the air, until their skin smoked and they had to step back.

Gisela reached out, but couldn't leave. Couldn't stop dancing.

Trapped.

Needed help—but not theirs. They were princesses too and might get trapped alongside her.

No, she required a compeer, preferably the one who'd proven himself able to match her and magnify her power.

"Get Stevan!" Her throat hurt from her scream.

Danissa nodded and ran off.

Gisela set herself to dancing and keeping herself alive until Stevan could arrive.

If he did.

From the first he'd struck her as solid and reliable. It was she who'd been skittish and unpredictable, as though a leaf plucked from its tree and set to tumble head over heels through the air, blown this way and that.

Or a seed, seeking fertile ground.

Which was not that on which she danced, but she might find that with him if she could only let go of the sorrow and bitterness she lugged with her ever since her life went awry.

She'd tried to make serving as a princess ease her pain over her lost fertility—and failed. They were two different things. Linking them did nothing to ease the one, just reduced her ability to explore and take joy in the other. She had to let them be separate. Allow the one grief to hurt and ease with time. Open herself to the opportunities being a princess brought.

Her vision began to waver. Waves of heat made the dust-and-ash-filled air shimmer and sway around her.

She closed her eyes, the better to dance the inner workings of her heart.

The air thickened. Her breath reduced to pants, lungs unable to draw in more than a gasp at a time.

The ground beneath her feet grew hotter yet, almost molten. She kept her feet moving, never resting too long on any point, but her arm gestures drew from a different type of dance. One of grief and resignation. Of finding possibilities and embracing them.

Her head began to droop, body succumbing to heat and suffocation.

All at once, hands wrapped around her waist and lifted her high.

She went slack, arms falling down at her side and head lolling back.

Moonlight poured down on her. Separation from the heated surface let her breathe easily.

"Dance with me." Stevan lent her strength.

He'd leapt into the poison. It grew thicker. Foggy. Hard to see, but three forms stood on the other side.

"You shouldn't have come. You'll be trapped too." Fear burned Gisela's throat.

"Then let us die dancing."

Again and again he supported her, proved himself reliable and stalwart.

The least she could do was be the partner he deserved.

As he moved around to keep from getting burned, he held her high.

She reached up and lured down cool breezes to ease the heat and reduce the motes of poison filling the air. They cleared from the center of the Shadow, but thickened around the border.

Gisela and Stevan might not survive passing through.

So they danced together. Without words, letting their feelings show. Hope filled her as she opened herself to the new possibilities before her . . . love, magic.

With every step, their alignment increased and rapport grew. Awareness of his body pressed against her bloomed and heated her blood in a way far more welcome than the sullen heat of the Shadow below.

Under the almost-full moon, they danced as they had at their first meeting.

Until their hearts beat as one. Then they danced to that single beat. Hands joined, bodies pressed close, and gazes meshed.

The ground quaked beneath them. Stevan lifted her as cracks formed in the stone.

Energy swirled in the air. Crackled in their ears. Slid along their skin, making the hairs on their arms and legs stand straight up.

Gisela focused on the beat of two hearts joined in one.

He pulled; she pushed.

She led; he followed.

The earth shook more. Cracks widened, splitting the circle into three parts.

A wisp of steam escaped at the point where they joined.

Stevan swirled away, but Gisela was unable to avoid breathing in a little steam.

A sudden urge flooded through her.

Twirling around, she gathered energy into her hands until they overflowed.

Stevan lifted her high again, retreating toward the edge and the circle of poison around them.

Arms shaping the energy, Gisela aimed it at the central crack and let fly.

A bolt of lightning crashed into the earth. The force sent them flying through the air—over the poison.

Gisela landed the soft grass, but the impact drove air from her lungs. The instant she could move, she rose to her feet and reached for Stevan to find him likewise seeking her. They stumbled to their feet, clinging tight—then froze.

The red cast on the Shadow melted away, leaving chalky gray. Stone crumbled and turned to dust then merged with the poison dust circling at the edge.

A whirlwind from on high formed and lifted the poison and dust. Carried it up into the sky, where it shimmered and vanished in the moonlight.

Layer after layer disintegrated, wicked up by the wind, until only a perfect circle of earth remained, dark brown save where lay two immaculately preserved bodies. They lay face down. More notable than proportions or lineaments were the wounds and bloodstains at the center of each back, as though they were pierced through at the same moment.

The whirlwind abruptly stopped, then reversed direction. Curved beneath the bodies and lifted them high. Cries of gladness and gratitude broke the silence before the bodies, too, vanished into the moonlight.

All Gisela's bitterness and anger seeped away, leaving her light-headed and so light of heart she could float after them. But Stevan's hold grounded her. She squeezed his hand as plants burst forth through the circle of earth and grew at an accelerated rate. Midnight-blue stalks bore leaves unfurling in shades of deep blue green. Then buds appeared, opening into blooms of dark blue and silver.

Life returned to the former Shadow of the Moon.

CHAPTER 25

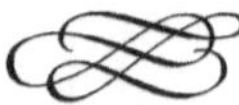

*H*igh on a rooftop, Stevan had an excellent view of the palace compound. No Gisela in sight, but plenty of others traipsing about.

A lovely sunset shaded the sky overhead with pinks and blues, although nowhere near the beauty of the sunset two nights earlier. Few signs remained in the palace of the recent storm. Crafters had repaired the broken shutters and servants cleaned the courtyards. The palace returned to normal, although the same was not true of the city.

Stevan stood close to the protective wall at the edge of the roof. The rough stone remained warm under his hands after hours of soaking in the sun. His light blue tunic and darker mantle fluttered in the breeze. Bands of green-blue and copper embroidery edged the hems of both. The ornate twining vines matched well with the formal circlet resting on his brow. Heavier than he'd expected, it kept his hair back from his face.

He wore good sandals on his feet, set with polished stones but not so light as he was accustomed to. He'd declined the loan of any other adornments, so no bracelets or anklets weighed him down. Time enough for that after he'd adjusted to the minimum requirements of formal attire.

The zest of clover honey lingered on his lips. He'd eaten well, but not heavily, at the banquet—well aware of the need to keep limbs loose and ready for the ball. High, sour notes carried across the distance as the harpist and other musicians tuned their instruments. Stevan could be there, on the floor. Or still in the banquet hall. He'd retreated to the rooftop for a respite instead.

As a compeer, he was expected to attend the ball and not sit out more than one or two dances. This had been made very clear. Idan, Amara, Nefeli, and others had all indicated that although he might choose to dance with whomever he wished to ask or was asked by, he needed to be present and accounted for whenever the Terparchon glanced around.

He hadn't found Gisela to ask yet. She'd been huddled away with other princesses preparing some special interlude to present before the dignitaries at the ball.

His vantage point offered clear lines of sight in two very different directions. To the one side, servants bustled about making the last decorative touches to the open-air dancing floor. On the other, irregular groups of palace denizens snuck out to the far clearing amidst the wooded garden to see the recent changes.

Guards had been assigned there, but they only kept people from drawing too close—and allowed viewing otherwise.

The former Shadow of the Moon had become quite popular. The more so since the Terparchon's and her daughters' reaction to the news of the change the day before ensured everyone who hadn't already heard about it did so. The Terparchon reputedly blanched, older daughter froze, and younger daughter turned red with fury.

Just as well he wasn't there.

A hint of unease followed him wherever he went. Not merely because he hadn't seen Gisela to speak with—viewing her across the room at the banquet barely counted. They'd all agreed to keep their involvement in undoing the Shadow of the Moon as secret as they could, but Gisela had seemed unsure.

No matter how he scanned the throngs of gaily clad nobles and notables filtering out of the buildings in the direction of the dancing floor, he found no sign of her. From the distant sense of her footsteps, she lingered somewhere in the banquet hall.

A cough behind him set him whirling around. Elbows clamped to his sides, but arms raised and hands ready to join a fight if necessary.

His brother stood there, in the same outfit as Brenn wore to every dance. Knee-length tunic showing off shapely calves. Red mantle complementing sun-warmed skin. Brow and sandals adorned with the signs of his rank in the guards.

And a broad smile stretching his face, showing sharp, bright teeth.

"Startled you, did I?" Brenn's sandals crunched against the roof tiles as he approached further.

"Is it just you?" Stevan stretched out his senses, broadening them to note the presence of anyone in general rather than searching for Gisela in specific. Better not to allow anyone to sneak up on him. They had the roof to themselves, with no one closer than two floors below.

"No one else." Brenn drew close.

Stevan narrowed his gaze, searching his brother's smile and keen eyes for any hint as to what brought him close when they hadn't seen each other in nearly two days. "What news?"

"None so far, and that's to the good." The older man patted Stevan's back, hand warm and comforting. "No whispers anywhere, that I can hear. Everyone was too busy dealing with the aftermath of the storm to notice who went into the wooded gardens or came out after. Even the gardeners—and believe me, I talked to near all of them, nor was I the only one—were busy with the plots closer by and didn't check the woods until well after daybreak."

Stevan and the others had all fled the scene well before then. They'd walked back in company. Stunned, then shaky. He and Gisela had clung to each other, to reduce the chills rattling their teeth and toes. Danissa and Jola had done much the same, with only Brenn on his own. He'd felt the least of the power released—but even he stumbled on his words more than once.

Jola had worried the most over how the royal family would react.

She held no hope whatsoever they'd consider it good. Yet Brenn had talked her into keeping quiet, that they all do so.

All five of them.

"Can five keep a secret?" Stevan glanced again at the trickle of courtiers and servants stealing out to view the flowers that bloomed in place of the Shadow.

"Any five? No. This five? Perhaps." Brenn leaned a hip against the stone wall. "We all have good reasons to keep silent. For now."

"For now." A hint of last night's chill rippled through Stevan. He set his teeth and pushed it back. Refused to allow the honey of dessert to sour with fear.

Brenn nodded. "I happened to run into Jola earlier, not by chance—"

"Jola?" Stevan asked. "Not Danissa?"

Brenn shook his head. "Jola has the better connections, and the greater fear. I'd judge her the most likely to break, but she seemed calm. Said the Terparchon's ordered an investigation but, most interesting, not by anyone here. The Chief Librarian at the winter palace is to send someone. By the time they arrive, memories will be even more muddled. Most people blame the storm. Think it was a freak of nature. They'll talk themselves into impressive signs and signifiers, and lightning strikes that blazed across the sky."

"You sound very certain." A layer of tension slipped from Stevan's shoulders and arms.

"I have some experience in investigations done after the fact." Brenn made a face. "Don't you?"

"I've written them up, but never done them." Stevan broke off. He sensed rather than heard two people climbing the stairs. One, Idan, stopped at the foot of the last flight while the other continued upward.

Gisela.

He turned to watch as she emerged from the doorway. Every step brought her closer, allowing him a better view of her shapely figure and the light fabrics billowing around her. Thick bands embroidered with vines bedecked her pale blue tunic and darker mantle. Her hair wrapped around her head in thin braids, half-covered by a wide gold-and-silver circlet. Matching bands hung about her right wrist and ankle.

Her colors meshed with his. Accident or choice?

Again Brenn clapped a hand against Stevan's back, this time giving a light push. "Good fortune to you, brother. I'll see you at the ball."

He walked off, exchanging nods and smiles as he passed Gisela. Teasing on Brenn's part, tentative on Gisela's.

"Come to view the sights?" Stevan gestured at the many views: ball, sunset, trickle of viewers heading to or from the former Shadow.

"No." She ducked her head for a moment, then looked him square in the face. "I came to find you."

THE SUN still rested above the horizon, and summer's warmth lingered. No matter that a light breeze tugged at the hems of Gisela's tunic and mantle, by all measures she should be warm. Yet a thin layer of perspiration dampened her skin and left her chilled. Her toes curled against the soles of her sandals.

Even weighed down by lengths of leather on her feet, she walked lighter. Stood straighter. Found the very air easier to breathe. The sun shone brighter, and the moon gazed down at the world with greater beauty than before.

On the other hand, despite drinking amply of watered wine at the banquet, the better to wash down the few dishes she'd found to her liking, her mouth was dry. She played with the bracelet at her wrist, a gift from the Terparchon for her first successful Dance. The twined wires of gold and silver chafed skin unused to such adornment.

Nearly all Gisela had done for the last moon was adjust to change and newness.

Time to take a more active role.

Swallowing a rush of fear, she searched Stevan's face for response. Found the glimmer of hope, but also wariness.

Fair enough, given how she'd blown hot and cold.

"You've come in search of me so many times. It's my turn to do the seeking." She shifted to stand directly before him, separated by only a hand's breadth. Close enough for the warmth pouring off him to warm her. "It wasn't easy, either. Compeers may have the gift of tracking people by their steps, but not princesses. I had to ask for assistance."

"Idan and Brenn are at the base of the steps." Stevan didn't glance that way, surety in his voice regardless. "They can't hear us, not if we keep our voices down."

"Idan offered to keep anyone else from coming up until we'd had a chance to speak." Gisela sighed. "He doesn't know what happened the other night, at least not from me, but he knew I hadn't had a chance to talk with you."

"If you're afraid of word leaking out, we're safe, for now, from the Terparchon's ire. Brenn assured me, so long as we all keep quiet."

"That's not why I'm here." A flash of shame flicked Gisela, that he'd think her first concern on speaking with him would be safety.

At the farther end of the sky, the full moon started its ascent above the horizon. Soft silver light meshed with the fading glimmers of the setting sun.

Taking his hand, she urged him to turn and view the night ascending. Everything on land differed from the night they'd met, at the last full moon. There was to be a ball, a dance, but it would little resemble the festival at which they'd first danced.

He'd sought her out then, for she would have retreated without his encouragement to dance together to the end. Though he'd turned down her offer to walk aside and lie together under the moon, time and again he'd come through for her.

She took his hands in hers, sliding fingers under, over, and through. "You told me that if I made the offer again under another full moon, you'd have a different answer."

"Is it the same offer?" His hands trembled, but his voice remained steady.

"It can be, if that is all you want. But I am willing—desirous—of more." Gisela breathed deep and blinked back impending tears. "You know where I am from, what I can bring and what I cannot. I will never be a princess such as some of the others seek to be. Never a power, except as needed to protect those I love. And never able to bear you a child."

"I need no children of my body. I'm sure my family and your people will provide more than enough for us to love and cherish. I don't wish for power, never did." Stevan lifted her hands to his lips. "Only a sufficiency—enough to live and love and flourish the rest of my days."

"A sufficiency sounds lovely. May I share it with you?" Gisela slipped her arms around his waist, drawing close.

"I would have no other."

Their mouths met in kiss after kiss, two bodies close entwined.

Until the harsh sound of a gong summoning celebrants to the dance floor broke even such a reverie as theirs.

"Come dance with me, this night and always." Gisela asked and offered.

"If it's a life of dancing you desire, I am your man."

CHAPTER 26

$\mathcal{A}$t the end of summer, Amara slipped from her room in the dark of night. Her long, dark gray tunic and mantle enveloped her in shadows. Matching cloth wrapped around her hair, hiding every strand lest any glitter and give her away. Her skin she'd touched with ashes stolen from the kitchen hearth. Only so much as needed on face and hands to let her slip unnoticed through the darkness. Nevertheless, ashy dust covered her fingers and got in everywhere, bitter to the taste.

Regularly oiling the hinges of her door had benefits. It opened without sound. A quick glance up and down showed no one about. Someone might go to lengths, as she had, to hide in the dim corridor, but she doubted any had. The one most likely had rooms elsewhere, and no reason—Amara hoped—to wander those parts of the complex where former princesses and compeers resided.

Indeed, Amara had little company here. Most who left the ranks of the princesses also departed from the court to live in the cities of their birth or choice. Or, if they opted for other types of employment with the court, did not travel with it from city to city and palace to palace but remained in considerable comfort in one or another. Only a few remained to serve in one capacity or another.

Then again, the others who left had choices not allotted to her. She knew her place. It chafed, but it always had.

She checked the hall anyway. Best to take extra care, and give no cause for complaint or suspicion. She did not work against the well-being of the Terparchon, after all.

Only for the peace of mind of those no longer able to dance for themselves.

For them, she ventured out after resisting the urge for weeks on end since the Shadow was banished.

She had only this chance. In the morning, most of the court would leave the summer palace. Two entourages, led by the Marchon and Terparchon, would take separate routes to visit various villas, towns, and castles, before rejoining at the winter palace.

Now—or wait nearly a year to stand witness.

The latch barely clicked as she closed the door.

She left her sandals behind. Went barefoot, the better to walk in silence. She tiptoed down, hand light upon the railing lest she leave any trail of ashes behind to mark her passage.

Out into the night, finding her way by memory and starlight and a sliver of moonlight. A few clouds flitted across the sky, the wind brisk up high but warmer and lesser down low. A hint of chill mingled with the warm gusts doing their own dance above the flowers and paths. Autumn remained distant, but not for long.

Keeping to the shadows and the edges of paths, rather than strolling down the center, she wove her way through the gardens. Her passage kicked up a light layer of dust which the winds blew about. No doubt her feet and ankles would be coated when she returned, but a damp cloth would make short work of cleaning.

Thin candlelights flickered in windows along the way. From the Terparchon and Marchon's quarters and their son's in the royal residence, but not their daughters'. A few of the windows of the princesses and compeers likewise were lit, not least Idan's, but he had confessed to finding sleep more difficult of late.

Of more interest, no lights glimmered in Gisela's chambers or Stevan's above, though these past weeks they'd often shared one or the other. More than once their laughter broke the night in the princesses' quarters, albeit not this night. A good sound to hear, even if it did make many a heart ache—not out of jealousy but the wish such fortune might favor them.

Including Amara, if only for a few moments here and there. Bittersweet memories wakened, but she stuffed them back down. All it took was a moment or two counting her years on her fingers and toes and back and forth. She'd borne too much for too long to waste time remembering certain things.

Yet here she was, visiting a site she'd avoided: the former Shadow of the Moon.

Changed utterly, she'd been told. Everyone wanted to tell the story, especially those who hadn't been there in the moment but stopped by afterward.

"You wouldn't know it." one of the cooks had told a new arrival, waving a dripping ladle, as Amara stole through to take up ashes. "Flowers such as even no gardener's ever seen. Blooming fierce as any garden, or something fiercer as though it had decades to make up."

Or centuries.

Amara drew the skirt of her tunic close about as she hustled down the path through the woods. Made it almost all the way, until exhaustion set in and she had to stop and rest.

How had she grown so old without noticing? She'd missed the signs, until they bore in on her all at once as though she stood within a hollowed-out house waiting for the roof to cave in. Her chest heaved and lungs ached. She had to force herself to drag in deep breaths—she who once outlasted all her fellow princesses in capacity to dance on a single, long exhalation. Much as she wished to blame the thickness of the air, she knew the weakness was as much internal as external.

Digging her fingers into the bark, she let her head fall back. The folds of her tunic hid her slender figure from others, but no longer concealed the truth from Amara herself. Eyes open at last, she noted how her limbs withered. Body contracted, drawing inward. Shoulders began to slope and curve despite long years of keeping herself straight.

Even her hair changed, growing brittle. She still kept it long, and usually braided, but if strands kept breaking, one of these days she might give in and chop it off. A sorry day for one who'd once gloried in her long tresses. Then again, those days were well and truly gone. She could think of no one alive who remembered when her hair was not white. No one who'd care.

Not even the Terparchon, although Amara had occasionally taken turns among the princesses dancing before the current ruler assumed her throne. Only in the decade since had she withdrawn completely from the field and contented herself with teaching in hopes she might find pupils willing to learn what she sought to share.

They learned, but never enough.

Yet she kept trying. Hoping. Praying. With so little to show for it. Everyone else seemed so young these days.

Then a light, buoyant perfume reached her. She drew in a deep breath, near tasting a scent bright and sweet beyond compare. All her weariness dropped away, banished by the flowers even at a distance.

Memories of her youth flashed back. Of running through a thick forest, branches catching at her tunic and scraping her arms and legs. Hiding in the underbrush to watch people dancing in a ring. No drums but the clap of their hands. No flutes or harps, but voices raised in a single tune although sung in several different languages or dialects.

Being caught out, and dragged into the center as face after face turned down upon her. Eyes staring. Lips set.

Until one broke out in giggles, and another followed.

And somehow she knew matters would work out all right. They had, that night.

The laughter, joyous cascades of mirth, echoed in her ears as a chilly breeze passed by. Returning to reality, she found the giggles repeated.

Slipped onward through the wood to the edge of the clearing, then stopped in the shadow of a tree.

At the center, there remained no sign of the chalky soil, or the murdered bodies once laid there and unceremoniously covered in such a way as to poison the soil.

Instead, wildflowers filled the circle. Such a profusion of blooms, for so late in the year. Perhaps the cook was right and no gardener had ever seen them, though Amara doubted it, but sooner or later someone would recognize them. Match them against drawings and descriptions in books.

Nightbells.

Far more, and fuller grown, than Amara would ever have expected —but she doubted not. The reason why lay clear before her.

Two figures in plain tunics and bare feet. Arms entwined. Bodies in harmony. Smiles clear even at this distance.

Gisela and Stevan whirling around and around.

They danced for joy. Their pleasure fed the earth, furthered the blooms, in turn contributing to their joy. A wondrous cycle seen too infrequently.

All the court might wonder how the change had come to pass. No whisper of a credible explanation had reached Amara's ears, though she usually heard all manner of gossip. She'd pondered the matter herself. Worried. Fretted.

No more. These two must have played some part.

Rather than proceed anywhere nearer, she retreated. As she left, she Danced just a little. A minor jig upon the path. Unbalanced she might be, but she still had some power to dance magic and so she laid a confusion around the clearing and its occupants—that no one else might spy upon them this night, or make the connection.

They never knew, but their laughter lightened her steps as she left, and for many a day after.

Their delight fed the flowers.

SNEAK PEEK

CHAPTER 1

*B*e among the first to learn of new releases: sign-up for her newsletter at https://BookHip.com/PCSWMCK. Book recommendations, updates on stories, and snippets from works-in-progress—plus a free Dancing Princesses story for signing up!

THE WORLD of the Dancing Princesses continues—read on for a peek at *A Healer Princess*!

LEANDER FOLLOWED the hum of bees to the scene of the crime. Or the mystery. No one seemed sure which term applied.

He slipped out first thing in the morning, when the dew still lay thick on grass and late-summer flowers. The sun barely poked above the horizon and the air remained cool, almost still. The long swath of his mantle wrapped around him from mid-chest to lower thigh, with ample left over to toss over one shoulder and fall to mid-calf. The light green contrasted with the darker shade of his knee-length tunic. Although clean, both bore stains along the hemlines and the tunic an ill-mended rent from knee to hip on the side. He slung over his shoulder his usual work kit, a stoutly woven bag of dark gray.

His steady pace down the stairs kept him warm. Legs pumped, arms swung, and strands of wavy, brown-black hair got in his way since he hadn't visited his barber before being sent off on the trip to Yaras and the summer palace.

Even this early, the air had a thickness to it, a degree of moisture beyond what Leander was accustomed to. If it did get hot—and given the heat of the last days of journeying, he now believed every florid description ever written about this part of the country—the humidity might make merely breathing troublesome.

Then again, the climate also allowed for lush gardens everywhere he turned. Even inside the lesser section of the palace where he'd been granted a room. He passed at least three immense pots overgrowing with scented greenery and purple flowers before exiting the building and crossing the courtyard. Few of the plants blooming here grew at all in the winter palace gardens, and in far less profusion.

His environs were at once familiar and strange.

Simple gray-pebble mosaics laid out clear walkways to and from different parts of the palace complex. Much as he looked forward to viewing the many ornate, full-color mosaics for which the summer palace was famous—not to mention visiting the local palace library and librarians—he preferred to get started on his investigation first.

He took three steps away from the library path toward the gardens, then stopped at the faintest creak of hinges. The hairs along his neck prickled.

Early-rising birds called overhead. Blue-and-white lakelurkers spread their wings wide as they soared over the palace complex. Many smaller birds with gray coats and speckled chests darted among the eaves. A couple gave a ululating screech as they plucked insects from between the stones.

Although he heard nothing to indicate a human followed him, certainty flooded through him. He shook his head and strode off as if untroubled, only to whirl after the fifth step.

His sister froze a few measures from the open door. Her solid body canted forward as she balanced on her tiptoes, hands raised. A pale-blue mantle covered her from neck to knee, but the hem of her matching tunic fluttered around her bare ankles and feet. She'd chopped her hair off at shoulder length a few weeks earlier and burnt the lengths as a declaration of independence.

Whether or not they shared a sire remained a mystery to them both, for their mother hadn't ever let slip so much as a hint, but no one ever doubted their relationship. Both had round faces, snub noses, and medium-brown complexions, though her eyes seemed bigger and darker brown, especially when trying to convince him to change his mind.

He motioned for her to return to the room. She would legally come of age in a few months but remained under his care until then.

For a moment her body remained raised, then her ankles wobbled. She dropped onto her flat feet, shoulders slumping.

"Keep to your studies." His lips twitched at the heavy droop of her body, every line suggesting dejection. "Enough progress, and perhaps I'll permit you to help later."

She maintained a woeful expression for a few seconds longer, then flashed him a brilliant smile and skipped back into the building. The door shut with a firm click behind her.

No one stirred in this corner of the palace. All the same, Leander watched the windows two floors up until Edrena appeared there and gave a wave.

Nodding, he continued on his way toward the middle of one of the gardens. He'd caught a distant view out the window of his third-floor chamber the night before. Slipped a coin into a few servants' hands in exchange for directions on how to locate a spot amidst the palace's pocket wilderness that had once hosted one of the famed Shadows of the Moon.

All the servants gave the same instructions. At the time, he'd considered them overly simple, being no more and no less than walk out a specific door and take the garden path directly ahead, never turning aside.

Yet what constituted directly ahead? The mosaic path gave way to one of gravel, then even the stones vanished leaving a track of trodden vegetation, narrow to the point only one person might walk at a time. It appeared to be a servant's path, a back way that courtiers likely never noticed.

By implication, the servants who'd provided directions still recognized him as one of them. That, or librarians were considered servants at the summer palace. Denizens of the winter palace, servants and members of the court alike, considered librarians as both necessary record-keepers and bloodsucking parasites determined to extract detailed stories from anyone foolish enough to fall into their clutches.

Still, the librarians had accepted him into their ranks and given him a place on the ground. Falfor, his mentor, had seen value in nurturing his intense desire to uncover answers.

Trees rose high to either side, their branches and thick foliage blocking out most of the growing sunlight—and also the heat—but many dripped water although it hadn't rained the night before. Though the path showed evidence of regular trimming by gardeners, they failed to keep up with the growth. Several times, Leander pushed through thick greenery even when turned sideways.

Dozens of different shades of green flourished along with sprays of small flowers amidst mosses marking the many places where the path crossed another or split in two. The crossings, even when at acute angles, he navigated well enough. The splits he found trickier to interpret and guess which counted as straight.

All the while, the moisture in the air condensed into droplets coating him to the point he couldn't tell the difference between his own honest sweat and the wooded garden's dampness.

Fortunately, the current chief librarian had allowed him time to pack, and even given a bit of warning about the kind of climate he'd find. He'd possessed only one outfit when he first climbed down off the city roofs, but now he had tunics and mantles suitable for all kinds of occasions.

If his closest rivals among the ranks of ambitious sub-librarians had been sent here instead of him, both would surely wear long tunics and mantles in light yellow or pink and come back complaining about the stains and how hard it was to get weeds or other plant matter out of well-woven linen.

Likely one reason the chief had chosen Leander.

Then again, this particular assignment also involved direct service to the Terparchon. He'd have to be polite and keep his mouth shut and his opinions to himself, save when asked for, and then delivered in the most circumspect and diplomatic manner so as to let no detail slip without due thought.

Leander couldn't make out whether this was the chance of a lifetime—or a dangerous slide set to send him back to his former life atop the winter palace roofs.

Probably both in one, all of which made it interesting, at least. A nice change from reading over reports from the chief's official and unofficial correspondents and writing summaries and annotating reports.

Plus the chance to get out of the city and see more of the countryside at its greenest—and hottest.

Alas, sneaking out first thing meant delaying breakfast. His stomach protested, having gotten used to regular meals since promotion from mere scribe to third assistant librarian for court affairs, then second. He could practically taste getting the raise to first if he managed to navigate the tangle satisfactorily.

He only needed to figure out what would constitute a satisfactory result and how to ensure it manifested *without* lying or faking evidence or making a big fuss that turned out to be no more than a bag of wind.

First, however, he needed to see exactly what it was he'd been sent to investigate.

The summer palace contained one of the odd geographical sites poetically called the Shadows of the Moon. One and all—no one seemed entirely certain whether there were twelve or thirteen—took the form of perfect circles of chalky white stone in the middle of otherwise lushly grown gardens.

Many Shadows lay within the shifting borders of Codaros. The winter palace boasted one and he'd stolen time from packing for a quick visit before departing. Although reportedly popular as a place to picnic on hot days, he'd failed to appreciate the fuss over the ghastly thing.

Every time he'd seen a Shadow, his mind started asking questions. How had the makers managed such perfect circles? Where did the stone come from? How deep did it go? Why did the stones' color remind him of nothing so much as the layers of ice left by the worst winter storms, a substance known to cause frostbite within moments?

Hardly thoughts conducive to rest and relaxation.

Evidently, the Shadow at the summer palace had vanished overnight.

A very particular night, given the few details the chief had entrusted to Leander, for it had disappeared immediately following one of the killer summer storms that regularly rolled off the lake waters around this time of year. Even when the dancing princesses eased a storm's wrath, it still leveled much damage. Leander had done his time sorting and organizing weather and damage reports in past summers.

Still, if the storm were to blame—a lightning strike, perhaps— there should be bits and pieces of the stone left behind. Scattered debris or some such, and the spot itself, the Shadow, surely would be blackened or in other ways blasted.

Instead, it had turned to full-grown flowers.

This unsettled the Terparchon to the point she considered no one at the summer palace exempt from suspicion, except perhaps herself, and sent to the winter palace for a librarian to investigate.

Hence Leander's presence, although the importance of the Shadow's disappearance still escaped him.

With the end of the path in sight, he twined his fingers together and committed himself to the service of truth and justice and asked that they guide his inquiry.

"May I not mar or stain any reputation unduly, but only gather and sift through what is known and suspected to piece a tale that rings with veracity."

Nothing and no one answered, as expected. Librarians regularly debated the existence of Truth, whether divine being or earthly force, separate from the messy realities they faced on most occasions. The discussions Leander had participated in—usually involving copious amounts of intoxicating beverages—never came to any conclusion other than a general preference that they serve Truth without ever having to discover the answer.

His breath escaped in a huff, a brief tremor of relief slipping over his skin—and another runnel of moisture down his spine.

Then he left the cool of the woods. The sudden press of sunlight across his body dispelled any remaining chill. He halted and blinked, shading his eyes with a hand.

In the moments of mixed light and shadow, a whiff of something bright and sweet reached him. A flower of some kind, with a buoyant scent and flavor that reached deep within him and struck an unexpected chord. As though the aroma touched his soul and extracted all weariness to leave him refreshed.

The instant his eyes adjusted to the sunlight, he pulled a thin stick of charcoal from his kit. He scribbled a few phrases on a piece of old parchment. Rubbed them out and tried again, and a third time, before he gave up finding sufficient words to describe the new, strange aroma.

Sweat trickled along his spine.

A wide clearing stretched out before him. Stone paths bisected swathes of well-trodden green grass and blue-green mosses. One traced the circular perimeter close to the edge. Others headed to the center and no doubt formed a cross shape, although he couldn't see the far side due to the upwelling of flowers at the center.

Such blooms. Stalks of deep blue with long blue-green leaves and topped with petals mixing dark blue and silver. The blossoms glowed with the beauty of a star-lit night sky.

All the while giving off an aroma that lured him close and closer. He crossed the clearing without any recollection of doing so. One moment he'd left the woods, the next he stood only a hand's length away from the flowers. They swayed in the breeze atop their slender stalks, rising nearly as high as his hips.

Even among the wealth of plants he'd never seen before, these stood out.

He shook, hair tangling, and found he still held charcoal and parchment. Setting to work, he sketched the flowers with detailed notes that, as with the scent, were at best an approximation far removed from the visceral reality. He even bent to check the earth from which the stalks sprung, finding it a rich, brown loam that trickled through his fingers.

"Pretty, isn't it?"

Leander jumped to his feet, elbows clamped tight against his side. His hands clenched around charcoal and parchment. Uncricking his neck with a crack, he turned to discover who'd managed to creep up on him unnoticed. He was far more accustomed to the reverse.

An elder stood there. Once a half-head taller than Leander but now stooped so they had the same height. Skin of light brown save for their bare feet, covered by such a thick layer of grass and leaf clippings as to appear green. A knee-length, once-white tunic likewise bore numerous stains of green. The elder wore it in an old-fashioned style tied over one shoulder rather than both. Lacking a mantle or a proper cord or chain at the waist, they used a length of fraying gray cord to belt the tunic across a rounded belly. Their bald head boasted big green-brown eyes, a nose as short as Leander's, and a scraggly beard. A long stalk of grass bobbed between their gums as they chewed.

Overall, the stranger presented as a man but might be an eleee, the term favored by many, albeit not all, who found the terms men and women inaccurate or insufficient. Some eleee were rumored to be able to change anything about their bodies that they wished, though Leander doubted any willingly chose a body such as this unless they wanted to pass unnoticed.

"Beautiful. I've never seen the like." Leander tucked his charcoal and parchment safe within his kit bag.

"I wouldn't think anyone'd have." The stranger settled hands on hips, ducking as they scanned the blooms. "I only ever heard stories about magic flowers, myself, but these are even better than any tales."

The two watched several golden butterflies dance across the petals. The other huffed and angled their body to face Leander.

With minimal movements, Leander mirrored the other's stance.

"You're that librarian sent to find out why this changed overnight?" The grass stalk jerked this way and that as dark eyes bored into Leander.

"Yes."

"Thought so." A short nod. "Came out to find you."

"Did you now." An additional pang struck Leander at not having noticed, but he let it pass. Only a fool let slip an opportunity to gather information.

"Figured I ought to tell someone where no listening ear might hear and start rumors." The other removed the stalk and brushed the tip against a wrinkled temple. "I wouldn't like that."

"A good librarian respects their sources." Leander's fingers twitched to retrieve charcoal and parchment. He resisted, trusting his memory to retain what mattered.

"So I heard. Well, I got a little tale for you then." The elder stuck the stalk behind an ear and crossed their arms over their chest. "Mind, it wasn't me that saw this. We had us a couple three extra pairs of arms and legs to help tidy up some of the branches lashed down by the last big storm. One of them, he told me later about seeing someone running through the wood over here that evening after the storm and before anyone found the shadow changed."

"So this man . . ." Leander tilted his head and left an opening for the gardener, given their description of their laborers, to offer additional details. The other scuffed a knobby foot against the grass and said nothing, so Leander continued, "saw someone running away."

"That's about the size of it."

"Nothing more?"

"Not really. Just that I figured she might've been here when the change took place and might be able to help you figure out everything what happened." The grass stalk moved from behind the ear back to dipping and rising out of one corner of the gardener's mouth.

"Who did you say saw this?" Leander asked.

"His name don't matter. He were up from the town, cheap labor, and I heard got hired on with a trader a couple day back."

"Convenient." An apt word, for Leander didn't miss how little the gardener shared.

"That's what I thought."

"And the woman he saw?"

"He didn't know her," the gardener said with a shrug.

But Leander caught a glint in their eyes, and the way the corners of their lips twitched into a smirk for a moment before returning to work away at the stalk.

"*You* do."

"Maybe I do, maybe I don't." The other tilted their head back for a long moment, then gave a decisive nod. "It were twilight. He said she were short with plenty of curves, lots of black curls, and dark skin with glittery bangles at her wrists. Young and bouncy with energy even as she ran." A hand with dirty fingernails stroked the short gray and white hairs sprouting from their chin. "Only one I can think of fits that description. She's a sweet thing, too. I've seen her over the summers grow from a little toddler turning circles on the green to as lovely a dancer as you'd ever want to see. You treat her well, you hear?"

"Of course. Her name?" Flickers of energy surged through Leander's body. Young, bouncy, sweet, curved, lots of curls. The winter court held several matching such a description, but only one he knew had come with the Terparchon to the summer court.

"She's one of them princesses, now. The youngest, though not the newest anymore."

"Good to know." Leander swallowed, mouth suddenly dry. More warmth welled within him, beyond that of the air and the sunlight. "Her name?"

"That's enough for you to find her." The other grinned, showing every one of their remaining teeth. "No doubt she'll tell you all you need to know, mind she might need a push. You just talk to her daddy on the quiet, and say old Natter pays his debts."

"Much obliged to you." Leander managed to smile and nod as the stranger turned on his heels and stalked away—quite fast at that. He hadn't missed the gardener's reference to himself—assuming Natter was, indeed, his name.

Likewise, he noted the old man's skillful avoidance of true details, the kind Leander would need for any report. Leander extracted his parchment and took notes, wondering if the tale were true, and if Natter meant the princess well or had a score to settle with her father. The gardener would bear further investigation in addition to those he'd so carefully kept from naming.

Still, he'd given Leander another place to start with his investigation.

And a reason to introduce himself to a certain princess. Unfortunately, as an inquisitor with questions rather than merely an admirer.

THE STORY CONTINUES!

FATE TURNS

LEANDER LOVES THREE THINGS: information, truth, and his sister. For her sake, he clambered down off the palace roofs to take a place as a sub-librarian in the library. He earns their keep in a world of books, papers, and the pursuit of answers to any and all questions. One more successful mission means promotion to full librarian—cementing his and his sister's place on the ground.

But at night in his lonely bed, he dreams of a woman as far out of reach as a star in the sky. Seen and admired only from a distance: Danissa, the youngest of the magical Dancing Princesses.

Sent to the summer palace to investigate a mystery—the destruction of a royal treasure—his investigation leads to Danissa. Promotion hinges on extracting vital information, but gaining her love requires restraint and secrecy. Work or love? Or find a way to win both?

Two cautious hearts collide in a sweet romance in *A Healer Princess*.

ABOUT THE AUTHOR

Alea Henle writes non-fiction by day and fiction by night. Contemporary and historical fantasy, fantasy romance—and more! Check out her website www.aleahenle.com.